AN
INCH
OF
SNOW

William E. Cobb

AN INCH OF SNOW

JOHN F. BLAIR, Publisher   Winston-Salem   1964

TO THOSE
who do more than find fault with their government

AN
INCH
OF
SNOW

1

YANKEES

are no good in general. One by the name of Horatio
Bunker is no good in particular. There is nothing narrow-
minded about me, but experience has convinced me that Yankees, Republicans, and foreigners are not to be trusted.

About a year before the accident, Horatio Bunker came to
Jeffersonville. He did not intend to stay, but he is still here, and
I can see no hope of his ever leaving.

On first meeting, Horatio Bunker attracted people to him.
More accurately, it might be said that he compelled people to
listen to him, for there was nothing about his appearance that
was magnetic in itself, except possibly his attire. His long, slender frame was accentuated by loosely-fitting clothes. They were
not loose enough to be baggy, but there was sufficient surplus
cloth to let the observer realize that he was not likely to fill out
any suit. In style and color his clothes were extremely conservative, beautifully tailored. It would be obvious to anybody that
they were custom-cut and that the tailor had misplaced no
stitches. His shirt was not like that normally worn by those who
wear shirts and neckties in Tarvania. It was slightly off-white,

like those recommended for television. The collar was secured below the necktie knot by a gold pin. The tie was of a small paisley pattern, in good taste and obviously costly. His shoes were of a subdued Scotch grain, giving off a sheen characteristic of high quality leather. Altogether, Bunker gave the appearance of an impeccable New York executive, or a London con-man.

Possibly the perfection of his attire seemed unusual only because it was uncommon in Jeffersonville. He appeared comfortable and accustomed to what he was wearing; there was no affectation, or pride of appearance, such as you find among more successful traveling salesmen.

Bunker was far too thin ever to have been an outstanding athlete, except possibly a track man or basketball player. Nevertheless, he gave the impression of being physically fit. He was broad of shoulder, considering the rest of his frame, and he moved with a springiness characteristic of a man who makes a point of keeping himself physically in tune.

These impressions were formed when he was at some distance, and were forgotten when you met the man face to face. His long fingers gave him a firm handshake; his hand felt dry and clean.

I've been shaking hands with politicians all my life, and I know of nothing more devastating to political success than a limp handshake. Except for the ready smile, there is no more valuable accessory to success at the polls than a good handshake.

Horatio Bunker had the ready smile characteristic of successful men and women in every field. It was encased in a lean face, narrow at the jaw, so that his smile covered most of the lower half of his face. His nose was long and sharp and straight. Finely-textured brown hair, thinning on either side, was combed from a point that gave an arrow-like impression. It was greying around the ears, offsetting the impression of youth that his slender figure implied.

Out of keeping with his hair were heavy eyebrows and an apparent heavy beard. Although cleanly shaven, he would have made a good model for those five-o'clock shadow ads used by razor blade manufacturers.

Bunker's complexion was clear, although slightly mottled and sallow without any indication of ill health. There were no lines of worry on his face. The wrinkles that were noticeable were around his eyes, as if he had smiled a great many times at a great many things. All these facial characteristics were secondary to his eyes.

I don't know the exact color of Bunker's eyes, somewhere between hazel and brown I suppose, but I do know that his direct look held me attentive to his every word. He might have been lying in forty different directions, but you could never detect it by his intensity.

A man would have to be mighty deaf not to clearly understand Bunker. Although the New England accent was objectionable to me, there was no misunderstanding each word, for it had plenty of volume and a precise enunciation. Altogether, he made an extremely effective presentation, if you like overconfidence.

Part of this impression of confidence was due to his being well over six feet tall, which allowed him to look down upon most people to whom he talked. Provided he isn't too tall, a man enjoys the psychological advantage of height. I chuckle remembering how Harry Truman avoided being photographed while standing with taller men. They say Tom Dewey used to carry a wooden soft-drink crate to stand on at every public appearance.

From the start, I concluded that Horatio Bunker was not a

man to be trifled with. He didn't utter a lot of words, but those he did speak were short on adjectives and strong on meaning.

His actual character was less obvious. Bunker might either be an intensely sincere young man or extremely skilled in planting that impression.

Jeffersonville would be described by most Northern visitors as a typical, sleepy, Southern town. That's the way they always characterize anything south of the Mason-Dixon, and there is some truth to it. The ancient brick courthouse sits in the center of town and is surrounded by hickory and gum trees under which loafers of both races pass long, warm hours. Around this there are parking meters on streets that are more and more "one-way" to traffic. Across from the courthouse square the four sides are commercial, where hardware and general merchandise stores, like Webb & Sons, are slowly yielding to Woolworth's and other big chain operations.

Town consists of ten to fifteen thousand people making up the incorporated City of Jeffersonville. We call it fifteen thousand due to a loose concept of the city limits and an affection for stray cats, goats, and darkies. The census always limits us to something under eleven thousand people.

All Jeffersonville is divided into five parts, the central one being "downtown." To the south of town, more or less along the Yatawba River, it is mostly industrial, featuring a lumber mill, two furniture plants, one feed mill, a textile dye plant, and Opulant & Company's hosiery plant. The other three parts are residential, which is to greatly dignify Negro and poor-white housing. Then there are middle-class white homes, wherein live most of our people, not spectacular as individuals but making up the average, the moral fiber of Jeffersonville, and the dutifully voting population. Finally there is the well-to-do, or once well-to-do, white residential. This is marked "Residential

A" on the new zoning maps. In "Residential A" are found members of the Jeffersonville Country Club, the original owners of homes, the new car buyers, and the stockholders of Opulant & Company.

I suppose Bunker and Jeffersonville had as little in common as is possible between a man and a town. They hardly spoke the same language, Bunker's English having been thoroughly corrupted by generations of New Englandism.

Jeffersonville, lying in the rolling Piedmont of Tarvania, has somewhat its own language, and beautiful it is to hear. Some of it is aristocratic South, some of it is Dan Boone mountain, and it has a fair share of African-Tarvania.

The language barrier was a minor difference between Horatio Bunker and Jeffersonville, and it didn't cause him to feel unwelcome. As I understand it, he inherited almost half the stock in Opulant & Company from way back when the company's interest was in cotton ginning and land stealing for the Southeast Railroad. Later it evolved into a respectable hosiery business, employing about five hundred people. Bunker's family had never taken any interest in it as long as it was paying dividends by which the Bunker tribe could live well in Worcester, a place in Massachusetts.

After World War II, the local management of Opulant & Company made some mistakes, one of which was serious. As a small stockholder myself, I tried to tell them that seamless hosiery was what women wanted. Regrettably, they bought machinery for full-fashioned stockings while women were becoming too lazy to keep the back seams straight. All this was regrettable because it deprived me of dividends and because it brought Bunker to Jeffersonville.

Horatio Bunker showed up unannounced early in 1959, just a few days before the annual stockholders' meeting of Opulant

& Company. He checked into the old Yatawba Hotel and immediately began his dirty work, which consisted of contacting a goodly number of minority stockholders. He did not even bother seeing Grandin Opulant or Sharster Queems, who just about controlled the Company and had managed it for a quarter of a century.

"Mr. Anchor," he said to me, "I understand you would like to make a profit on your investment in Opulant & Company." This was said in the lofty air of a lord of the manor speaking to a land-owning peasant.

"Don't much give a damn if I do or don't," I answered. Horatio Bunker seemed neither taken aback nor nettled. Instead, he turned on the big smile of a used car salesman and gave me his pitch.

"Mr. Anchor, you have the reputation of being a gambling man. They say that you bet two hundred horses against Sedge Hildebran's brickworks on a poker hand in 1922."

He had me there. I had lost the herd while holding three of a kind.

"Yes, Mr. Bunker, I've been known to make a small wager from time to time," I said.

"Then you are the man to talk to about getting rich with no investment," said Bunker.

I had to listen him out. He proposed that I elect him, myself, and some other small stockholders as directors of Opulant & Company. These new directors would elect Bunker as president of the company. This didn't appeal to me in itself, but he wasn't finished.

"I am willing to bet a thousand dollars that the company earns at least $1.36 a share after one year under my management," said Bunker.

Opulant & Company had been returning less than fifty cents

a share, when it wasn't showing a loss. It looked like a good bet, if Bunker paid his gambling debts. It didn't take any figuring to know that my old friends Grandin Opulant and Sharster Queems would be out of management, and quickly. Upon reflection, that wouldn't be too bad. The two had outsmarted me enough in the past fifty years.

"Put your thousand up in escrow at the First National Bank, Mr. Bunker, and I will do the same," and that ended my comment. Usually such a deal would have taken six months' haggling.

"Mr. Anchor, it is a pleasure to do business with you. Already I am enjoying the fancy women and fine beverages your generosity promises to provide." With that comment he took his leave.

Bunker was moving too fast and a damn sight too directly to suit me, even if his proposition was too good to pass up. It's just that we give new ideas time to ripen. It's the way of our place and it's the right way.

2

ORDINARILY

the Directors' Room at Opulant & Company would have been adequate for the annual stockholders' meeting, but not so this year. Word had made the rounds that something was about to happen and all stockholders showed up, so the meeting had to be moved to the Community House.

Correctly for once, rumor had it that Grandin Opulant and Sharster Queems didn't have the Bunker proxies in their pockets. In such case they couldn't count on control of a majority of the stock, and even the smallest stockholder might hold the votes that would decide the future management of Opulant & Company.

Grandin Opulant held the largest number of local shares and retained the title of President as a matter of tradition. Sharster Queems had nearly as many shares and was considered the leader of the two. They worked as partners not only in Opulant & Company but in many another venture, primarily real estate, lumber, and banking. Each served as a director on the two local bank boards, and when they agreed on something, it usually assured its success. Also, when they agreed on someone, it assured him of plenty of credit, favorable business contacts, and complete social acceptability. Contrariwise, they had the power to break a man, and had been known to do so for the "good of Jeffersonville," as they explained it.

The influence of O&Q, which is railroadese for Opulant and Queems, extends beyond ownership and control of a lot of Jeffersonville. They are also the big wheels of Jefferson County's political machinery. They have never fought for public office and they've held no official titles in the Democratic organization. Opulant holds the Mayoralty more by tradition than by contest. Notwithstanding their apparent political obscurity, nobody enters a Democratic primary without trying to get the support of Opulant and Queems. It takes a miracle of good luck, a lot of hard work, and plenty of money to win without their blessings.

Grandin Opulant's a Methodist and Sharster Queems a Baptist, and they both give generously to their churches. Incidentally, these two denominations take in three-quarters of the church-goers of Jeffersonville. Opulant and Queems always support fund-raising efforts in a big way and were the prime movers behind our YMCA and YWCA. The only time I've seen them downright niggardly was in the payment of taxes. Since they more or less control the Courthouse gang, their land evaluation is always reasonable. My own land evaluation is also reasonable, so I do not join those who say that O&Q's are ridiculously low.

O&Q have an inner circle of which I am a part-time member. It meets about 10:00 A.M. over coffee at the Jeffersonville Grill. Nobody is excluded from the big round table, but the good tips on over-the-counter stock or inclusion on a land trade are not discussed until the inner circle is alone. Opulant and Queems don't try to rush anybody away; they just argue the virtues of athletic teams or complain about the conditions of the golf fairways until only the chosen few remain. They outwait even me on major deals, not to exclude me so much as to save me embarrassment when a lot of money must change hands.

I make a contribution to the partners in exchange for choice tidbits of information gleaned from meetings of the inner circle. My voting precinct, Stony Creek, which is just north of town, is about half Republican. Not only have I tried to lead our people in the right direction at Democratic primaries, but I have to fight like hell to keep the Republicans from taking Stony Creek in the general elections. I haven't failed since Al Smith ran against Herbert Hoover in 1928.

As the day for the stockholders' meeting came up, I realized that Horatio Bunker had taken me in. For a thousand-dollar bet I had bartered the life-long confidence of Opulant and Queems. Anyway, I couldn't live many more years and I had salted away enough to make it. Maybe my ill-considered bet with Bunker was just a compulsive reaction to a lifetime of being a second-team man. It couldn't be helped now unless I asked Bunker to call off the bet and I wouldn't give him that satisfaction. As it stood, I had to support him in taking over the direction of Opulant & Company. I wondered how many other little stockholders were also committed to Bunker.

At Opulant & Company the profit picture wasn't too good. A small dividend might be voted by the Board of Directors, but it wouldn't be a proper return on investment. We had listened to Grandin Opulant make the usual optimistic approach about a better year coming up, when Bunker dropped his stink bomb.

"Mr. Chairman, for many years my family has taken no active part in the management of Opulant & Company, even though we have owned close to half the outstanding stock. My father sat on your Board of Directors as long as he was able and he seemed satisfied with your profit picture and your management. I greatly appreciate the resolution you have passed noting his death, but I do not appreciate the way this company is managed," said Bunker, pausing for a moment.

All eyes went to the chair, where Grandin Opulant flushed visibly for the first time I can ever remember. Nobody had publicly criticized Opulant and Queems since their lumber competitor left Jeffersonville.

Bunker continued, "It occurs to me that one of the reasons for an inadequate profit is that one or more of the executives of Opulant & Company are drawing excessive salaries and expenses. Will you give the stockholders of this company the total and breakdown of the salaries and expenses of the officers of the company?"

Sharster Queems, Treasurer of Opulant & Company, rose to his feet. He had a pleasant smile on his face.

"Mr. Bunker," he began slowly, "we greatly appreciate your attending our stockholders' meeting. The wisdom of your father has been carried to his son. We hope and expect that the stockholders will recognize this when the time comes for the election of a Board of Directors.

"In answer to your question with reference to salaries and expenses, I regret that I do not have these figures at hand. Even if I did, it would be in violation of the instructions of the Board of Directors of Opulant & Company for me to make them public at this meeting. Let me ask for your patience in this matter, Mr. Bunker, and I believe you will be reassured that the officials of this corporation are reimbursed in a most moderate way for the services they render you and all other stockholders."

This statement was intended to leave the impression that an

uninformed boy had made a fool of himself before older and wiser heads. I wasn't sure that the minority stockholders were convinced.

At 11:15 A.M., Robert Huey moved that the present Board of Directors of Opulant & Company be re-elected with the exception of Horatio Bunker, Sr., and that he be replaced by Horatio Bunker, Jr. A second to Huey's motion came forth promptly, and President Grandin Opulant asked slowly and carefully for further nominations. There was clear warning in his voice that there should be no further nominations.

Horatio Bunker rose and the stockholders waited as if the voice of prophecy were ready for a pronouncement. As for me, I wished terribly that I were home under the bed, or better yet, in Florida fishing for marlin twenty miles offshore.

Bunker read clearly and loudly the names of ten men and one woman. It was a sure bet the lone woman would never again serve as Register of Deeds for Jefferson County. Another name was that of the plant manager. He was gambling everything. Only the Secretary of Opulant & Company was on both slates for Board of Directors. The name of William Anchor came last and I wished it had never been uttered.

Grandin Opulant turned towards me. His words were not said aloud, but "You son-of-a-bitch" was clearly on his lips.

The vote was close, but when it was over, Grandin Opulant, Sharster Queems, and three yes-men walked from the room without bothering to adjourn the meeting.

3

THEY
    say that dogs love people and cats love places. I have always thought of myself as a lover of my fellow-man, and looking back on my life I can't say that I've ever hated anybody very long. That doesn't mean I haven't insulted 'em, slandered 'em, and occasionally fought with 'em. More often than not it was a political row and after the affray was over we were still on good terms.

    Now it's different. There are not many of my contemporaries left and those few are hanging on by the rear teat. It's hard for me to get close to anybody under sixty years of age. They call you "mister" and "sir" and wouldn't think of threatening you with physical violence.

    I like people all right, but I've gotten to love a place, and that place is Jefferson County. It contains most of the memories of my life, and for an old man or woman, memories are life. Oh, I'm not dead yet, and I'm still in political affrays. I still detest my neighbor. I still perk up at the sight of a pretty shape. Yet most of the time I think about the things that happened long ago, and most of them happened right close to Jeffersonville.

A brief sojourn at Tarvania University is hazy in my memory. It's like some of the national conventions I've gone to, when too much alcohol and too little sleep left only the recollection of a wonderful time. It was about the same way when I went to France in World War I. Glorious and terrible, but hard to remember. The rest of my life has been spent in Tarvania, mostly in Jefferson County, and most of that in Jeffersonville. Everything that I've known is related to this little town, and when my time comes, I want to be buried along with Emmy Lou and my old friends at the Forest Grove Cemetery.

Back in McKinley's time, Jeffersonville was about half its present size, and in those days a town of five thousand was a big city. We had the tannery and the sawmill, and most of all we had the railroad. Before they took the curves out of the Southeastern tracks, extra engines were put on in Jeffersonville for the heavy pull over the mountains westward. I guess my first hero was old Bluechin Ball, who was engineer on "No. 11." Who can ever forget the sound and sight of the great black machines as they chugged in and out of Jeffersonville?

Things were much the same through the administrations of Teddy Roosevelt and Taft. The town's streets gradually got paved as automobiles made their appearance. Sidewalks got new wooden slats; the Jeffersonville *Democratic Bugle* became a semiweekly instead of a weekly, and circulation reached two thousand. A lot of the kids in the county were now going to public schools.

Even the World War didn't change things much. There were more cars, Wilson died, and electric lights got pretty common in town. Governor Torrence started the great highway program that was to link every county seat with a paved road. Even the hosiery mill didn't change things much. Most people still farmed for a living.

Although we had a few telephones, and radio started coming in during Coolidge's time, there was little contact with the outside world. Even the great depression of the Hoover administration didn't affect us much. Only a few people owned stocks, and everybody else could live pretty well off the land.

Franklin D. pretty near tore the state apart with the minimum wage of 40 cents an hour, but after the storm broke and things settled down everybody was about the same as before, except maybe the niggers were making a little more money here and there, and some of 'em began to vote.

Things really began to change in World War II. A lot of our boys went off and a lot of 'em had settled in other places when it was all over. It was the same way with the girls. Jeffersonville girls are spread all over the country now. In their place came newcomers, some from the North and others just moving around the South looking for better opportunities. By the time Truman was elected, television had hit Jeffersonville, and we became part of the world.

By 1952, I was getting towards the end of the prime of life. Emmy Lou got sick and the Republicans elected Eisenhower to the White House. New ways and new ideas were becoming harder for me to accept. I think it was better for everyone when we were a provincial little town that lived in itself and leaving it was never seriously considered by anybody.

Despite the waste of human resources, which the world had never known on so vast a scale, the doughboys of World War I never quite lost the crusading spirit. It took a lot of zeal to be enthusiastic about a conflict that consisted mostly of waiting or walking, punctuated by bad food and lice-infested bedding.

From the beginning, those responsible for the management of the United States Expeditionary Forces appeared to be idiots. I was assigned to Field Artillery, and they attempted to teach us the art of gunnery with field pieces that should have been discarded at the end of the War Between the States. Even if the azimuth and elevation scales had been accurate, no amount of ballistic skill could produce accuracy with the muzzle-loaders with which we trained. When we reached France we were given French 75's, and no man who had ever held a rifle could fail to love those perfect field pieces.

Elementary school and one year of college soon caused me to advance to top-sergeant. My French was limited to little more than "comment allez-vous," but I had a considerable advantage over my fellows in understanding the instructions of the French officers who taught us to use the 75-millimeter field guns.

My influence in the Company extended far beyond rank in that I was greatly sought after as a companion in sorties into the villages. A slight working knowledge of French was of great value in dealing with the maidens of the provinces and those who dealt in alcoholic beverages. I was not ashamed of my nickname, Le Bon Vivant.

France was mostly mud until the action in the Champagne Sector, noted for its chalk soil and expanse of red blood poppies. It was July, 1918, and I was one of those who made up the Rainbow Division. Our battery was placed maybe four hundred metres from the most forward German trenches. Our trenches were in between. Our orders were to make shambles, softening the enemy for the zero hour when our men would go over the top.

The Lieutenant in command of the battery was a grass-green West Pointer. I never learned whether he was fanatically patriotic or determined to be the first General of his class. It's hard to believe that an officer could be a martinet in the field, but the Lieutenant had us saluting and cleaning up as if we were back on the parade grounds of Fort Sill, Oklahoma. In spite of this, he was a good officer and one whom we respected. For example, he made us dig gun pits deep enough so that only a direct hit in the battery would hurt anybody. He made us put enough drainage around the shelters so that we were about the only men near the front lines who weren't soaking wet throughout the battle. As I look back at it now, he was the man who made me a hero in Jeffersonville.

About 4:00 A.M., the barrage began. The long guns in the rear were the basses of the discordant symphony. Howitzers closely behind us joined the long guns. Machine guns and rifles occasionally punctuated the clamor to our front. The Germans seemed to be in strength equal to ours, and their guns, though more distant, seemed to respond in ever-increasing frequency.

Our pieces were fired almost simultaneously. A French 75 may not be a great big cannon but it sure can make a helluva racket. The fast-acting breechblock could throw shells in fast enough to melt the barrel, and that's what the Lieutenant told us to do.

There may have been some science to our frequent changes in range, although I'll never know how observation could be made with everything going off at once. It was apparent the Germans were doing the same thing, because their guns were closing in on us. We got used to the whine of shells going over-head, but no gunner will ever get used to an explosion within a hundred feet. A man can get on his face real fast when hot shrapnel is seeking his scalp.

A few of the men had been hit, but we were all alive when the big one found us. Half of the battery was killed outright and another fourth was so badly wounded as to be as good as dead. I was one of the lucky ones—merely had a couple of teeth knocked out by the right wheel of my 75, which took most of the force of the explosion.

The Lieutenant had been knocked out of his perch in a tree and was moving around trying to help those who were worth helping.

The medical boys were nearby and they quickly moved out the seriously wounded. Those who were just bleeding a little and cursing a lot, like myself, had to stay. A man had to be gushing blood for the Lieutenant to send him to the rear.

We hadn't finished tossing the dead into a crater before the Lieutenant had the one remaining gun in action. I was glad, because the action and explosion of the gun were a lot better than listening to the moaning of our men.

If the ammunition had lasted, I guess we'd have fired that damn gun till Armistice Day. But our lines broke up front. The Germans came directly into our guns and threw themselves into the gun pit. With an indeterminate front line, we were catching bullets from ally and enemy alike.

"Fix bayonets and prepare for attack," shouted the Lieutenant. Those West Point boys might not have known much, but what they did know, they knew awfully well.

The Heinies were upon us in seconds. I got mine from a bayonet. It hit a rib so I wasn't quite dead. I sure as hell thought I was dying. I wouldn't be the only one. The Germans were methodically slaughtering everybody in the gun pit, not even sparing the hopelessly wounded. Being under the French 75 meant only a temporary haven.

Folks back home thought the war was being fought by airplanes, balloons, and tanks. At the front it was being fought by man and mule. If a squad of British infantry hadn't arrived, there wouldn't have been a man left of our battery. The British were using sabres just like Alexander used against Darius and they worked right well against the German bayonets.

Less than half a dozen Germans were left standing when

their remaining officer surrendered. I doubt if it ever went down in any record book and it's too late to make any difference now, but when the German leader was three feet from our Lieutenant, he died. The Lieutenant's fury over the killing of his wounded men caused him to shoot the Hun as you would a mad dog. I heard that our Lieutenant was killed later at the front. I expect he was glad it happened.

After three weeks in the hospital, I was ambulatory and stood with a hundred others to be honored by Black Jack himself. General Pershing didn't pin on each medal, but he said a few words that sure classified us all as heroes.

Back in Jeffersonville things were pretty much as I remembered them except that I felt a proprietary interest I had not known before. This was the place and these were the people I had fought for. The little honors accorded the returning warriors were received with gratitude, and I never felt they were inappropriate. Even after the failure of Wilson at Versailles and after it became obvious that nations were arming themselves once more, I always felt I'd done the right thing and a little more than my share. I suppose I'm just an old-fashioned flag waver, but I'd have gone to war again in 1942 if the artillery could have used me.

The war caused something else to be important—that was an awareness that our politicians dictate much of the course of our country. At first I didn't particularly enjoy fooling with elections, but I felt it a duty that should not be put aside. It wasn't long before I knew that I would never be a man elected to any worth-while post in my own right, so I got to being more of an unpaid campaign manager for one candidate, then another, who had a chance of going someplace.

After a few years it got to be a habit and I was always involved with a faction during the primaries and then hell bent to beat the Republicans in the general election. They think they had it rough during the Roosevelt days, but it wasn't any better for us when Harding, Coolidge, and Hoover were taking the country no matter what they did in office.

One reason I never got too far was that I wouldn't join one faction of the Democratic Party and stick with it for successive elections. When I thought the other crowd had a better man, I would switch. I can say with honesty that I never saw the day when the Republicans had the best man.

Over the years I was often against Opulant and Queems, the exceptions being when they split among themselves. This was when the outcome was seriously in doubt. It may seem impossible, but it happened many a time that Democrats would be fighting each other with everything they had during a primary and then be bosom buddies for the general election. It's kinda like being in a rough family row when a common enemy, like the sheriff, arrives. We Democrats come together like a closely-knit family when the Republicans are at the door.

If you want to be successful in climbing the political ladder, you not only have to stick with your Party but you also have to work with the same crowd within the Party. This I wouldn't do, maybe out of plain orneriness, or maybe because I thought I ought to be helping the best man we had. Had I had more sense I might have wound up as a member of the Council of State or in some other high-paying spot that requires very little effort beyond campaigning a little every four years.

They tell the story of Andrew Jackson being harassed on his deathbed by his preacher to ask forgiveness for any misdeeds he might have committed during his political lifetime. Andy Jackson wasn't the apologetic kind, but after enough prodding by the preacher he sat up and said, "Yes, preacher, if I had it to do over again I'd have shot John Calhoun."

If I had it to do over again I'd have stolen enough votes to have carried Tarvania for Al Smith in 1928. That was the only time I ever failed the Democratic Party.

When I was a boy there were no such things as juvenile delinquents in Jeffersonville. A father wouldn't think thrice about thrashing his son for getting out of line, and a mother could take him in hand if the old man wasn't available. Oh, we had our share of adult crime, but not much from boys living under their family roof. We didn't have cars, and liquor wasn't convenient either, so maybe we didn't have the opportunity to get into much trouble.

But today, I guess, it's different. We sometimes have almost balmy nights in the middle of winter. It was warm enough for Mrs. Coggins to sit on her screened-in porch, which is how I got my information.

Bunker was visiting Betty Ray Cline when the incident took place. Three young hoodlums had parked their souped-up Chevrolet next to Bunker's Bentley. They were sort of pawing over the fancy car when Horatio came out of the Cline house, sleepy looking and doubtlessly fatigued. Mrs. Coggins is keen of ear as well as of eye.

"Hey, big boy, have a good time tonight?" Mrs. Coggins quoted one of the boys. He was the Creed kid, which is a pretty good family.

Bunker responded with a grunt and a glare and started to open the door. Young Creed leaned against it, preventing it from opening.

"Thought you might take us for a spin. We can open her up on the by-pass. No patrol out this late," said Creed. The other two boys jumped into the back seat of the Bentley.

"Gentlemen, remove yourselves from my vehicle immediately," said Bunker in slow cadence, loud enough for Mrs. Coggins to hear.

The boys started to get out, but Creed was the leader and, with a few beers in him, he had to continue the fool. "Beanpole, you don't look as if you could do much about it."

With that Bunker went to the rear of the Bentley, opened the trunk, and pulled out the lug wrench. He was beginning to swing it at the boys when they scrambled to get out of the car. Creed wasn't much of a sportsman either. He picked up a brick from those serving as a sidewalk border.

It must have been quite a fracas, a joy to behold, and one that I shall forever regret having missed. There was no police report, but all four of them turned up at Memorial Hospital for sprains, lacerations, and one broken wrist. Each claimed to have fallen on the ice. There wasn't any ice that night, and no such luck as Bunker busting his long, straight nose.

The boys reported for school the next day, which was not too usual under the best of conditions. They stuck to their story that they had fallen on the ice, despite Mrs. Coggins having disseminated the true version. Nobody could guess how Bunker made them turn up at school and keep their silence.

It taught me something else about the man. He might not fight clean, but he sure as hell would fight. I decided not to insult him thenceforth, unless I could call for nearby assistance. I wouldn't put it beyond him to beat a pitiful old man to a pulp.

World War I was important beyond my conceit in being a hero and having a great adventure. Let nobody think that war isn't fun, provided you didn't get maimed, or gassed, or saddled with a permanent malady. That's one of the reasons every generation is ready to go. They know not war's devastation but only the challenge of strange lands and great deeds.

Things are different now because personal conflict is disappearing and individual courage is less and less an asset. I guess my war was about the last when the majority of combatants were actually in the fray, when you saw the whites of their eyes, and when a butchering Hun was really alive and ready to butcher.

War as Bunker knew it in Korea may have had some of the old-time hand-to-hand combat and there may be brush wars to come that try the physical strength and personal courage of men to their limit, but it appears destined to be different.

I remember how we hated the butchers of Belgium and how our GI's hated the Nazis and their crimes of Jewish extermination. Everybody recalls how our Marines hated the dirty yellow Japs and their brutality after Corregidor. But how can we hate people working in factories, or causing mass death by the selection of electronic switches for long-range destruction?

Maybe the hate wasn't good, yet every American soldier felt it personally. Somehow the hate became devotion to country that can not be duplicated by propaganda skill. In World War I we knew we were making the world safe for democracy. The boys in the second world war believed that dictatorships would be ended by their sacrifices. When the Korean action came, the desire to fight evil was less compelling. Americans used to volunteer; now they had to be drafted. They used to die before surrendering. In Korea too many sold out to the enemy rather than face the hardships known to unfaltering prisoners of war.

Such thoughts are characteristic of an old man. Possibly the good old days never really happened and the young American male is still as ready as ever to go to the defense of country and ideals.

Regardless of his all-too-numerous faults, there is one characteristic of Bunker that I shared. It is his outspoken devotion to his country.

While I am not overly sympathetic with the flag-wavers of the American Legion, the Veterans of Foreign Wars, and the Disabled American Veterans, I like a man who is outspoken in his loyalty to the country which has provided him natural wealth and unlimited opportunity. Bunker had no sympathy with those who regarded their American citizenship lightly. He felt, and I feel with him, that when war comes it is the privilege of every young American to join in combat. Bunker and a lot of other smart alecks could well be removed from peaceful civilized society, but we sure are lucky to have 'em when our country is in hot water.

It really isn't the draft-dodgers and the sore-backed, flat-footed jellyfish who worry me. It's smart young people like Susan Ponticorn. A lot of them really believe that good works, the love of fellow man, and tolerance of the wrong-doing foreign powers can provide peace. I don't object to their being Christian in attitude; I just hate to see 'em try to carry it into practical application in our international dealings. It wouldn't be so bad if it were just the young women who had these crazy notions. They've had 'em ever since I can remember, but now we find a lot of our best-informed young men thinking the same way. When the majority of Americans capitulate intellectually in preference to taking their chances in an all-out war, we are finished as a nation.

It's old saw to talk about walking five miles to school, but it damn well makes me sick to hear today's parents demanding that school buses stop within a quarter of a mile of their homes. It is also revolting to see a healthy young man of sixteen immediately become incapable of getting himself from one place to another without a personal automobile. President Eisenhower had his faults, mostly being a Republican, but he hit it on the head when he said that American youngsters are becoming weak and soft. I suppose they say that Ike is just another old man, outdated and way out of touch with modern youth. If Emmy Lou and I had had any youngsters you can bet that they wouldn't have been raised to be rowdy softies.

I never think of Emmy Lou without recalling how she got me right after the War. Going to war had been a lot of fun, but getting back from it was even more fun. Being slightly wounded and a hero, and being back home before the rest of the boys, really put me in an advantageous spot as far as courting the girls of Jefferson County was concerned. In those days when she was only twenty-one a woman was pretty well written off as a spinster, and there sure were a lot of girls in their late, late teens. I really took advantage of my opportunities.

I had known the White family all my life and I guess I'd been aware of Emmy Lou when she was a little girl. It hadn't meant anything to me any more than knowing the name of the schoolmaster's horse, but when I got back from France Emmy Lou took me over before I knew what had hit me. She wasn't the prettiest girl in the world and I guess she didn't have the very best figure. My old man always said, "Marry a broad-bottomed girl who can cook, and you'll be happy, son." Emmy Lou fitted those requirements.

The most objectionable thing about her was that she was from a damn Republican family. Being a Republican in Jefferson County is kind of a hereditary disease with some families. There's no rhyme or reason why they should be Republicans. They just vote that way year in and year out for pure damn meanness. Of course I felt it would be a relatively simple matter to convert Emmy Lou over to the Democratic Party. I don't think I ever succeeded, although I worked on it for a lifetime. Not only did she vote her father's politics, but she evidenced the same stubborn streak that would cause him to argue for hours about the virtue of Republicans and the evil of Democrats and how they were someday gonna beat the hell out of every Democrat in Tarvania. Emmy Lou was the same way. She might have been short on logical reasons for being a Republican, but she sure didn't give an inch when it came to being one.

The most unpleasant thing in our premarital days was the fact that Warren G. Harding really swamped James M. Cox in the 1920 elections.

Another big factor entered into our courtship, and that was the persistence of Frank Alsobee. He was a war veteran, and even though he did nothing but shoe mules, he could make his experiences sound like he personally won the war. I might add that I could make it pretty clear that it was my work that saved thousands of Americans at Champagne. I had a medal to prove my heroism; Alsobee was pretty heavy on conversation and had awfully strong forearms. I learned very early in life never to push a blacksmith too far.

Religion never entered into our contest for the hand of Emmy Lou, but Frank sure could come to the aid of black Republicans when we got on politics. Of course, Emmy Lou was always on his side politically, and I felt for a long while that I never would get anywhere beyond holding hands and swinging on the double-seater that old man White had on his front porch.

What finally gave me some advantage, other than my personal charm, was that I got a hankering to be better educated. Both my brothers had done well in school. One was about ready to go into medicine in Mecklenton and the other was already trading profitably in tobacco in Moravaton. You know, a man can love his brothers, yet downright dislike them. I guess that's the way it was with me, because it made me green with envy that they were doing so well and I was nothing more than a general clerk at Webb & Sons. I took to studying and went at it like Abraham Lincoln except that maybe I didn't know where I was trying to go, other than to be as learned as my brothers. Guess maybe I had my eye on being a big-time politician back then because I got to know about as much of the law as the boys from the University. Nobody does it any more today, but back then most lawyers got their education by working for an experienced lawyer. I was all set up to go with old Counselor Kornegay when Emmy Lou agreed to marry me.

With more and more houses in town, and more people working at the plants, the ice and coal business looked like a coming thing. Iceboxes were getting common and we had no local deliveries. Convenient timber was about gone, and the lumber company was making a mighty poor job of giving service on its coal. Maybe my idea wasn't exactly original, but when a man starts a family he also starts a need for some steady cash.

I suppose I threw some dreams out the window when the Anchor Ice and Coal Company came into being. I knew even back then in the early twenties that when I gave up studying law I probably gave up a chance of ever being governor of Tarvania.

Looking back across nearly forty years I think I made the right choice. I doubt if I ever would have been smart enough to make the Governor's Mansion, although I've seen some of 'em come and go who were damn sight poorer men.

4

MOST

of my adult life has included the daily reading of Ham Fisher's comic strip, "Mutt and Jeff." Certainly in appearance Opulant and Queems are those timeless comic characters. Contrasted to Opulant's tall, stately figure is that of Sharster Queems. Back in the days when he could barely afford a square meal he earned the nickname of "Pearshape," and that describes him about as well as it can be done. With all his accumulation of wealth, Sharster Queems never ventures outside of Jeffersonville to buy a suit of clothing. Cohen's Ready-to-Wear can be made to fit most anybody, and while I have no figure of a sixteen-year-old football player, Cohen's manages to make me look presentable.

Not so with Queems, for no amount of altering can make a man's standard suit fit a shape like a big ripe pear. It takes a lot of fabric just to cover his oversize hips, and somehow the pants can never be gathered below that point to resemble anything but an empty potato sack. Sharster believes in a vest, except for the summertime, likely because it comes with little additional price. No amount of Cohen's skill can make the bottom of the vest and the top of Queems's pants get closer than two inches from each other. Covering that unsuited band of circumference is a shirt of questionable cleanliness more or less tucked into the trousers.

Other sartorial obstacles are revealed at his neckline, where no collar seems quite able to reach around Sharster's well-padded neck. As if to emphasize the unkempt attire, the collar tips always point upwards and outwards like a bird in flight. Three or four overly bright and multihued neckties are his only variations in wardrobe.

To further Queems's appearance of being more wide than tall, he uses all pockets as portable filing cabinets. These are none too tidy, as they also contain stubs of pencils and other items such as glasses, a pocketknife, a large assortment of keys, and a tape measure for checking real estate and property lines.

In the best caricature of short, fat men, Sharster Queems is mostly bald. His face usually contains the punctuation mark of a brown cigar, which more often than not is unlighted. As Sharster had emerged from his rural environment, society had more or less forced him to give up chewing tobacco, so he had taken up cigars. Actually, he doesn't smoke them. He merely chews them, working his way by chewing towards the end that would normally burn. While not otherwise noticeably fastidious, Sharster never spits. When you chew a wad of tobacco you damn near have to spit. When Sharster had been convinced that he could no longer chew tobacco in public, he had also been convinced that he could no longer spit. Where the juice goes I suppose I'll never know, and if he's man enough to swallow the stuff he should go down in medical history as one of a kind.

Queems's ears are prominent, his nose globular, his skin somewhat splotchy. These things you rarely notice because of his twinkling blue eyes, mounted in reddened and well-watered sockets, yet quick and keen of movement. They are jolly eyes like those we associate with old Santa Claus himself, whom Queems regularly portrays at Christmastime.

How deceptive those eyes can be. The old bastard can tell the blackest lies with nothing but innocence and purity. When he's about to close an important deal, his eyes get a vacant look as if he's confused and out of his depth and should immediately back out of the proposition. What they really indicate is that he's ready for you to take the hook. When he's about to "con" you into something, those blue eyes of Queems take on the roguish look of a fellow-conspirator. When the eyeball liquid nearly brims over, Sharster Queems is about ready to tell some aging widow that he must foreclose on her family home.

Most of my description is told from envy. If the whole truth is ever known, Sharster Queems will probably have done more good than harm across a life of nearly sixty years. He certainly made whatever he has the hard way. His mother was deserted with a brood long before state welfare was concerned with such matters. He was out wooding for the tannery by the time he was twelve years old. His formal education had been scant prior to then, when it stopped completely.

Sharster and I shared one thing in common; we were going to learn as much as we could out of books. Of course I had the advantages of a good preparatory education and year of college, which possibly made me make the effort to learn something besides the intricacies of a balance sheet. Anyway, Queems learned what he did learn thoroughly and was well on his way to becoming a successful businessman when he and Opulant formed their enduring partnership.

What a partnership it has been. Opulant does the speaking

for the two and always makes the first contact with new out-of-town business prospects. Queems calls the shots, does the thinking, and then takes just slightly more than half for his share of the proceeds.

The partners are together at least five times a day under normal working conditions, and their wives are pretty good friends. In Jeffersonville, the social position of wives is somewhat regulated by financial status. The only time the partnership suffers is when Grandin Opulant is obliged to invite Sharster for an annual week end at Vanderbilt Hills. Even though Sharster Queems makes a serious attempt at tidiness by buying his annual new suit for the occasion, his efforts are unsuccessful and cause Grandin Opulant to go through a humiliating two and one-half days with all his friends from Mecklenton and assorted Yankee cities. Sharster Queems doesn't give a damn about high society or the houses and gadgets of good living, but he likes to be on a first-name familiarity with people who count in the business world. That means that Opulant has to invite all his prominent friends to two nights of cocktail parties, one with formal dinner.

Despite the sacrifices, the partnership is well worth it to both parties. It has endured for more than thirty years, and I am sure that when I am long since gone it will be flourishing until the day one of them finally dies. I privately doubt that Opulant and Queems will ever die.

Who is Mr. Jeffersonville? Who was the first Man of the Year for Jefferson County? Who has served four terms as Mayor of Jeffersonville? Who twice has headed the Chamber of Commerce? Who has been Chairman of every fund-raising drive from the Tarvania Symphony to the Yatawba Valley Orphans' Aid Society?

Grandin Opulant, former President of Opulant & Company, is also a Bank Director, Director of Jeffersonville Lumber, and a member of the County Board of Education. The son-of-a-bitch has been President of the Golf Club, the Elks Club, the Moose Lodge, the American Legion, the Industrial Research Commission, the Art Institute, the Rotary Club, and the Society for the Prevention of Cruelty to Animals.

He also owns a summer home in Vanderbilt Hills, which is a mountain resort and available to only a few Tarvanians and a very few rich Yankees. Part of the act includes a diamond-studded, fur-bedecked wife and an annually-replaced, long, heavily-chromed Cadillac.

All this costs money, which makes Grandin Opulant an ideal partner for Sharster Queems, who is concerned with making money for its own sake, rather than for that which it will buy. If I sound critical of Grandin Opulant it is because I am envious, except in one respect.

He is not an evil man, nor one desiring all things for himself. He has formed a pattern of what he believes to be Southern aristocracy, and to this pattern he is a slave, doing more in the world by his devotion to his ideal than would have been possible had he been satisfied with mediocrity.

Grandin Opulant looks his part as well as acting it. He reads *Fortune* magazine, more to emulate the clothing than the management skill of the industrial giants featured therein. Fine pin-striped suits, elongating a tall, dignified figure, are a part of his personality. His head is classic with a mantle of grey hair, adequately flecked with the dark mane of his youth. A complementary moustache completes the façade and hides a mouth that is not strong.

"To the manor born" would be appropriate of Grandin

Opulant, for in truth his family was important in Jefferson County when the Cherokee were making raids in Tarvania. Courtly in manner, slow to anger, and of sound opinion is this man whom I detest.

Though I've said it's mostly envy, I still say I detest Grandin Opulant. I would rather live and die as Bill Anchor. I couldn't pay the price he pays, for it is too great for the reward. Never can he make a decision without calculation. All things must be immediately or ultimately profitable.

Thus has Grandin Opulant become the partner and confederate of Sharster Queems. One needs a brain of dependable fiscal avarice. The other needs a front, an always acceptable personality by which acts of avarice may be concealed in a vehicle of highest respectability.

Who is slave to whom? Is Grandin Opulant the chattel of Sharster Queems, who creates the schemes of gain without which the life of Opulant would be ordinary and pinchpenny? Or is Queems the slave of Opulant, plotting and working so that his partner enjoys the glory while he accumulates only wealth that serves him little on earth and can serve him not at all in hell?

Possibly people such as I are the true victims. We envy and dare not defy them. We fall in step with their plans, we reap small compensations for conspiring with them, and we remain subservient to them all our lives.

Such is the leading citizen of Jeffersonville, and to him I pledged my fealty until Horatio Bunker came to look more aristocratic, own a bigger house and better car, and challenge the citadel of political and economic wealth personified by Grandin Opulant, Mayor of Jeffersonville.

Two months had passed since the momentous stockholders'

meeting of Opulant & Company. Horatio Bunker had been installed as President of the Company and had assumed active and undisputed management.

Meanwhile, I was paying the price of a double-crosser. Opulant and Queems met at the Jeffersonville Grill as always, and they spoke to me as always, but it wasn't with the hearty "Here comes Old Bill" any more. The talk around the big table wasn't free and easy the way it used to be. I was among the first to leave, and I knew that I would never again be in the inner circle.

Exclusion wouldn't bother a lot of people, but it represented a great deal to me. When you are seventy years old the associations of a lifetime are important. New friends don't come readily.

I hadn't seen much of Horatio Bunker since our new directors had elected him President. I didn't want to be around the leader of the conspiracy.

Apparently Bunker had no family. A heavy-set man named Marcus, of about fifty years, seemed to be his only close personal contact. We first saw this person when he drove into Jeffersonville in Bunker's expensive English-made sedan. The combination was another detail that made Bunker just a little more objectionable.

People in Jeffersonville also own automobiles and there are a few high-priced new ones in "Residential A." Grandin Opulant's son has a little foreign sports car, but nobody has ever had anything like that leather and wood and high-polished Bentley belonging to Bunker.

People in Jeffersonville also have servants, and some of the old families have several darkies working around the place. But nobody, except this Bunker, ever thought of having a uniformed white man in constant attendance. He was swarthy, silent, and observant. He looked like an older version of the Secret Service men who are always around the President of the United States. A character like Bunker probably needed a full-time bodyguard.

At Opulant & Company the cold-blooded tactics of the new President were paying off. Bunker's new machines, new methods, and new personnel had caused a great deal of unhappiness among employees, as do most slashing changes. Men and women who had been on the payroll for years and could not adapt to the changes were being dismissed without mercy. Other employees were resentful of the fast pace demanded by management. Opulant & Company was ripe for unionization.

The AFL-CIO has made little ground in the South compared with the rest of the nation, but its most fertile field has been in textiles. It is always trying to organize workers in Tarvania. The unions haven't been notably successful. One reason is that most of our plants are relatively small, and workers have ready access to the owners. Differences can be ironed out without resorting to high-pressure union tactics. Local management tends to be easygoing and tolerant of employees' problems. Indeed, they are often blood relations.

Another obstacle to unionism is the independent nature of the worker himself. He feels he can tell the boss to go to hell without outside assistance. He more often than not owns a little land, which gives him a security not found in northern cities. And he can always resort to making liquor or cutting pulpwood. Mountain folks just don't take kindly to being regimented, and neither do the rest of us Tarvanians.

Bunker's changes at Opulant & Company were enough to create a lot of interest in worker protection, and the union organizers were ready to fill the need. It wasn't long before they had enough names on a petition to call an election. Bunker was not surprised.

By this time restrictions upon management imposed by the Wagner Act had been mitigated by the Taft-Hartley Act. Bunker called the entire plant personnel together about a week before the decision on unionization was to be made.

Effer Vestal quoted Bunker's entire statement in the Jeffersonville *Democratic Bugle*:

"An election is facing the men and women employed by Opulant & Company. The union organizers have promised an average wage of $1.40 against your present wage of $1.26. They have promised you augmented group health and accident insurance, and pension benefits which will amount to another nine cents per hour above direct labor costs. These things you naturally would like to have, and if I were a decent sort of fellow I would give them to you without your having to pay union dues.

"For the immediate future I have no intention of complying with your wishes without being forced to do so by a union. That would likely involve a strike in which management would ultimately be forced to yield. You would get your wage increases and the promises of the union organizers would be fulfilled.

"In addition, they have promised job protection by seniority, which I understand would be retroactive and would apply to those employees we have recently laid off. Indeed, I understand that those dismissed employees are actively supporting the union organizers. We shall assume that all the promises of the organizers will be fulfilled. I must join with you in support of having a union and I will tell you why.

"I am pretty tired of struggling with Opulant & Company already. I take little joy in telling loyal employees their services are no longer wanted. The often expressed dissatisfaction of our stockholders concerning profits is boring at best. I don't like having to put up with your disgruntled acceptance of the numerous changes I have felt necessary. Unaccustomed as I am to working, the thought of spending twelve to fifteen hours a day struggling with the problems of Opulant & Company is onerous to me and I shall be glad to see them end. Even greater problems lie ahead now that we are starting to show a profit. I shall have a hard time keeping the profit-sharing plan in effect. I know full well that the Board of Directors will think it high time for it to end so that the owners can realize some substantial benefits.

"Of course I am paid a handsome salary. Based on my hours of work and the tax situation, my take home pay is twice yours on the average, and I could improve this by having a family. Unfortunately, I haven't had time to hunt for a partner for this purpose. Under present working conditions I doubt if I could keep a wife.

"You can see that the coming of the union would be of great benefit to me, as well as to you. It would permit me to leave Jeffersonville for the Riviera, which is beautiful this time of year. I can visualize a sun-soaked piazza overlooking the Mediterranean at this moment.

"My departure might not be graceful, but it would be with good reason, for the union would not let me run this Company as I see fit, and that is the only way I can run it so that it will not go broke. My departure will gladden not only your hearts but also people such as Opulant and Queems, who also have your best interests at heart.

"You can see we all agree that the union is the best answer to the needs of Opulant & Company. I urge that you support it in the coming election. Thank you for your kind attention."

Effer Vestal dutifully reported that there was no applause and that nobody took the rostrum to add to Bunker's statement.

I don't suppose you can be sure that the employees thought

of their own future beyond the union promises. Maybe they saw a chance to make Bunker miserable. Whatever the reason, the union was soundly beaten and Opulant & Company continued to operate as usual. The employees continued to be sullen, but not quite mutinous.

5

HORATIO BUNKER,
from the first time I had met him, showed a surprising knowledge of Jeffersonville. He had a speaking familiarity with leading citizens and he even knew something of the history of Jefferson County. Most of his information would not have been recorded anywhere, so I was curious as to how he became so well informed.

The secret of his information sort of slipped out when we were talking about the by-pass highway extending past Opulant & Company. I was telling Bunker that the only way it could be accomplished was through the Highway Commissioner, and he in turn would be highly influenced by Sharster Queems.

"But Miss Ponticorn told me that her father could do a great deal towards getting this highway properly located?" queried Bunker.

So Horatio Bunker knew Susan Ponticorn. This was a surprising tidbit, and I immediately pressed unrelentingly for the full details. Bunker told me that he had been seated in an adjoining space to Miss Ponticorn when flying South from Washington. He readily admitted that he had struck up a conversation with the pretty girl and had learned quite a bit about Jeffersonville.

"Of course I told her that I was from Worcester, Massachusetts, and neglected to say that I had just moved to Jeffersonville," chuckled Bunker. "Miss Ponticorn hadn't been home for many months and she had no idea of my existence as a citizen of this fair city. I assumed the pose of a Yankee who had a lot of misconceptions about small Southern towns. I might have overdone the part because she seemed to have the impression that Yankees thought that slavery was still a common practice away from the large Southern cities. I never saw anybody do a finer job of defending her home town, and by the time she was finished I was really convinced that Jeffersonville was about as good a place to live as anywhere on earth," said Bunker.

"It's just your nature to deceive most anybody you encounter," I stated with vehemence. I thought an awful lot of Susan Ponticorn and I just didn't like anybody putting anything over on her. I would assume that Bunker would try to extend his deception further but I was glad to learn that Susan was wary of overly-friendly males.

"When we arrived at the Mecklenton Airport, Marcus was there with the Bentley to bring me on home. Naturally I offered Miss Ponticorn a ride, since otherwise she would have had to take a taxi into town and await a bus. She certainly was suspicious of me at that point, and I finally had to show her the registration card for the Bentley to prove that the vehicle really belonged in Jeffersonville. Then she got awfully curious about my connection with Jeffersonville and I went through a cross-examination such as you haven't heard since Army psychologists were trying to prove that you were insane. I didn't take too well to the questioning and provided as many evasive and misleading answers as possible," said Bunker.

"You sure do stay in character," I said, slightly amused at Bunker's discomfiture during the ride from the airport.

"By the time we arrived in Jeffersonville, Miss Ponticorn had found out that I was a resident and connected with Opulant & Company. She had recalled some comment made by her father in a letter, and I gather that it was not entirely complimentary," said Bunker.

"I'm sure the good Judge did you no injustice," I said with conviction.

"Miss Ponticorn certainly holds very strong opinions. She told me she had heard of me and, while she appreciated the ride home, she trusted that the association with me would be terminated at that point. In fact, we cruised the last five miles without a word being said by anyone. Marcus isn't very talkative at best," concluded Bunker.

Horatio Bunker's lack of tolerance for Southern custom displayed itself even when Jeffersonville was at its best. I was puttering about the yard and enjoying the repetitious creation of nature, aiding it slightly with a load of manure. Some of the flowers were perennials long ago planted by Emmy Lou, blooming again to remind me of pleasant days long past.

"A shabbily run town if I ever saw one," said Bunker, having entrenched himself in my favorite porch rocker. This was without invitation, Bunker having made me his friend and confidant without my being slightly interested in reciprocating.

"What unpleasantness springs from thy craw this day?" I asked.

"Why doesn't anybody run against the Mayor? Grandin Opulant has held the office four consecutive times and, despite his incompetence, gross inefficiency, and nearly criminal conduct, nobody even challenges his re-election," said Bunker.

It's true that our leading citizen is a damn poor mayor. Examples of municipal waste are too numerous to enumerate, but I recall one example that is typical.

Curbing street gutters is not complicated, requiring just enough engineering to drain water. The job is more or less dictated as new streets are opened, or old ones repaired and changed so that even larger automobiles can get around corners. Our guttering would be hilarious, if it weren't so expensive. You see eight men on the job, of which no more than two are in motion. Mass production may be impractical for street curbing, but our methods were antiquated when the Parthenon was built.

Jake Mokaby was supervisor and as such was in charge of the entire operation, so he could not be expected to do any manual labor. Under him were two white foremen, one handling the laying of the steel forms into which the concrete would be poured. This entire part of the operation, including its three niggers, who did the work, was suspended due to an argument with Mrs. Tillard. She was fearful that the excavation had damaged, or might damage, some roots of her prime magnolia tree. Therefore, she wanted the curb to encircle the tree. Jake Mokaby carried on the town engineer's side of the debate while the workers observed.

Meanwhile, the other white foreman was engaged in waiting for the ready-mix concrete truck. He also had a crew of three niggers, not because they were required to spread the concrete, but because he would lose status if he had less than the form-laying crew.

Only old Jeff Davis, who is one of the best niggers in Jeffersonville, was doing any work at all, and that was putting the final rub on half-hardened concrete. He was going at it as if he were patting his coon dog. Soon it would be dinnertime and all work would stop sure enough. I often thought that municipal labor in Jeffersonville might make the subject for a political-sociological-economic study of American decadence.

Horatio Bunker had suffered similar municipal ineptitude in getting extra electric power for the plant. The town somehow wired in inadequate transformers, so that knitting machine motors had irregular voltage causing them to gallop, then crawl. Finally the transformers burned up completely and the plant had to be closed awaiting major electrical repairs.

"Every man and woman in the plant has been fully impressed as to the cause of the lay-off, and I expect Grandin Opulant will have an opponent in the mayoralty race. By the way, who is on the Town Council other than the Mayor?"

"Four good men and true: Jimmy Wells sells shoes throughout Tarvania, so he rarely attends a meeting, although he's pretty good when he's there. Rufus Jones is a good man when he's sober. It is regrettable that he is well satisfied with the town administration so long as the illegal whiskey confiscated by the police chief is turned over to him for safekeeping. Blanden McTatetor is Sharster Queems' son-in-law and his position as Councilman is his only useful occupation. The brother of Jake Mokaby, Director of Gutters and Drains, completes the Council. To put it briefly, Opulant and Queems run the town and one of their chief interests is to see that they own property on streets that the Council decides to pave."

"Doesn't anybody ever try to throw them out?" asked Bunker.

"No. For one reason, hardly anybody wants a job on the town council. There's no pay, which isn't so bad in itself, but anybody elected has to listen to complaints day and night. John Barefoot served one term and damn nigh lost his mind listening to gripes, since he was the only one worth talking to. He tried to put in a town manager and that nearly brought on a revolution. In the end, the old department heads kept their jobs and Barefoot refused to run for re-election," I told him.

"Could try to get a competent mayor at least," grumbled Bunker.

"Nope, nobody could beat Grandin Opulant. He may not be much of a manager, but he hasn't been caught stealing. You have to admit he looks like a Mayor and would probably be elected in a lot bigger city," I added.

"It would seem to me that the people would evidence a little opposition," muttered Bunker.

"They probably would," I said.

During the next few weeks rumor reached me that Bunker was trying to get up an opposition ticket. He succeeded to the extent of getting his office manager to seek a seat on the town council, promising him time off from his regular job to perform this civic duty after election.

There was no doubt that Bunker's man was the best on the ticket, but interest was negligible, with only about ten per cent of the eligible voters bothering to go to the polls. The incumbents wanted to stay in office for one reason or another, and campaigned at least among their relatives. Also, Opulant and others wanted to give Bunker a lesson in humility. A few people were promised curbing and a few more were promised an extended sewer line. The mayor made a speech before the Garden Club implying that the ladies should take the lead and he would provide the funds to beautify Jeffersonville. And, oh yes, he joined with a vice-president from the Southeastern Railway in proclaiming that the ancient depot would be completely remodeled, which meant putting on another coat of yellow paint.

When the votes were counted Bunker's man wound up sixth in a race with five winners.

"The next time around it will be a different story," quoth Horatio Bunker to my great amusement. He added he might head the ticket himself. This caused derisive sounds from all interested. Our people may not vote in town elections much, but they are all interested observers.

This defeat in the town election was galling to Bunker, and he got to seriously talking politics.

"I might as well be a Republican," said Bunker.

"Yeah, ya might as well. Then you'll enjoy the fun of a general election, and you'll have even less chance of being elected," I said.

"Just assuming that I could somehow get nominated as a Democrat, wouldn't it be hard to make any radical changes in the Democratic Party's way of doing things?" asked Bunker seriously.

"In a way you are right, Mr. Bunker. Democratic appointees are pretty well entrenched, and an elected public official has a hard time changing things unless he's repeatedly re-elected and knows the ropes. In a way he owes something to the people working around him because most of them have contributed to the Democratic war chest and insured his election against any Republican challengers. You don't throw your friends out of their employment. As long as they are under state employment, or county employment for that matter, they do the day-to-day work and handle it pretty much as they always have," I said.

"In effect you're saying that we do need a Republican Party in Tarvania—one that can win elections and throw these entrenched employees out in the street," said Bunker.

"No, I've never said any such thing. You forget that I'm pretty well satisfied with the way the Democrats run this state, and I'm not a damn bit anxious to see any Republican make any changes. We'll make the changes within the Democratic Party, though they may be a little slow in coming. You know there has never been any appreciable amount of government scandal in Tarvania, such as you read about in Louisiana and Georgia. We have good clean government, and I think the people want to keep it that way, and that means keeping with the Democratic Party," I said. I felt pretty virtuous.

"Well, admit that it would liven up things if the Republicans made a serious race," said Bunker.

I couldn't deny this. I wasn't thinking about politics at the moment, but about the days of my courtship with Emmy Lou and how that dern Frank Alsobee sure had made me active as a competitive suitor. Maybe Tarvania really does need another political party that can actually threaten Democratic control and keep us on our toes. Many times I'd wanted to get rid of some lazy ne'er-do-well working on the sheriff's payroll but couldn't really push his dismissal because he was a good Democratic worker. I can imagine the fun the Republicans would have putting in their own set of ward-heelers. Of course, we would come back the next election, as we always do, with somebody who could beat the tar out of 'em.

Horatio Bunker didn't say much more. He just sat there leaning back in my favorite chair with his long legs across the porch rail. I wondered if he had such illusions of grandeur as to think that he could someday be elected to any public office. We don't elect Yankee carpetbaggers to represent us in Tarvania.

I began talking about the 1928 Convention, and it was well worth remembering. The Republicans had just nominated Hoover and Curtis; the scandals of the Harding administration were still fresh in the public mind, and silent Cal Coolidge had done little besides be silent. It looked like a good year for us when we boarded the train for Houston, Texas. Three Pullman cars originated in Tarvania loaded with Delegates, alternates, hangers-on, and enough illegal liquor to fire the boilers of the giant locomotive that pulled us westward.

A Delegate is a big man at a National Convention, being one of a handful who selects the President of the United States. Sure, the people vote in the general election, a few states even have presidential primaries, and theoretically nobody is bound by the parties' choices. In practice about a thousand Delegates from each Party get to a hall in some big city and pick somebody to be President. Even then it isn't the choice of the Delegates, but of a few strong men who pretty well control the big states or blocs of smaller states. It seems like a haphazard kind of system, undemocratic at best. Yet the best man usually gets nominated at a Democratic Convention. We have to get somebody good or the damn Republicans will eat us alive in the election.

Anyway, every Delegate is a potentate, and none enjoyed his hour of glory more than I. It was as obvious as the fact that Houston is hot in June that it would be difficult to beat Governor Al Smith of New York. I was one of the hold-outs, knowing that Tammany Hall, legal liquor, and the Roman Catholic Church would be hard to sell in Tarvania.

There are several ways of swinging an obstinate Delegate; each is effective, and sometimes all are used in devastating combinations. Sometimes you can straight-out buy a Delegate, like they do Southern Republicans at their conventions. No Tarvania Democrat gets bought for cash. He's sent to the convention because he's a good man among a lot of good Democrats.

More effective is the promise of federal patronage, and who can resist a Federal Judgeship, or a lush postmastership, or being Assistant to the Secretary of War? I wasn't either fit or interested in much that was offered. Anchor Ice and Coal was prospering and I liked living in Jeffersonville.

When a political mission can not be accomplished by the high road of persuasion, there is another avenue of success. Either I was too fond of Emmy Lou or maybe those Texas women were too damned big, so that method failed. That girl could have thrown a full-grown steer, but damned if she seduced this Southern gentleman.

Only once in my life has liquor been my downfall and then it took a lot of outside encouragement. Every big shot in the Democratic Party personally invited me to his suite, "to get your opinion, Mr. Anchor," they said. What they did was propose a toast from their own private stock. The last drink I remember was in the Arkansas headquarters, where I was saluted by Senator Joseph T. Robinson. I am one of the few who remember he wound up being the Vice-Presidential candidate.

I didn't hear Franklin D. Roosevelt nominate the "Happy Warrior," and I didn't hear the roll call, but I found out later that William Anchor had helped nominate Alfred E. Smith on the first ballot.

"Reminds me of the 1952 Convention in Chicago," said Bunker.

"And what know you of a national convention?" I asked irritably. Not everybody attends the big shows. They are events that set a man somewhat above his fellows. A Republican National Convention may not be much, yet it aggrandizes those of such faith. Bunker minimized the entire system by his casual announcement.

"My father was a Delegate from Massachusetts and managed to get me appointed as an Honorary Sergeant-at-Arms. I was on the floor and saw the whole thing," related Bunker.

"You had quite a fight," I admitted. Taft was the Party's

logical choice and Eisenhower was a political unknown. I remembered the speech of Senator Dirksen. It was right forceful as he pointed to Governor Dewey of New York. "Twice you've led us down the road to defeat. Don't do it to us again," was the way I remember it.

"I learned that great speeches don't nominate the President. I learned that just because you best represent your Party you aren't necessarily its choice. I also learned that a Southern Republican Delegate is not a highly respected animal in the councils of the Party," said Bunker.

Taft should have been nominated, and would have been were it not for five long terms of Roosevelt, Roosevelt, Roosevelt, Roosevelt and Truman, and finally Truman. Ike looked like he could win and the Republicans needed a winner. They were willing to put aside a proven Republican if it took that for victory. Typical political opportunism, I thought, and was glad I was a Democrat.

"My father believed in Robert Taft and wanted to vote for him," continued Bunker. "I can remember one night we were returning from the International Amphitheater."

"Sure does smell around those stockyards," I added.

"Everybody was tired from a long session of speechmaking, procedures, and irrelevant entertainment," said Bunker.

"Before television we just sang a little bit and politicked a lot," I recalled.

"One Ike supporter was a little noisy, feeling was running high, and he got to calling Taft a second-rate Senator," related Bunker. "My old man was tired but he got to his feet and made a five-minute speech about how the Republican Party owed its character and integrity to Bob Taft. Then the Ike man made his rebuttal, which included 'to hell with Ohio and to hell with

Taft.' Father was kind of stuffy but he kicked his fellow Delegate in the butt. The bus lurched at the same time so they both went to the floor."

"Would certainly like to see a Bunker laid flat," I chuckled.

"Turned out that the Delegate was a Boeing executive from San Francisco. Sent dad a gold-plated model airliner after the convention. Responsible people do funny things at conventions," said Bunker.

"We threw firecrackers in the stockyards at Houston. Stampeded half the town and made those damn Texans do something besides brag about Texas," I said.

"Dad wound up voting for Ike, but he nearly broke down. We were at Taft's last meeting before the balloting. Taft knew the vote would be against him, and while he urged that the fight continue, he was really just thanking his friends who had stuck by him."

"So your father voted for Ike," I mused.

"Finally—you know Massachusetts," Bunker rationalized.

"I know Republicans are compromisers," I said, even though it wasn't necessary.

"You old faker," replied Bunker, "you are in bed with Jack Kennedy, those spendthrift Harvard crackpots, and every screwball socialistic scheme ever invented, and you call yourself a Jeffersonian Democrat. Compromise is a mild invective. Political promiscuity is too gentle. Devoid of principle doesn't describe some Democrats," said Bunker heatedly.

"There is a little give and take in politics," I added gently.

"Anyway, Dad's vote didn't defeat Taft," continued Bunker. "It happened in the Credentials Committee when they refused to recognize the Georgia delegation supporting Taft. Money, influence, or something had got into Georgia and an Eisenhower delegation was born, bought, and delivered to Chicago.

The entire operation looked bad and I lost confidence in all Southern Republicans," said Bunker.

"For once, you're right," I added. "Until the Republican Party can clean up its own house in the Southern states, it can hardly expect the support of Southerners at the polls."

"Maybe I shall work towards that end," said Bunker, just as if he too were a Republican.

"No damn Yankee will do it," I said, but I felt bad about calling Bunker's father a compromiser. In politics you're not supposed to hit a man when he's down, much less when he's dead. I then admitted I had read all about the dedication of the Taft Carillon in Washington.

"This memorial to Robert A. Taft, presented by the people to the Congress of the United States, stands as a tribute to the honesty, indomitable courage, and high principles of free government symbolized by his life," I quoted from memory.

6

LATE
summer is hot in Jeffersonville. On one of the hottest
days Bunker came out to the house demanding a mint julep.
It's been said that my skill in the concoction of this potion is
justifiably lauded. Actually all you do is throw some crushed
mint leaves in a glass, a bit of sugar, mull together and fill with
crushed ice. My fame is really based on tall glasses and generous
portions of bourbon therein.

I wasn't pleased to have Bunker consuming Anchor's best,
but he was better than nobody to talk to.

"Mr. Bill, one can not help but admire your skill in concoct-
ing this beverage. It is a masterpiece of individuality, a trait of
yours not evident in other fields," said Bunker.

The bait was offered, but I approached cautiously. "Young,
impertinent man," I said, "if you had fought the Battle of
France, counting on your individual skill for survival; if you
had started a business, made it grow by your individual labor
rather than that of others; if you had controlled the political
future of this County, possibly the state and nation," I became
flamboyant; "if you could look back on a life of individual accomplishment; then, I'd say, the words you utter might have
some authority."

"How then, aged braggart, can you espouse this political party that refutes all that you say?" asked Bunker.

"Your ignorance appalls me, unwhelped youth. While there may be a group in temporary control of the Democratic Party, the core of the Party is here in the South and that core is still Thomas Jefferson. It is merely a matter of time before these Yankee Democrats turn to the Radical Party, which you call Republican."

"I'm really not concerned with Party labels and have little esteem for the Republican Party either," said Bunker haughtily. "What concerns me is the drift away from the concept of the freedom of the individual, and that seems to be most advocated by the Democrats."

"What freedom was lost under Roosevelt or Truman?" I asked.

"No part of the Bill of Rights was repealed, no legal recourse abrogated; instead it was by the slow strangulation of taxation. Each time taxes were added, some direct, many hidden in transportation or elsewhere, the individual lost a little of his freedom. The deception was carried so far as to cause the public to believe that heavy taxation of corporations was something other than a tax on every consumer, passed on in higher prices. Each siphoning of profits, whenever it occurred, meant that the individual had less to use of what his labor earned. When a man is robbed of the fruits of his labor he becomes even more a servant to the will of the majority, the government of the United States, in this case."

"Your point is true, but most of the services were desperately needed, Social Security, for example," I added.

"Was it needed?" asked Bunker. "Were not the vast majority of the people able to save for their old age? Had there never been a program of over-all, government-enforced, public self-protection, would the old people of Jeffersonville be hungry and without shelter? Of course not, except for the indigent and improvident. For them, their families and public charity would suffice."

"Rich people, especially those inheriting wealth, Mr. Bunker, can be extremely objective in evaluating the shortcomings of those who are of limited background and ability," I said. "Even if the people of Jefferson County could take care of themselves and their own, the problem of the landless workers of your industrial North would remain unsolved."

"Oh, I would not deprive the unable of the necessities of life, nor do I expect the revenues from inheritance or gift taxes to be reduced; I merely maintain that every service provided to the people is not the blessing its advocates maintain. For the good it might do, those who labor for its cost pay dearly in a straw-by-straw reduction of their expendable income. This is also their freedom," said Bunker.

"You fail to note that the people have more free cash today after nearly thirty years of Democratic policy, with or without control of the White House, than ever before. Whoever heard of the working man having one hundred dollars a month, much less a hundred dollars a week, back in the Hoover days?" I pointed out.

"Figures lie, as you well know, old hypocrite. Granted the slow increase of real wealth for the individual began with the Industrial Revolution, one hundred years before FDR. But how much more of the individual's wealth is drained off by government than he has gained? Where once it was two or three per cent, it is now one-third of all that people earn. And I am particularly disturbed at your use of dollar figures as a measure of improvement," said Bunker.

I patiently awaited the onslaught about inflation and the fiscal irresponsibility of Democrats. It's the perpetual conversation of Republicans.

"Inflation is the most insidious of all taxation," said the pious Bunker. "Those who saved and wisely invested in safe securities were literally robbed by their own government by the calculated devaluation of their holdings. No alibi can exonerate those who made paupers of others who valued the freedom of their latter years."

"Assuming that some of your ideas have merit, Mr. Bunker, you remind me of the crackpots soapboxing in Union Square. Your convictions dominate neither political party, not that you claim allegiance to any. If you actually hold your beliefs beyond the braying of a backward mule, I would humbly suggest you get elected to Congress and do your bit. Needless to say, if you want to pursue such a course, you would wisely stop berating the Democratic Party. For all practical purposes it is the only vehicle by which a citizen of Tarvania can activate any political concepts."

"For once you speak wisely, and it would be well for me to heed your words," said Bunker. He didn't exactly win his argument, but he didn't lose it either.

He had about as much chance of being elected to public office as I have of being seduced by "Miss Tarvania."

On one of those fall afternoons in Tarvania that make you glad you're alive, I had been reading of the early snows and freezing weather up North, and here I was raking leaves in my shirtsleeves.

We had built the house soon after Emmy Lou and I were married. It was kind of an old-style frame now, but I kept it painted and it still looked a little bit more magnificent than the neighboring homes. We were out about three miles from the center of town, which was mighty inconvenient when I was running Anchor Ice and Coal Company, but Emmy Lou never wanted to move into town. I guess she was right.

I had just told Heliotrope to go home early and not take any of my supper with her. She'd been stealing from our household so long that she considered it more of an obligation than a crime. Of course, I only pay her $15.00 a week, and under present wages she'd have a hard time carrying as much away as she could have made working for somebody in town. Nobody else but me would want her anyway. She'd been keeping our house twenty years before Emmy Lou died and she does keep it pretty well, despite her mean disposition.

Heliotrope made it feel more like home with her nasty innuendos about my conduct. When she was alive, Emmy Lou always felt it her bounden duty to criticize me when there was anybody else around. I hated this and even went so far as to slap her soundly, a long time ago. It didn't do any good.

Of course nobody else knew what a wonderful woman Emmy Lou was when we were alone. She never complained about anything and knew how to keep me happy even when things were going pretty badly.

I remember when the icehouse burned down soon after it was built back in 1923. That icehouse wouldn't amount to much now, but then it represented every dollar I had saved during the war and after. I came in wet and cold from fighting the fire and trying to move some of the ice to another building.

Emmy Lou was opposed to liquor in any form, but she got out some peach brandy I had tucked away, mixed it up with some cloves and sugar and hot water. Meanwhile she was heating water for the old galvanized tub. She scrubbed me like a baby, which was something new in our married life, and then put me right to bed. Before she finished with me I forgot about supper, the icehouse, and everything else, except that Emmy Lou was a mighty good woman.

Next morning I got up hungry as a wolf. Before the day was over I had acquired enough building material on credit to rebuild the icehouse.

Emmy Lou and I never had any children, but she manifested her motherly instinct by harboring every objectionable child from both our families when its parents took off on a trip. She also harbored unrelated waifs from time to time until we were pretty old.

I didn't so much mind Emmy Lou giving me hell right regularly, but I sure wished Heliotrope didn't feel that she was obligated to carry on this chore in Emmy Lou's place. Heliotrope is especially suspicious of other women. If I so much as look at one of the neighbor's daughters, she reminds me of what a good, faithful wife I had.

I wouldn't tell the old nigger crone for the world, but when I die she and her family are going to inherit this place. Her kinfolk are bound to be more appreciative than most of mine.

Incidentally, it would be a wonderful way of paying back old Jim McAllister. For thirty years he's been my next-door neighbor and I've been hoping every minute of it he'd move away. A houseful of niggers next door will damn near kill the old goat.

To keep the afternoon from being too pleasant, up drove Horatio Bunker in that fancy English Bentley.

"Hey there, Mr. Anchor, we'll have a two-man directors' meeting. I've got some problems down at the plant I want to discuss with you," said Bunker.

"Come on up and sit on the porch," I said with no great hospitality.

Bunker did have some problems at the plant. Turned out he'd fired one of the Henkles, and the other three who worked at

Opulant & Company were doing a lot of talking and destroying what morale there might have been left. I told him to fire the whole tribe and he wouldn't be losing anything. I'm sure he had this in mind anyway, but he wanted some confirmation.

More than that, Bunker just wanted to talk to somebody. His chauffeur, or bodyguard, or whatever he was, was clearly no conversationalist, and I don't suspect that Betty Ray Cline's greatest asset was discussing national affairs.

Bunker got to talking about his ideas of business, which I assumed were pretty much a summation of those of the Harvard Business School.

"Mr. Bill, people have the wrong idea of the purpose of a business today. It wasn't that way back when you were running the Anchor Ice and Coal Company. Nobody ever questioned that the sole purpose of your conducting a business was to make a profit, but that seems to be a serious objection in 1959."

I was forced to agree. Back in the old days it was considered honorable and proper to get every possible profit out of the fruit of your labors. Now, people expect the owners and management of a business to give away anything they earn. People have forgotten that for every four businesses originated, three go broke within five years. Those that are successful have to reap the rewards for the risks they have taken. We were talking about small businesses, which are a lot more vulnerable than the big corporations which could survive hard times and forty-hour-a-week executives.

I baited him. "You are an exploiter of the masses."

"Nobody is going to exploit the masses except their government," said Bunker. "Government can't exploit high-income groups. That has already been accomplished. In fact, they are reaching a point of diminishing returns. Some of the men who graduated a few years ahead of me at the Business School have already retired. They have enough to do what they want to on unearned incomes, and can profit not at all by using their talents to earn additional income. As a result, some able minds are spending their time devising patios on small islands in the Bahamas."

"A lot of people enjoy their work for its own sake, regardless of return," I said.

"The business world of today is not like that of more casual times," said Bunker. "All the excitement of building a railroad or inventing a new cotton process is there, as it always was, but the competition is cut-throat. Every small business is under terrific day-to-day pressure just to survive. The price of survival is ulcers and premature death for the men in responsibility. Government has taken away the financial rewards. The joy of having done a good job or created a new product does not equal the price that must be paid."

"There ain't much room at the top, Mr. Bunker, and I'm sure there's always somebody below who's ready to get there, regardless of the price," I said.

"You speak with the wisdom of many years, old man," said Bunker, "and yet your talents have gone into hibernation when this country needs them most." Unpredictably, Bunker would flatter a person, for reasons unknown.

"At least the average working man is a lot better off than he was when I was in business," I said.

Bunker agreed. But he pointed out that the gains in real income made by individual workers would be a third more if it were not for the government.

He sounded like a damn Republican.

7

IT

was hard to believe that Bunker had been in Jeffersonville a year when I received notice of the annual stockholders'
meeting of Opulant & Company, called for January 11, 1960.

Although I was now a Director of the Company, there had
been no meetings of the Board since the previous January. I
seemed to know as much as anybody about the condition of the
Company, which was nothing except that the plant was still
running and its creditors were not howling for money.

One rumor making the rounds was that Opulant and Queems
were quietly buying up stock. I went to see my old poker pal,
Frank Alsobee. He was in the hospital and thought he had
stomach cancer. Anyway, he was always glad to see me and
would tell me if anything was afoot. It was.

"Yeah, Bill, Queems was in here about two weeks ago and
bought my two hundred shares for about three dollars a share
over their value. My hospital bill was outrunning my cash and,
since he is a trustee of Memorial, he knew it. He made one condition on the sale. I was to sign the stock over to him, but he
wanted the transaction to be absolutely confidential. He said he
would have the transfer recorded on the company books before

the stockholders' meeting but I had to promise not to say a word in the meantime," said Frank. "And I haven't told anybody but you."

I don't know why Frank Alsobee told me. I had always liked him, mostly because I had won out when we were both courting Emmy Lou. Maybe he was glad she had married me. She gave me plenty of public hell for nearly half a century.

"Just got curious, Frank," I said. "If many of the small stockholders have done the same thing, O&Q have absolute control. I'll give you a report on the meeting if you're not up and disturbing the peace by then. Keep fighting, old friend, and you'll be at my funeral yet."

I left Frank Alsobee and felt bad all day. Too many of my old friends weren't around any more. At one time I could stand their dying off. In fact, I was a bit proud of outlasting some of 'em. Especially John McTateton, who beat hell out of me in the fourth grade.

I didn't see Horatio Bunker until the annual meeting, and he didn't look well when he gave the President's report.

I guess I was the only one in the room who didn't want a good profit picture. He had bet me a thousand dollars that earnings would be better than $1.36 per share. He won the bet and had seven cents to spare. I would make a profit on the deal if I lived another four years, and by God I was going to do it.

With the union defeated and the profit picture good, even after profit sharing, I expected Horatio to be his usual gloating self. When the holdings of the stockholders were read, I knew why he was sick looking. O&Q had managed to buy enough shares and held just enough proxies to control the meeting.

Grandin Opulant's aunt, Mrs. Corday Opulant, nominated the Board of Directors for 1960. She made only two replacements from the existing Board. The former Register of Deeds and I were to be replaced by O&Q. Even with us gone it meant that Bunker's supporters would control the Board, indicating that O&Q wanted to keep Bunker on as President. They just wanted a front seat in the balcony and to slap down a couple of traitors in one blow.

Bunker was ready as usual, but uncharacteristically tense and apprehensive.

"Stockholders of Opulant & Company, you have heard the nominations. Before further consideration of the slate I call to your attention that the present Board has, in my opinion, served in the best interests of the stockholders. If they should be replaced at this time I would consider it a reprimand of the management of this Company. In such case, I would be obligated to refuse to serve in any capacity in the future management of this Company," said Bunker.

Maybe he was bluffing. He had most of his net worth and a hard year of his life tied up in Opulant & Company.

A dozen sets of angry eyes glared at Opulant and Queems. It had been a long time since the Company had provided any joy for its owners. O&Q were oblivious of the animosity. They were huddling to discuss this unforeseen development. If they failed to fully support Bunker, they would lose a profit-making President. If they failed to back up their motion in the voting, they would lose a lot of careful labor in preparation for this day. In addition, they would lose face. Of course, if Bunker was bluffing, they could go through with the plan and still let him run the Company. O&Q were in a helluva dilemma. They had to choose between greed and pride.

"Are there any further nominations?" asked Bunker. His voice was nearly inaudible.

Old lady Hart stood up. She owned about ten shares of stock, which wasn't even worth asking for in a proxy fight.

"Mr. Chairman, I move that the present Board be re-elected without change," she piped in a voice accustomed to parliamentary operations in the Women's Club.

Bunker asked for further nominations. Directors would have to be elected individually. The others would be elected without contest, but the former Register of Deeds and I would be against Opulant and Queems in the voting.

O&Q had walked to a corner and were still whispering vigorously to one another. I thought back to a conversation with Horatio Bunker a few weeks ago. It took place in Webb & Sons on a cold rainy day just after Christmas. I was warming my backside and giving Eisenhower the devil for playing golf at Augusta. Bunker must have been walking because he was wet and took time to back up against the stove.

"How are things at the plant, Mr. Bunker?" I asked. I expected no significant reply.

"Your money seems to be safe for the moment," he said, "but I'm worried about my attitude."

"What's that got to do with profits?" I asked, properly business-like as a Director must be.

"Mr. Bill," said Bunker, "I have found myself trying to hire back some of the old hands we fired earlier. Of course they are coming back at lower pay and doing less demanding work, yet it bothers me. The only purpose of a business is to make a profit, and when that ceases to be paramount you are no longer a businessman. You have become a sentimentalist and your competitors are still businessmen."

"In Tarvania a helluva lot of businessmen are pretty close to their employees," I said. "Most of them die at their desks rather than let their men risk chances with a new boss."

"I'm not that stupid, Mr. Anchor," and Bunker went his way. I wondered, and my mind returned to the stockholders' meeting which was still in progress. Candidates for the Board were about to be voted upon.

Grandin Opulant rose to his feet.

"Mr. Chairman, let me preface my vote with a remark. When my name was put in nomination, I failed to consider that my old friend, Bill Anchor, might be eliminated from the Board. My confidence in him has always been great and I would prefer to have my name withdrawn than to vote against him."

It was a damn lie. O&Q were capitulating to Bunker. Greed had won over Pride. For the first time I was glad I had double-crossed O&Q over a year ago. The rest of the proceedings were quickly concluded. Even the former Register of Deeds was re-elected, although Queems had left the room and was not voted aye or nay.

For the first time I was pleased to see Bunker win a battle. It was complete. Queems even had him elected to the Board of Directors of his Bank.

O&Q had lost a big contest. Or had they lost? They had practically wedded Bunker to Opulant & Company, and the Yankee schemer would make a profit for them from now to eternity.

Horatio Bunker was now a big man in Jeffersonville and I had helped bring it about. I was to regret it deeply.

The accident occurred on an April day that couldn't have been prettier. I had just left the Jeffersonville Grill in a de-pressed state of mind. I was headed towards Webb & Sons with the uninspired intention of buying a new paintbrush when I stepped out against the traffic light right in front of Bunker's Bentley. I remember I was hit hard and that is all.

When I finally came to consciousness at Memorial Hospital, I learned that I was in bad shape and it had been touch and go as to whether I would live. Both legs were broken, one so badly

I would never be able to put weight on it again. The fractured rib wasn't too serious but it hurt like hell to breathe. A brain concussion still left me groggy, as if I were half-awakened from a drunken sleep.

Immediately after the Bentley hit me, the whole town had turned out to watch the proceedings, which is standard practice for such incidents. Police waved at the traffic, Dr. Bernhardt came down from his office to fumble around my battered body, the Green Funeral Home ambulance made as much noise as possible. It advertises by siren, which is cheaper than radio or newspaper space.

Having been raised on a lot of black-eyed peas and a little corn liquor, I had never been hospitalized except in France during the war. Except for the fact that I was suffering "excruciating pain and great mental anguish," as Lawyer Leon Combes so well phrased it, the experience was not altogether unpleasant. Three enchanting nurses were regularly in my room, and just for added interest others came in from time to time. The matter-of-fact way in which they handled my personal needs was disturbing at first, but when I got used to having my back rubbed with alcohol, my original embarrassment was gone. Had Emmy Lou still been alive, I would have had to fake terrible pain to get such attention.

No visitors were allowed at first, likely because Doc Bernhardt was afraid he would lose his practice if the public learned of my appearance. Both legs were in casts and one was pulled towards the ceiling with a Rube Goldberg contraption of ropes and pulleys. My chest was generously wrapped in adhesive tape, causing me to scratch like my prize beagle during rabbit season. My head was bandaged to the extent that I looked like a Pakistani potentate.

The food came often and was good. Flowers were plentiful

and I was surprised to see a big display from Grandin Opulant and another from Sharster Queems. Another was from Lawyer Leon Combes, who was no special friend during my healthier days. Others came from old employees and customers who remembered me from the days when the Anchor Ice and Coal Company was a pretty big business. A few came from old political friends, most of whom would be coming up for election in the approaching months.

Only one gift was resented. That was the one marked "H. Bunker," and it came every day. I told the nurse that Bunker's flowers should be given to Frank Alsobee, who was dying of cancer down the hall. Not only had Horatio Bunker caused me to turn on lifelong friends, then run me down with his automobile, but now he wanted to avoid an all-out lawsuit. The nurses told me he came by Memorial every day to see me. I soon learned that all my hospital bills were being paid by Bunker. It occurred to me that the young smart aleck must not carry public liability insurance.

The first person I wanted to see was Lawyer Leon Combes. His interest in my welfare would be multiplied many times if he had a large damage suit. He didn't waste any time in arriving when Doc Bernhardt let me see visitors.

"Yes, Mr. Bill, we have a good case. A dozen witnesses will testify that Bunker's Bentley was racing down Main Street when it hit you. I wouldn't be surprised if that fancy chauffeur has a police record already. No matter how you look at it, Bunker won't win a popularity contest with the jury," said Combes.

"What's he done now?" I asked.

"For one thing, he's setting up a piece-rate system at the hosiery mill, and you know how much take-home pay that will mean with some of those old full-fashioned machines. They stay broken down more than they run. He has given severance notice to some of the eldest workers already, in anticipation of new equipment that will eliminate a lot more. He is wasting a lot of money and once again inviting a union to come in. Opulant & Company could be broke in a year," said Combes.

"Rush the suit so we can get him before he's insolvent," I said.

"You know it will sound like small change to sue a man for a hundred thousand when he owns a twenty-thousand-dollar personal vehicle," chuckled the lawyer.

"And I suppose you expect half the settlement as your fee," I said, knowing it was the going rate. "Take your pound, chaser-after-ambulances, and leave me in peace," I said. The conversation tired me. Now was a time in my life when I was more interested in revenge than in money, although I was not one to ignore the latter. I was really in the mood for a fine old-fashioned hanging.

Memorial Hospital became less pleasant as time went on. The food didn't seem quite so good and I no longer needed the pleasant company of the full-time nurses. What got me most was the loneliness.

All my life I've been a sociable creature. Jeffersonville was a little smaller when I was a boy than it is today, and at one time I could tell you the full name of every man, woman, and child in town and from most of the county to boot.

We had mostly private schools back in those days in Tarvania, and they were a clearing house for personal information, so that I knew most every family right intimately. My paw, who was better known as Old Man Anchor, believed in education and, even though money was scarce, landowner or not, he gave his three boys a crack at college. Of course the two girls didn't get much education and they really didn't need much. There was no such thing as a University for Women back then.

The condition of my staying in college was that I had to be

in the top half of my class at the end of the first year. Otherwise I would come home to work to give the other boys a little help. My two brothers finished college. One year and I was home from the University.

The University of Tarvania wasn't much before World War I, but it specialized in education instead of victories won by recruited athletes. We were supposed to be studying English, the languages, mathematics, the Bible, and history. I regret that I studied the booming tobacco town of Brightburl too much.

You could easily ride a horse to Brightburl in half a day, and you could do a good deal of riding of another nature for half the night. I learned that women didn't necessarily spend all their spare time at church circle meetings. I also learned that a boy doesn't stay in the top half of his class without considerable study. Anyway, I made a lot of friends at the University and I still keep in touch with a few across the whole state.

Tarvania is funny that way. Until recently it was made up of mostly little towns, and pretty much still is, compared with other states. Anyway, a certain few people in every town go to the University, Deacon College, Triniton, or Wilsonia College. They belong to the "club." Or, if you own enough land or a sizable portion of a textile mill, furniture plant, or tobacco company, you belong to the "club." If your family has lived long enough in Tarvania, you belong to the "club" without ownership or education, provided it is certain that at least one ancestor died fighting for the Confederacy.

Membership in the "club" entitles you to entry into the top social strata of every Tarvania town. Once within the special halo, you can call a lot of people by their first names all over the state. I guess I'd be considered a better than average member because I could call more folks by name, or at least know the immediate ancestry of somebody, in every town of five thousand or more in Tarvania.

A bounden duty of every club member is that somebody in every family participate in politics. Of course the leaders shoot for governor or United States Senator, but you are carrying your responsibility if you are merely a Democratic Precinct Chairman. I've always done my part and even represented Jefferson County in the General Assembly during the 1945 session. I guess I knew half the men elected that year, even before we were sworn in. I was even on speaking terms, though not pleasantly, with the seventeen Republican members of that session.

Liking people and politics go pretty much hand in hand, although I really enjoyed being friendly more than being a political wheelhorse. All this getting around and knowing people for a lifetime became important when I was stuck in a hospital bed. A lot of my old friends came by and visited once or twice, but as the weeks wore on, fewer and fewer were the calls.

I guess after what had happened I shouldn't have expected Grandin Opulant or Sharster Queems to come by, and they didn't. Their wives came in and talked about how they missed Emmy Lou, as if she hadn't been dead a full seven years.

Meanwhile, Horatio Bunker called every day asking that he be permitted to see me. For the sake of surface courtesy, Doc Bernhardt continued telling him that no visitors were allowed.

I was wondering what was happening in my lawsuit against Bunker when Leon Combes finally came back and his face didn't have that cheerfully-greedy expression it had had before.

"Mr. Bill," said Combes, "the brilliant minions of the law made a blunder. It didn't occur to me that they wouldn't press charges against Bunker's driver, especially since they charge nearly every accident down to 'Reckless Driving.' Chief Mull said there would be no charges unless Bunker charged you with willfully bloodstaining his Bentley. I would have brought the bad news earlier but didn't want to be charged with giving you a heart attack."

It was just possible that the fine touch of Opulant and Queems was operating in the Police Department.

"What about the witnesses?" I asked.

They too were unwilling to testify helpfully. The whole truth was that I had been absent-mindedly jaywalking and had stepped out into slow-moving traffic from behind an ice cream truck, which completely obscured me from the view of Bunker's driver.

"Did you talk with Judge Ponticorn?" I asked, seeking a last straw of hope. Opulant and Queems wouldn't try to influence the old Judge. James Ponticorn didn't sit on the county bench any longer, but he had been there off and on for thirty years. He was a good friend, he had fought me, and he had worked with me, as we sought control of the Party over the years.

"He seemed to feel that we had no case, Mr. Bill, and that makes it pretty final. He offered to help you without fee at the beginning, and then found out the case wasn't worth attempting to bring to court."

So that's the way it stood. Nothing would be recovered from Bunker, and he had literally added insult to injury by paying for a lot more medical expense than I'd ever have authorized with my own money. The bastard! Now I was obligated to pay him every dime he had spent in patching up what he had damn nigh destroyed.

"Judge Ponticorn told me to pass a message, Mr. Bill," said Combes. "The old man has been down with arthritis a lot this past winter but said he would be up to see you as soon as he could. He had something else on his mind besides your busted legs. He said for you not to make any political commitments until he could see you."

I wondered what the old boy was up to now. He certainly wouldn't want to run again himself, and it was a little late for him to care who would be governor. And what could I do to help him anyway? I had been an influence as to the way the Democratic Party moved for a long time in Jefferson County. But this year would be different, with me laid up and helpless at least until Christmas.

I moved into a ward the day after learning that I, instead of Bunker, would owe the hospital bill. Maybe I should let him pay, since he wanted to, and I have little cash at best. To be truthful with myself, it was a choice of overcoming my established fondness for spending a minimum amount of money or of accepting something that would not permit me to blaspheme Bunker for the rest of my days. I decided I would prefer freedom of vitriolic speech to saving several hundred dollars.

Shortly after moving to the men's ward, a gift arrived in the form of a wheel chair that was almost a miniature automobile, altogether in chrome. By this time I was being pushed around a little in the hospital chairs. I had also pinched two nurses and was definitely feeling better.

The shiny wheel chair was the gift of Bunker, although I was damned if I could see why, unless he hadn't learned he was free of liability. Maybe he had a conscience, which I doubted. The wheel chair was superb. It ran under its own electric power, rechargeable in any household electrical outlet, and could be adjusted for comfort in almost any direction. It even had little compartments in the armrests for newspapers and tobacco— and a revolver, should I finally be goaded into murdering Bunker.

When Bunker next telephoned, I asked that he see me at his earliest convenience.

Horatio Bunker looked like a person from another world when he walked into the old men's ward. His face was darkened by the sun, and he looked like an Olympic discus-thrower when he strode among us of bent shoulders and tired old bodies.

"Mr. Bunker, you've about ruined me," I said. "My reputation, my health, and now my money is about gone as the result of your efforts. The less I see of you the better it will be for me."

Instead of showing concern about my health or apologizing for the general damage incurred, Horatio Bunker completely ignored my verbal onslaught.

"Mr. Anchor," he said, "you have incurred a debt to me of nearly three thousand dollars, including the cost of that chair you are in. You are not legally liable to pay me back because I paid out these monies without your knowledge, consent, or expressed desire. However, if you should desire to reimburse me, I have a proposition to make. It will cost you only your time and not a great deal of work."

"Mr. Bunker," I said, "I'm not going to owe you anything for very long, nor do I intend to work for you, or anything that you are promoting."

Bunker apparently took no notice of my reply but went on in his efficient, urban manner.

"I am opening a small office on the street floor next to Webb & Sons. I need someone with some sense to be in charge of that office. There will be almost nothing to do, but I am willing to pay four hundred dollars per month for the right man," he said.

He was thinking ahead of me again. Being next door to Webb & Sons, I would be right on the path of all my friends as they wandered to and from Trade Street. Being on the ground floor would enable me to get in and out of the office in the wheel chair. This was exactly what I needed, provided there really wasn't too much work involved.

"What's the purpose of such an office?" I asked Bunker.

"Mr. Bill," he said, casually changing from the formal approach as if we were already in business together, "I intend to run for office in the General Assembly in Tarvania. I am aware of your experience as a politician, and I believe your presence in my campaign headquarters would be helpful towards my victory."

A more unlikely proposal I had never heard. The possibility of a foreigner being elected from Jefferson County was as remote as my being appointed Ambassador to Japan.

"What brought about this project, Mr. Bunker?" I asked, wondering how such a ridiculous idea originated.

"There is much injustice in our tax situation, Mr. Bill, and in particular I have been outraged by the fact that some of our customers at Opulant & Company suffer discriminating taxation which puts them at a competitive disadvantage with vertically organized operations."

Not a bit sure of what he was talking about, I assumed that this was quite probably true. It was just one of thousands of small tax injustices that develop in a complex economy loaded with patchwork taxation, mostly designed to be as painless as possible. For him to think that as a newcomer in the legislature he could change anything was vanity at its most. To think he could get elected to the legislature made Mr. Bunker even more naïve. It went through my mind that Bunker's screwball whim couldn't hurt me in any way. I wouldn't even agree to support him.

"Would I be committed to support you, Mr. Bunker?" I asked.

"No, sir, Mr. Bill, I want you to vote the way you see fit and merely keep my headquarters open. Do I need to look further for a person to do this job?"

The last time I had taken Bunker up, I had barely survived to regret it.

"You don't expect to be elected, do ya?" I asked.

"Not exactly, Mr. Bill, but I do expect to open the eyes of a few of our people. It is amazing how little the employees of Opulant & Company know of their government."

"And care less," I said. "Mr. Bunker, this could be a very short-range job. What makes you think you'll get past the primary?"

"Let me worry about that, Mr. Bill," said Bunker. "You just keep the office open."

It would be criminal not to use this example of naïveté to my own advantage. It would pay off my debt, keep me happy, and be a pleasure to see Bunker get squelched at the polls. His running for public office was as sensible as charging a cat to guard mice.

I had been in the little office next to Webb & Sons most of two days before some signs went up and I learned that the whole County of Jefferson was laughing at William S. Anchor.

8

THROUGHOUT

Tarvania and including Jefferson County we are proud to proclaim that we have about eliminated the Republican Party as a political force. A most cursory review of the Reconstruction period will show any observer the moral correctness, as well as the political desirability, of having only Democrats in places of public trust in our great state. We look back askance to the late eighteen hundreds. We honor and praise the leadership of the Democrats from that time unto this day that all is well in the State of Tarvania.

It is well known that during the War Between the States Tarvania was among those states losing the most men fighting for the Confederacy. Less well known is the fact that we had a large number of men fighting for the Union. Here in Piedmont Tarvania we find descendants of families who fought on both sides in the War Between the States, and we find a damn sight too many Republicans. In fact, there are always about two Republican votes for every three Democrats in Jefferson County. This makes us nervous because they can turn the tables when we get careless, which happens about every twenty-five years.

They laugh like madmen for weeks after winning an election, and being laughed at by a Republican is not pleasant for a Democrat in Jefferson County.

Talk about a laugh, who would have guessed that Bunker intended to run for the General Assembly on the Republican ticket? While he didn't have a chance of winning in a Democratic primary, he had less of a chance on the Republican ticket.

"Did I say that I was a Democrat?" was Horatio Bunker's question to my barrage, which included words like "double-crosser, thief, nigger-lover," and assorted profanities.

The damage had been done. I was now established in the "Headquarters of Horatio Bunker, Republican Candidate for the House of Representatives for Jefferson County." I had already been publicly humiliated, and now I was prepared to see to it that the Republican Party took its worst beating in history.

Probably the Republicans would eliminate Bunker by having a primary election of their own. But I hoped he would win that fight. It would be more satisfying to beat the entire Republican ticket with Bunker as one of the candidates.

"All right, Mr. Bunker," I said, "you've tricked me once again. I shall not work against you while serving with you in this office, but I shall not help you win while here, and I shall defeat you on election day. I recommend that you terminate our agreement."

"Mr. Bill," he laughed, "we have made a deal. I'll live up to my part of it."

Later, when old Judge Ponticorn came by the office, he made me feel a lot better. He razzed me about changing over to the Republican Party, but I could tell he didn't take it seriously. He was always courtly in his manner.

"Bill," said the Judge, "it distresses me to the extreme to learn that such difficult times have befallen my old friend that he has seen fit to align himself with the forces we have opposed for so many years that the memory of man runneth not to the contrary. However, we perceive that this deviation is not of a genuine nature and that we can count on you to strike terror once again in the hearts of our opposition at the appropriate time.

"The real business at hand," continued the Judge, "is to see that I have no failing among my friends at the time of the primary come this next-to-last Saturday of May. It has come to these aged ears that young Counselor of the Law Sylvester Amchase seeks again the Democratic nomination as Representative from Jefferson County. This I would normally encourage were it not for the fact that I wish to serve one final time in that very same capacity."

So the old Judge wanted to go down to Tarvania City one more time and say good-bye to his old friends at public expense. He was too old to be of much use to the public, but at least he would protect us against screwball legislators.

"You want me to try to talk Amchase out of running against you, Judge? It can't be done," I stated with finality.

"Bill, I am prepared at the polling places to utterly defeat my youthful opponent. Indeed, my charming daughter has returned from an assignment with the State Department to take care of the details of my campaign. For such a minor office and for a man of my unusual talents, such preparations would seem superfluous. However, one can not take lightly the advantage of an incumbent, nor ignore the fact, alas, that the people of this great County may have forgotten the excellent services I have rendered over the decades past."

"Sounds like a lot of trouble to get paid just less than expenses, Judge," I said. "You aren't being corrupted by the soft drinks lobby boys, are ya?"

"From other than you, such implications would be the occasion for a challenge. The truth is that I am an old man and don't want to lose a race just before I cross the Bar of No Return. Thus, I am hiring my daughter at an exorbitant salary, which she is well worth, regardless of inheritance taxes." The old man's eyes twinkled.

I waited for him to come to the point.

"Many have been our battles, old friend," said the Judge, "but this time I really need you. Young Amchase has already said he could carry the county if for no other reason than that I am too aged and infirm to get to the voters." The good Judge's hands shook and there was no mistaking the depth of the appeal.

When you first hear Judge Ponticorn speak, your reaction is that he is a hypocritical old fraud with too much education and too little sense. I've never known him to say anything the easy way. Instead, he makes it as flowery and as long-winded as possible. I remember one time some young drifter through Jeffersonville had gotten a job as grease-monkey at the Judge's favorite service station.

"Young man," the Judge said, "we welcome you to the fair city of Jeffersonville, which is a place of great and noble history, and which, despite its limited size, houses not only some of the finest people in the world but some of those important indeed in the affairs of the state of Tarvania and of the country as a whole. I hope that your stay here will be most pleasant and most permanent, and I hope that I shall never see you in my professional capacity." The Judge laughed.

The boy was flabbergasted. "Yes sir, your honor, sir, what can I do for you?" asked the boy.

"My vehicle is in need of maintenance. From below its steel frames there come sounds that lead me to believe that all is not well. It is much my own fault, for many thousands of miles have I traveled without due care for the joints of my trusty carrier. It now needs the trained hands of a man educated in car lubrication. I trust that you will fail not to ferret out every joint and see that it is properly and generously supplied with the appropriate lubricants," said the Judge.

"You just want a regular grease job?" asked the boy, mostly in bewilderment.

"That's right," the Judge said, and went on his way.

When the Judge was young he finished his law schooling at Triniton College, and after he had passed the State Bar he observed too carefully those who were successful in politics. Grandiose expressions were the order of the day, and Judge Ponticorn learned them so well that he never forgot them, nor did he ever fail to use them, regardless of how inappropriately. In addition to this auspicious start in life, the Judge married the last survivor of the Belmont clan. The reason she was the last survivor was that they were so damn snobbish they wouldn't cohabit with anybody, much less marry 'em. Marjorie Belmont was no beauty and the family wealth had largely disappeared even before the 1929 stock market collapse. Yet she had qualities of aloofness and superiority that no reverses could destroy. She and the Judge were well fitted for each other.

The advent of little Susan Ponticorn was a surprise to everybody, most of all to the Judge and Marjorie, who were well past thirty-five when the glad tidings became obvious. Maybe it was the strain of birth, maybe too much inbreeding in past generations, and maybe too much age, but Marjorie Belmont Ponticorn was never the same after the birth of little Susan. For years the Judge managed to keep her in private hospitals, but finally, because of dwindling resources and the improvement of State care, she was transferred to the State Hospital for the Insane. The Judge never mentions his wife and I don't know whether she's still alive or not.

Susan Ponticorn grew up as an only daughter, and except for the fact that in place of her mother there was a high-class Negro housekeeper, her life was about the same as everybody else's growing up in Jeffersonville. The Judge did his best to be mother as well as father and did a good job of it. Susan was particularly bright, and by the time she was in high school the Judge had begun to try to save enough to send her away for further education. Maybe he had other reasons as well, because I sure can't imagine the Judge explaining the facts of life in that stuffy vernacular by which he always communicated.

At Martha Washington's School for Girls in Richburg, Susan proved her earlier promise and later was admitted to Southeast University for Women. She did so well that she had the opportunity to transfer to Barnard College in New York, which I understand is about as intellectual a place as you can find in the country. For women, that is. I guess she learned a lot of things, because she could speak French and Spanish like a native and read a balance sheet damn nigh as well as old Sharster Queems. But the most outstanding thing I noticed was her damn fool attitude about the place of niggers in society. She was worse than the Yankees when it came to integrating niggers in the schools, the churches, the swimming-pool, and anything else where they should damn well be separated.

She had a lot of other crackpot ideas. One of these was that everybody who wanted to go to college ought to, and the public ought to pay the tab. She believed that nobody should go hungry, regardless of whether or not he was willing to work. She believed that where unemployment was a problem the government should subsidize industrial plants so that there would be work for everybody. While all these noble ideas were nice listening, she never quite explained to my satisfaction who was going to pay the bill.

As might be expected, Susan and her father didn't see eye-to-eye on most of these issues, but she held her old father in such tremendous respect and love that she never expounded when he was around. Most of the time she was out of the country working for the State Department in far-off places like Ethiopia, Surinam, and Haiti. From the way she talked, I was pretty well convinced that she'd like to see all the wealth of the United States equally divided between these godforsaken, underprivileged nations. I guess everybody in the State Department feels about the same way, and if it weren't for men like Senator Byrd this country would go plumb to hell sure enough.

While Susan was off getting more socialized, liberalized, and internationalized, the Judge was carrying on back in Jeffersonville. He was a good man and about the only vice he participated in was poker playing, and he was pretty good at that. The rest of the time he practiced law, or served on the bench, or politicked.

Often we fought each other. Whenever there was a primary, he seemed to be on one side and I on the other, but I never lost my fondness for the old windbag, and we were always shoulder to shoulder come the general election when we were out to get the Republicans' scalps.

Of course the Judge had ambitions for himself, and I think when he was first elected to the County judgeship he believed that this was the first step that would lead him to the governor's mansion. He made the second step without any trouble and found he could be elected as Representative for Jefferson County any time he wanted to go to the General Assembly.

When he ran for Congress he got out of his league. Scott

Deyton was too well entrenched. As Judge Ponticorn made a serious bid in the Democratic primary, a lot of dollars flowed from Scott Deyton's friends. Too many dollars were against him for the Judge to win. Had he waited for Scott Deyton to die, he probably would have made that next step and maybe gone all the way to the top in Democratic politics, but be made a tactical blunder. Instead of biding his time, he sought a Superior Court seat. In this he was dealing with one of the most unscrupulous politicians in Tarvania. Judge Hawke didn't even pretend to be ethical. He was so closely tied to the liquor interests that they wanted to keep him seated at any price. Judge Hawke won damn few votes, but he sure bought a lot and he sure stole a lot. Enough to beat Judge Ponticorn for the Superior Court seat anyway.

That finished the Judge for high political office. He suited Jefferson County and he served on the county bench or in the Legislature pretty much at his own discretion.

The Judge was a good judge. He could be mighty lenient when the defendant was a first-timer and the circumstances were provocative for crime. He could be pretty tough, too, and he would give the limit without batting an eye if the crime was vicious or the criminal a repeater. But most of the boys he sent on the roads didn't hate him very long. It's pretty hard to hate a man who has devoted his life to public service and not lined his own pockets at the same time.

Things were never financially easy for the Judge, and he moved out of the old Belmont mansion, which Bunker ultimately was to buy. He got Susan through finishing school, Southeast University for Women, and Barnard College mostly on credit. He stayed on the bench until he had paid it all back; then he retired.

That was an unusual thing about the Judge. He was about

the only man I ever knew who voluntarily left the bench. There's something about sitting up there and deciding on the lives of others that must get in your blood, because most of 'em hang on till long after they're dead. Retirement wasn't easy for the Judge, and I guess that's why he was now ready to engage in the effort of a political campaign when his only reward would be to join his old cronies down in Tarvania City. The Judge and I would be on the same side of the fence in this primary.

"What about Opulant and Queems?" I asked, continuing my conversation with the Judge.

"That's what makes it tough," said the Judge, turning to direct language for a change. "Opulant and Queems want a horse that will run a lot more races. They won't actually oppose me, but their just being neutral can easily defeat me."

"Who do they want for Governor?" I asked.

"O&Q have been so close to Investus Bragery, I expect they will want his Crown Prince, Trimlocke Lee," said the Judge.

"You're probably right. Madison Promisom should carry the county easily, so if you get on his wagon it would help. Who will Amchase support for Governor?" I queried.

"No doubt about it. When the chips are down, he'll be for Beauregard Rytewin. The boy believes in slavery at heart, and Beauregard is the only one in the crowd interested in stopping integration," said the Judge.

"It looks like the only candidate without a friend is Ward Taycare. Maybe the Republicans will adopt him," I ventured.

"Speaking of Republicans, Bill, how in the world did you come to be working for Bunker?"

I answered with a statement that was later published in the Jeffersonville *Democratic Bugle*:

"Bill Anchor believes in a two-party system for Tarvania.

He has done his share in building the Democratic Party in Jefferson County and is now working behind Horatio Bunker towards the strengthening of the Republican Party."

This innocent statement brought howls of laughter for weeks. It was said that I had invented a new weapon of internal destruction for the final end of Republicanism.

9

AS
the May Primaries drew closer, the Democratic Party came to life, as it always does in the South about six months before the November general election. In Tarvania, along with other Southern states, we think of the Democratic primaries pretty much as the rest of the country thinks of the contests between the two major political parties. Indeed, we say that we have the effect of two parties under the Democratic label because there are rarely less than two candidates for any public office of consequence.

For example, Judge Ponticorn was faced by another Democrat, Sylvester Amchase, in a contest for the Democratic Party's nomination for the Legislator from Jefferson County. There were also contests for most Congressional seats and several candidates in the field for governor and lieutenant governor. With the exception of a few counties where Republicans are a threat, Democratic candidates win or lose in the primaries. The general election is little more than a formality.

Because the election machinery is completely controlled by the Democratic Party in Tarvania, which is as it should be, we have no trouble keeping Republicans from increasing their vote

88

by means of questionable practices, which they would use with half a chance. Our problem in the primaries is to keep the Democratic election officials from stealing from each other in favoring one candidate over another.

The chain of control is important as to who will win an election in Tarvania. It starts at the State Board of Elections—a five-person board made up of three Democrats and two Republicans. The governor selects these members and therefore has a strong hand in influencing the next choice of governor by the chain of selection to the county level and finally down to the precinct level and polling places.

The two Republicans on the State Board of Elections are no problem. The governor just picks a couple of weak-kneed men who are registered Republicans. Even if these were persons selected by the Republican Party, they could never outvote the three Democrats on the Board, but we prefer the "least harmful Republicans we can find," as Governor Bragery put it. There's no sense in having a couple of loud-mouthed Republicans stirring up trouble after decisions are made. The three Democrats effectively control the State Board, and the State Board selects the County Boards of Election from lists submitted by the chairman of each county political organization. There are two Democrats and one Republican on each County Board. It doesn't make much difference who the lone Republican is, since he is always outvoted, but the Democratic members are important to any candidate in a close primary. The County Boards select the precinct judges, and contests are decided in the precincts. To phrase it as kindly as possible, precinct officials can do a great deal to influence the outcome of a Democratic primary.

If an incumbent governor carefully selects the State Board and it, in turn, carefully selects the County Boards, he has a great voice as to who will be the next governor, or who will be the next United States Senator. It is not uncommon for governors, who are limited to one term, to seek a seat in the United States Senate at the next election following their term in office.

In Jefferson County the Republicans rarely have a primary, conserving their energy for the general election. This is understandable, because the only way they can win is to have Al Smith run for President on the Democratic ticket. Although few in number and at great pains to round up a full ticket of County Commissioners and other county candidates, the Republicans showed no enthusiasm for having Horatio Bunker as their candidate for the legislature.

Tarvania law provides that people register Democrat, Republican, or Independent. Probably ninety per cent are registered Democrat, mostly because they get a voice in Democratic primaries, which determine all state-wide offices. In addition, all registrars are Democrats, and unless the voter is alert he will be registered Democratic regardless of his preference. It is a source of pride for a registrar to have an entire precinct free of registered Republicans. An unfortunate by-product of this practice is that so many Republicans are registered as Democrats that Democratic primaries are often decided by Republicans.

That the political picture is confused in Tarvania is doubtless one of the reasons the average citizen looks upon the entire structure with a feeling of helplessness. Not many understand the ins-and-outs, but those who do have a disproportionate voice in the government. As far as Jefferson County goes, few people fool with politics without consulting Bill Anchor.

So it was this year. All four candidates for governor and two for lieutenant governor had stopped by the little office next to Webb & Sons. Eleven aspirants for County Commissioner had been by. With only five places open, a few had to be discouraged.

This all took place behind a window painted "Horatio Bunker, Republican Candidate for House of Representatives." Needless to say, each Democratic aspirant had to have an explanation of my employment, and while I was less than wholehearted in my support of Bunker, there was an ever-spreading knowledge in political circles that the man existed. About two weeks before the primary election day it occurred to me that Bunker was no fool. By renting a small space and paying me a small salary, Bunker had established himself as a political identity in an incredibly short time. Because people kept asking me about my employer, it became necessary to learn something besides the fact that he was an undesirable alien.

During the pre-primary days I got to know Judge Ponticorn's daughter again, and there was a lot of difference from the little Susan who had stood out among others as the most scarred-kneed of the roller-skate set. Now she was about 120 pounds of young American womanhood and clearly distinguishable from the opposite sex at any distance.

Susan was really interested in seeing that her father went back to Tarvania City, and she knew that if he won it would be through her efforts. Arthritis was not going to permit the Judge to circulate much, and a lot of circulation would be necessary to beat young Amchase in the primary.

"Several things will make it tough, Susan," I told her.

"Papa's inability to get around is the worst, isn't it?" she asked. Susan had become familiar with international politics during the last five years, but she knew mighty little about Jefferson County grass roots.

"That's right, honey," I said. "The Judge has made a lot of friends and a few enemies over the years. Somehow enemies never die, and those boys remember serving a year on the roads as if they were terribly mistreated. Fetcher Guggencrow never has a new passenger in his taxi without trying to sell liquor, and failing that, he devotes his time to giving the Judge hell."

"But won't his friends protect him, Mr. Bill?" asked Susan. Her little-girl acute sense of right and wrong had not gone with her pigtails.

"Sure, honey, in so far as they run across slander, but they won't be greatly concerned whether the Judge is elected or not, beyond voting their immediate families. Don't forget a lot of old cronies are under the ground and a lot of youngsters your age don't know Judge Ponticorn."

"I'll have to be Papa's leg-man then," said Susan, a determined woman-look coming over her face.

Susan is an expressive personality to such a degree that every emotion seems translated into a new portrait. One minute she is a demure Southern belle accepting a flattering remark with a sweet virginal expression. The next she may see a new sports car and her blue eyes turn to avarice. When Susan has her determined look it is as obvious that she means business as it was when Carrie Nation used to break up saloons in behalf of the Women's Temperance movement.

At this moment Horatio Bunker strode into the office. Susan's face became Madam Suspicion. She looked like a pretty parakeet upon first being introduced to a lean tomcat. Anyone who might oppose her father's election had become an enemy.

Formalities concluded, lovable Horatio Bunker couldn't leave something disagreeable unsaid.

"It is with distress that I have learned that your highly esteemed father may be an opponent in the coming election. Please extend to him my good wishes for fine health in what I trust will be a campaign that will reach into every home in Jefferson County," said Bunker.

Susan correctly took this as a slur upon the vigor of the

Judge. She rose from her chair, and all five feet and three inches became a machine of offense.

"Young man, rest assured that Papa has not only the intention but the ability to terminate your political aspirations at an early date, and none too soon for the people of Jefferson County from all I hear," said Susan in careful, measured tones.

Bunker's eyes flickered with humor as he again mimicked Judge Ponticorn.

"The illustrious daughter of a revered sire does herself great injustice in so casually renouncing her reputation as a liberal and an intellectual, such as they be among the feminine gender. We understood you stand for tolerance and for political liberty throughout the World. Surely family greed for public office does not permit Jefferson County to be excluded from this concept?"

Bunker had picked the area of disagreement between friendly father and daughter. She was a one-worlder, a foreign-aider, and a champion of equal opportunity. Her father was an America-first, anti-union, anti-tax anti-integrationist. She was a Democrat in the Hubert Humphrey image; her father a Democrat in the tradition of Harry Byrd.

"Mr. Bunker," said Susan, "I am tolerant of all people except Yankee Republicans who now invade the South with money instead of guns."

Susan left the office with all the authority of a jet aircraft departing the Mecklenton airport. Bunker and I watched her departure with the eternal approval of males observing the exit of shapely females.

"Cute, isn't she?" said Bunker, showing a human trait not typical of the man.

My confinement to a wheel chair proved to be less terrible than I had thought, and I was the first to admit that Bunker had made this possible, although I am sure his motives were not altruistic. He had merely figured out another method of utilizing Bill Anchor. Reviewing the past made me aware that Opulant and Queems had always used me, although their methods had been less dramatic.

In the ground floor office of "Horatio Bunker, Republican Candidate for House of Representatives," I had easy access to the heart of Jeffersonville. The powered wheel chair could mount the curbs at certain low spots, so that I could tour the entire town square at will. Probably in the hope of squeezing more labor out of me, Bunker installed a bed behind the back partition of the office. My old Negress crone of a housekeeper, Heliotrope, caustically remarked on my spending entire nights away from home. I found the discomfort of transfer from town to Northside more difficult than just sleeping at my post.

Despite my years, I am not an unattractive individual. Not a woman, regardless of age, failed to chat with me during my ordeal of limited activity. Included in our discussions was a rundown on almost every human in Jefferson County, at least all those who had been caught in any kind of indiscretion. Were it not for my character as a gentleman, I'm sure I could have been the leading gossip of Jeffersonville.

My interest was more than mere curiosity, for much of the idle conversation held obscured information of considerable political value. For example, Mart Beard was thought to be fond of Marjorie Dale, a clerk in the Sheriff's Department, which is next door to the meeting room of the County Commissioners. County Commissioner is a position of public trust sought by said Mart Beard. By merely implying the distaste of Beard's wife for lassies such as Miss Dale, I convinced Mart that his services as a local campaign manager for "Promisom-for-Governor" would be the greatest contribution he could make to the Party, and to his own future. Otherwise it might be clouded by unpleasant rumors regarding his fondness for Miss Dale.

These and other minor political negotiations, all of which mean success on election day, occupied me completely. Yet in this pleasant work I was not altogether happy. Though not one to draw fine lines of loyalty, I had the increasing problem of serving two masters. It was difficult to be a keystone Democrat and work for Republican Candidate Horatio Bunker.

All I really did was hand out his political card to those who dropped by his headquarters office. It was pretty standard: "Horatio Bunker urges your support of his candidacy for Representative from Jefferson County." A head-and-shoulders photo reproduction showed the lean face of a young man with adequate hair on his head, and eyes that looked straight at you. There was no smile or frown to give a clue to his disposition. Typical of his sure-footed, straight-faced sneakiness, I thought. "Horatio Bunker, thirty-five years of age, was born in Worcester, Massachusetts. Graduate of Dartmouth College, Navy Veteran of World War II, decorated for action in the Pacific. Presbyterian. Businessman of Jeffersonville." That hardly told the story of the life of Horatio Bunker, which I had to pick out of him to get the brief biography. I had agreed to use only appropriate material, and there wasn't much of the usual "Past President Kiwanians," "Chairman of Jeffersonville United Fund Drive," "Debating Team at Tarvania University," "Sunday School Superintendent for ten years," or "Yatawba Fishing Club sponsor." His biography was hard to turn into votes in Jefferson County.

The Bunkers of Massachusetts were once big people in New England, starting a series of political and financial successes soon after the landing of the Mayflower. Those who signed the Declaration of Independence were intimates of the Bunkers.

While the family fortunes flourished in the early days, the twentieth century found them moderate. The family flourished numerically not at all. Horatio Bunker, Sr., died soon after the auto death of his infant grandson and daughter-in-law. Horatio Bunker was now alone.

All was not easy for Horatio despite his family's history of affluence. The Hoover depression left the family with a lot of New England textile stock and little cash. Dartmouth welcomed him with a partial scholarship and a chance to earn spending money through the laundry and cleaning monopoly.

Dartmouth gave up its undergraduates to the Korean War. Ultimately commanding a medium-sized landing craft, Bunker, as he put it, "saw a lot of Marines get killed." In any case the Navy Department saw fit to award him a DSC.

Postwar Dartmouth was like most colleges, divided between married veterans and callow youths, one group trying to get degrees and provide the livelihood for expanding families, and the other enjoying college life much as it had been before the war.

Bunker's wife and son were acquired while he was a veteran student. Like so many others who had faced serious challenges in battle areas, Bunker became an honor student and went on to the Harvard Business School. There competition was keen among the country's bright young future management potentials. It was while he was at Cambridge that tragedy struck.

Horatio's wife was as New England as he, dark and slim and aware of her primary responsibility as a family woman. Two years at Colby provided enough education for this role. She gladly made the educational and other sacrifices required for her husband's higher learning.

It was surmised that she was paying more attention to the activities of their little boy than to the STOP sign off the Cambridge Thru-way. She probably took her foot off the brake while struggling with the child inside their station wagon. The details didn't matter much after a Mack tractor and loaded semi-trailer hit them broadside.

Bunker graduated from the Harvard Business School in due course. Back home at Worcester, he tackled his family's textile holdings with energy and ability. When a merger became advantageous, he settled for cash and stock, and the Bunker name disappeared from industry in Massachusetts. With his parents gone, there was little to hold Bunker to Worcester. He was a little too prominent to engage in a local business as a future executive, and likely a little too lonely to be surrounded by a lot of boyhood memories. When the Opulant & Company stockholders' meeting was called, he got the financial statements out of his father's files. His training spotted a need for new management at Jeffersonville. What was more important, he had a place to go and a job to do.

The unusual and unpleasant character of Horatio Bunker was more and more revealed as he conducted the affairs of Opulant & Company. When Opulant and Queems were in control, things went along smoothly, with relatively little influence of management on the day-to-day production of hosiery. Now Bunker had his nose into every phase of the operation.

The knitters felt the impact first as new seamless machines replaced the old full-fashioned stand-bys. Production increased despite the loss of some knitters who could not, or would not, meet production standards demanded by Bunker. It was surprising that the union organizers had made no headway. Bunker told both men and women workers that survival of the Company depended on production. Most agreed to give him another six months of co-operation.

The finishing, dyeing, and packaging departments felt the

uncompromising knife of efficiency. Wounds were left among families who had worked for Opulant & Company over the years.

Salesmen felt the blow in new high quotas that would mean dismissal if not attained. One old traveling man put it, "When I am fired from Opulant & Company, Bunker leaves in a pine box." However, most salesmen went along with Bunker's plans, knowing that forceful measures were long past due.

Styling and advertising of Opulant & Company products had been dealt the strongest medicine. A new advertising agency was employed and "Opulant Color of the Season" became a well-known phrase in the hosiery industry. Probably the same old hose, but it sounded better with names like "Charleston Charcoal" and "Tidewater Tan."

The office personnel really caught hell. Some of us had suspected that the executive and semi-executive personnel at Opulant & Company spent a lot of money and played a lot of golf for the time they spent at work. Those who got the axe were not people other industries wanted at from ten to twenty-five thousand a year.

None of these had ever been interested in politics, but three of them made a special visit to our office next to Webb & Sons. They were willing to devote much time to describing Bunker in colorful language, the gist of it being that no matter how you looked at the man he was no good. A popular description was that he was a "revolving son-of-a-bitch," which is much more inclusive than a plain one. I readily agreed with these vilifications.

Yet, during this period, I did come to admire the foolish gall of Bunker. He had stepped on some pretty big toes and had anticipated the consequences. If his program failed, he would be finished for life as an industrialist, not to mention that his personal wealth would be largely dissipated if Opulant & Company went under. Folded hosiery plants are notoriously plentiful and very cheap in Tarvania.

Bunker's business techniques extended to his personal life. He bought the old Belmont place on Lee Road. It had housed a Governor, two Congressmen, and a list of less prominent Belmonts before the family deteriorated to the point of foreclosure by the bank. Then Judge Ponticorn married the last of the Belmonts. After some years he found he couldn't maintain the old mansion, and by agreement let the the bank take it over. Nobody wanted the beautiful old home except a few men who had climbed the financial ladder from a background of rural Jefferson County. They hadn't acquired it because they would have been socially ostracized for life if they had bought for cash the prestige that the Belmont place implied. This nicety didn't bother Bunker.

Six large columns and Georgian Colonial splendor describe the Belmont place, though run down and in need of the hands of a grounds-keeper. When Bunker wasn't working at Opulant & Company, he was supervising a half-dozen people in the renovation of what was now called Bunker's Place. If this man did nothing else decent for Jeffersonville, he had at least rebuilt a famous old show place.

Naturally, Horatio Bunker would create animosity even in renovating his own house. Dear to the hearts of all established social leaders in the South is furniture of eighteenth-century aristocracy. Contemporary or nontraditional styles are attractive and proper for those who come from the North and establish new homes in Tarvania. Those who have their roots here follow the styles established long before the War Between the States. Violating Southern tradition with such an edifice as the old Belmont Place was something only Bunker would attempt.

Word got out, as it does through the dark grapevine of the servants of the South, that much of the interior of the Bunker renovation was in vile taste. One room was in Italian style, and every decent woman in Jeffersonville had expressed disgust at the description of a nude statue that was part of the décor. Apparently one room was Japanese modern, whatever that might be. All I could make out of it is that you take off your shoes and sit around on the floor drinking rice whiskey.

These and other tidbits reached the ears of Jeffersonville's communication centers, which are book clubs, bridge clubs, church circles, and plant cafeterias. Each social stratum has its own facilities and there's enough overlapping to ensure total coverage of important information.

Most of Jeffersonville's females would have given a new hat to see the interior of Bunker's Place, but his occasional visits with Betty Ray Cline would have made an invitation unacceptable, even if Horatio Bunker had seen fit to offer one.

It seems that Horatio Bunker's Bentley was seen parked about twice a week, from about 7:30 P.M. to midnight, in front of Jesse Cline's home. Jesse died several years ago leaving a sickly wife, a teen-age daughter, and no insurance. Betty Ray Cline had to go to work to support her mother and herself, and it was not surprising that she needed income beyond that of a waitress at the Jeffersonville Grill. She was pretty and could be highly selective of those who offered favors, as many a traveling salesman had learned.

No man could seriously condemn Horatio Bunker for a bit of nocturnal relaxation, but Jeffersonville women, in the worldwide conspiracy against bachelorhood, were in a state of delicious outrage. Typical discussions overheard:

"Everyone knows that Betty Ray Cline has been a little tramp for years."

"It's terrible that a young man as handsome as Horatio Bunker should be taken in by her."

"Don't worry. He's too smart to get involved seriously with that kind of girl."

"If John didn't detest him so, I wouldn't mind having him meet Sue Ellen. He certainly can afford a decent wife."

"You mean you would allow your daughter to date a man with no morals? I just don't believe it."

"I guess you're right. I just couldn't permit such a thing. Still, he would make a good catch."

All the things Bunker had done in Jeffersonville made him a stinker for life, but after knowing his story I got to calling the boy Horatio. I'm a sentimental old fool.

10

THE FINAL

days of a primary are always hectic. More money was being spent in Tarvania than ever before and the gubernatorial contest was real interesting. For years Madison Promisom had groomed a personal organization for the big gamble of the Governor's Mansion. Trimlocke Lee was a relative newcomer into big-time Democratic politics in the state, having been appointed as Chief Counsel by incumbent Governor Investus Bragery. Also running were Beauregard Rytewin, the outspoken segregationist, and Ward Taycare, who had a record of a lot of political appointments and not much more.

I was a Promisom man, which proved to be a good choice. But I was really more interested in the Ponticorn-Amchase race for Representative from Jefferson County. Who the hell wants to be a good friend of the Governor when I'm not going to Tarvania City anyway, and I'm too damn old to want any appointment?

My old friend, Judge Ponticorn, was in trouble. Susan knew it, but didn't know how Amchase could have so many votes in his pocket.

"You're trying to make up for part of the trouble, honey, but the Judge has got to get around the county a lot more. Women can fool with politics here in town, but they hurt more than they help in the county," I told her.

"I know," she said. "I've started driving Papa over the county, but he gets so tired."

Susan Ponticorn looked pretty tired herself. Her plumpness seemed gone and there were lines around her eyes and mouth.

"What bothers me more are the promises Amchase makes everywhere. He can't possibly make good on them all," said Susan.

"No, he can't, and he hasn't made good on some of those from the last campaign. Yet you are going to have to fight hard, honey, or your father is beat, despite my considerable influence. You've got the goods on Amchase in the House Journal. Now is the time to use it," I said.

"His reneging on a teachers' pay raise is good, isn't it?" asked Susan.

"It's good enough in some quarters, Susan, but hit him hard on his vote for legal liquor in Milltown," I said.

"But I am for legal liquor, and so is Papa, if we have to have it at all," said Susan.

"Honey, are you trying to express your own sweet opinions, or are you out to win an election?" I asked. "For votes' sake don't mix up principle with public appeal in a close campaign. Young Amchase is smart, none too scrupulous, and very ambitious. It would be a feather on his pointed head to beat the Judge." I probably was too hard on the boy, but the Judge needed to hit hard above and below the belt if he was to win. Amchase would do anything but sell his law degree at this point.

"How many dollars do we need?" Susan asked out of the overcast sky. She had a little money and could raise some more.

The Judge wouldn't have cleared this action and she knew it.

"We could use about $300 for taxi drivers, and about the same for other handouts in the county. Buying votes is restricted to a few precincts and it would probably be cheaper to get with a couple of election judges. Iron Creek Number Two and Craggy Mountain can be bought for sure, if we get 'em first. A couple of my friends do well with liquor votes and we ought to spend $100 on half-pints. Altogether, $1,000 would be about all we could use to any real advantage. If that doesn't put the Judge across, $10,000 wouldn't either," I said.

"Disgusting, isn't it?" said Susan.

"Backdoor" Shepard was born Blackton Shepard and to one of the most important families of Tarvania. No war, no business, no high office failed to find a Shepard in the forefront or in the background. That was until Blackton was born in 1908, His birth marked a turning point in the family fortunes.

Death in war, bankruptcy in business, and defeat in elections began to plague those who bore the proud Shepard name. Blackton Shepard's fate was different, more lasting, and more terrible. Even at law school the signs were evident. Oversized and clumsy and something less than an average student, Blackton might have overcome the good-natured jibes of his classmates had his own family been more tolerant. As it was, they expected more than he could deliver. At home and at school he had no peace. He came to dread any kind of test. He failed in football, despite his size and strength. He failed in his college courtship. He even failed his oral test for the bar and was licensed to practice only because of the Shepard name.

As each big challenge faced him, his ability to meet it was reduced and his need for alcoholic courage increased. Somehow he never became a drunk, and he did title searches and other legal chores that proposed no court battles. He never married.

Slowly the Jeffersonville branch of the Shepards died away until only Blackton and his spinster sister remained. She, like him, had never found a suitor quite good enough to satisfy the pride of the senior Shepards. Unlike Blackton, his sister could stay at home, tend to the old house, and find her niche in life as housekeeper and genteel gossip.

Blackton Shepard was a figure of friendly ridicule. He walked with his heavy shoulders bent, looking at the ground, never speaking on his own initiative. He acknowledged greetings in a shy, grateful manner, whether slightly under the influence or completely sober.

He made a living, partly because of the name "Shepard" and partly because of his conscientious work and dependability, except under pressure. He was made Chairman of the County Board of Elections because he was honest as well as sufficiently capable, and there are no crises in that office. Because of his need to disappear when a courtroom appearance was inevitable, he came to be known as "Backdoor" Shepard. Unkind people often called him that to his face.

Opulant and Queems sometimes used Shepard themselves and sometimes encouraged a potential opponent to use him. Even though O&Q used me in a different way, I had a feeling of kinship with "Backdoor" Shepard. The big, stooped man was "Blackton" to me and I was his friend.

I was telling Horatio Bunker about the man. He had learned of the power of the Chairman of the County Board of Elections. In Bedlam County this power is used to what I might even call the extreme limit for the elimination of Republicans.

Up there in the mountains the Republicans had controlled every election since the War Between the States, until recently. When the Republicans in power in Bedlam County became pretty corrupt, the people up there became ready for a change, even if they had to vote Democratic to get it. In fact, it got so rough around elections, and so many people got hurt, that it became known as "Bloody Bedlam," and I can't say there's been any reason to change the name in recent years.

The way the Democrats got control, and keep it, was by careful scrutiny of the election laws. The legal wording provides that the County Board of Elections may choose as judges persons recommended by their respective parties. In practice, throughout Tarvania, it is rare for a County Board of Elections, except that of Bedlam County, ever to choose anybody who isn't unquestionably loyal to his own party. But because of the use of "may" rather than "shall," the law indicates that the provision is permissive rather than absolute, so that a County Board of Elections isn't actually required to choose judges recommended by the respective party leaders. Naturally, Republican judges must at least be registered Republicans, so it was very important that the Democratic organization in Bedlam set up some people as Republicans who might very easily be loyal to the Democratic Party. Registrations were changed from Democrat to Republican for the single purpose of getting people who would help the Democrats at the polls. Those who were loyal Republicans were, in one way or another, removed as judges by the Democratic organization. This takes the collusion of the Chairman of the Board of Elections, since he and the other Democratic member of the County Board can outvote the Republican on any issue. I've got to admit they've gone pretty far in Bedlam County. In the early fifties they started to refuse to accept the judges recommended by the Republicans and in their place put people bearing the registration "Republican" who could be counted on to swing the election for the Democrats. Since then, Bedlam County has gone Democratic and will keep going that way until the election laws are changed, or there is an armed revolution.

I'm proud to say we've always beaten 'em more or less fair and square in Jefferson County. I think it would be damn poor fun to just steal it from 'em outright. That's why we selected Blackton Shepard to be the Chairman of our County Board of Elections. Not only did the public trust him to give a fair shake to the Republicans with reference to their judges, but they could also count on him not to pack the boxes in favor of one candidate over another in Democratic primaries.

"I'm not telling you how to run your campaign, Horatio," I said, "but I'd get myself thoroughly familiar with the methods of the Board of Elections as quickly as possible. You'll find Blackton Shepard is a square shooter, and he's a better man half drunk than a lot who are sober all the time."

Horatio took my advice once again. He learned those election laws so well that he could even outpoint me, and I'm properly considered quite an expert. Apparently he made close friends with Blackton Shepard while he was at it. Rumor had it that Shepard was privately supporting Bunker for the general election.

You can say one thing with certainty about the outcome of the election. If Bunker wins, Blackton Shepard will no longer be Chairman of the County Board of Elections, and there will be one more to call him "Backdoor" to his face, namely me.

A history of politics in Tarvania during the twentieth century is mostly a history of the Democratic Party. Just before the turn of the century a Republican administration was elected through the combined efforts of the then powerful Populist Party and the Republicans. Since 1900 control of the state has never been successfully challenged by the Republicans.

To ensure its perpetuation in power, the Democratic Party has enacted legislation that gives the party in office tremendous advantages in the conduct of elections. Until recently, Negro groups have been deprived of the right to vote, partly because they might go Republican and partly because they might elect one of their own race to a county office. Political subdivisions, such as Congressional districts, have been grouped in such a way that the election of a Republican is nearly impossible. In the style of Gerry of Massachusetts, we have come up with some weirdly-shaped districts which always include enough Democratic counties to control the district.

For many years we referred to the Republican Party as the "nigger party" and, even though the appellation might not be quite accurate, it was effective politically. The entire psychology is referred to as "waving the bloody rag" and has been effective in eliminating Republicans in this state. I will never forget the wonderful speeches of Senator Clyde Calhoun, of neighboring Carolina, in which he always referred to the Southern boys coming back in their tattered, dirty uniforms from the Yankee prison in Elmira, New York. It is a fact that a lot of Tarvania men lost their lives dying for the Confederacy, and of this we have reminded the voters periodically. Lest some of our good citizens forget history, we have carefully placed permanent historical markers throughout the state commemorating the victorious marches of Northern armies through Tarvania during the latter part of the War Between the States.

In addition, we have wisely used state employment. Though Tarvania is far from the top in population, it is high-ranking in the number of state employees. We have avoided any Civil Service System or other means by which state employees can protect themselves against political dismissal. Our leadership has made it quite clear that those who are not registered and voting Democrats will soon be removed from the public payroll in Tarvania.

One device that has been extremely successful in preventing closely contested counties from going Republican is the use of the Civilian Absentee Ballot in the general election. As the law is written, it is not difficult to vote people in absentia year after year, though they may have died or long since left the boundaries of Tarvania.

In other words, we win a few, we buy a few, and we steal a few.

Of course we have had a few election scandals. Some of our loyal people became too flagrant in abusing the spirit of the election laws. However, we control the courts to such a degree that it's next to impossible to get a conviction for election irregularities. It would be difficult to condone such practices if it were not for the fact that the Democratic Party has served this state well. I can imagine nothing more horrible than to put a bunch of Republicans in control of Tarvania. We're gonna damn well do our best to see that it doesn't happen.

While we have generally been able to exclude Republicans from holding important offices by one means or another, a regrettable situation has developed in the Thirteenth Congressional District. There, in 1928, we lost the district to Cary Jones, Republican. Of course he went in on the coattails of the anti-Catholic, anti-liquor sentiment which characterized the Smith-Hoover campaign in Tarvania. Indeed, it's been the only time Tarvania has gone Republican nationally since the turn of the century. Of course we eliminated Congressman Jones in the succeeding election.

All was well in the Thirteenth District in Tarvania until the 1952 election, when a great many of our Democrats switched over to support General Eisenhower when he first ran against

Adlai Stevenson. At that time the son of Congressman Jones, Cary Plunder Jones, first entered the political arena. He, like his father, went in on the coattails of a popular Republican Presidential candidate. The regrettable thing about it is that we were not able to eliminate him in 1954.

The repeat contest between Eisenhower and Stevenson was damaging in Tarvania. Indeed, we were able to carry the state by only a fractional percentage. So, in '56, Jones again went in with a tremendous majority.

In 1958 things brightened a great deal. The Republicans had somehow put in 15 members of the General Assembly in '56, but we beat 'em down to a record low in '58. Only 3 remained out of the 120 members in the House and none remained out of 50 members of the Senate. But we still didn't get rid of Jones. By a narrow majority he carried the Thirteenth District for the fourth consecutive time.

There's nothing very promising in the Thirteenth District at the present time. Jones has the same opponent he had in 1958 when things were at their best for our Party. Unless lightning strikes, I'm afraid we're going to see Jones re-elected.

Because of the fact that Tarvania is going to lose one Congressman as a result of the 1960 census, we will arrange our Congressional Districts so that they will be twelve in number instead of the present thirteen. I have complete confidence that we can so gerrymander the counties as to eliminate Mr. Jones permanently. He originates in little Adams County, which is Democratic by nature, and by tying his county in with a lot more large Democratic counties he will stand no chance. At least that's our present plan and it should work.

Except for the cloud over the Thirteenth District of Tarvania, all seemed well for the Democratic Party when 1960 rolled around. We hold primaries in the spring so that any ill will developed among Democrats in scrapping for the nomination will be gone and forgotten by the time the fall elections come along. Of course, the big battle is for the governorship, and there were plenty of candidates in the field. Meanwhile, others were vying for a position on the state-wide level, although the significance of all of them combined is nowhere near that of the governor. He holds tremendous power in Tarvania. The gubernatorial office is the goal of every ambitious politician in the state.

Of course there were a number of hot races for congressional seats, and the usual close contests for various county offices. But the big thing is the governor's chair. The field was full.

The logical candidate was Ward Taycare. He had served in many capacities within the Democratic Party, including those of State Chairman and National Committeeman. He had been elected to the General Assembly on several occasions and had enjoyed a number of appointments over the years. He had a lot of contacts throughout the state and was at the right age, in his middle fifties, to rake in the big pot.

Late in announcing, but strong with the support of the incumbent governor, Investus Bragery, was Trimlocke Lee. He was appointed Chief Counsel by the governor, and had been spotlighted in the public eye through controversies over the KKK, unionism, and integration. He was personable and articulate, and, with the governor's help, looked to be a good possibility.

The third man was Beauregard Rytewin, distinguished professor and lawyer, and a real Conservative. He adopted a strongly segregationist position, although it was not nearly as strong as his admirers made it out to be. Because he formed an important influence in Tarvania politics, Mr. Rytewin posed a big threat to the fourth candidate.

This was Madison Promisom, who had literally devoted his life to becoming Governor of Tarvania. Now in his mid-forties, he was ready to take the big gamble. He had worked his way up to prominence through the Young Democratic organization and had sought public office only once and been spectacularly successful. He had no objectionable record, and what record he had was nearly ten years old. He was a skillful organizer and developed a pre-election machine that was the envy of every observer in the political arena. Though not a colorful personality or particularly impressive speaker, he had made thousands of friends throughout the state, and these he used to organize right down to the precinct level. In addition, he was a front runner from the very beginning. Anybody who seeks appointment or reappointment to a state office tends to support, personally and financially, the man most likely to win. Lobbyists and other pressure groups flocked to his side with money. It seemed highly probable that he would win the Democratic nomination in the first primary.

When the votes were counted, Promisom was well ahead, but he had no clear-cut majority. Mr. Rytewin trailed him by a large vote and had the right to ask for a second primary. Lee was third man in the running, and to my delight, Taycare, whom I've always regarded as a political hack, was bottom man on the totem pole.

Beauregard Rytewin exercised his right to call for a second primary. There ensued one of the most bitter, and probably the most expensive, contests ever seen in Tarvania politics. Every trick in the book was pulled, but Promisom's superior organization and the public fear that Rytewin's policies might close public schools won the nomination for Madison Promisom.

This should have been the end of the gubernatorial contest, but something happened at the Democratic National Convention in Los Angeles that drastically changed the picture. The Tarvania delegation was largely committed to support Senator Johnson of Texas. Promisom was not publicly committed to anybody when he left Tarvania for Los Angeles. Shortly after arrival, he showed his colors. He gave all-out support to Senator Kennedy of Massachusetts, although he could not bring all of the Tarvania delegates with him. It was a tremendous boost for Kennedy's nomination, as it enabled him to break into the Solid South. Wavering delegates outside the South quickly came into his camp.

Here at home we Promisom supporters were humiliated. Supporting ultraliberalism was bad enough, but supporting a Catholic was worse. We held our heads low, waiting for the sound and fury to die out.

Then columnist Draw Looklatter hit the newsprint with an article telling of the secret meeting between Senator Kennedy's Washington leg-man and Madison Promisom during the primary. Campaign money purportedly influenced Promisom for Kennedy. Before this part of the story was retracted, the candidate for governor had earned the name of "Purchased Promisom." All hell broke loose.

A "write-in campaign" for the defeated Beauregard Rytewin was immediately instituted. This didn't bother us, for it just wouldn't work. But something else was happening. A lot of good Democrats were talking about voting for the Republican candidate, Optimo Futrell. Spending enough time and money could undoubtedly defeat the Republican, but he'd likely ruin us in some close counties.

11

WHEN
the Republicans nominated Optimo Futrell at their
state convention early in 1960, it was given the same newspaper
prominence that would be given a replacement of the Minister
of Internal Affairs in Siam. Republican candidates for governor
of Tarvania are not taken too seriously, which is understandable
since they've not had a victory in the twentieth century. Optimo
Futrell was a good candidate, a respected member of the legal
profession from a family well regarded throughout the state,
even though the Futrells are traditionally Republican. After the
defeat of Beauregard Rytewin by Madison Promisom in the
second primary, a great deal of interest was generated in behalf
of Optimo Futrell. This enthusiasm increased because of the
affair at Los Angeles. Many of Promisom's supporters became
lukewarm to his candidacy.

"Democrats for Futrell" and "Citizens for Futrell" rapidly
developed in areas where regular Republican strength was
small. Although Futrell did not advocate the ultrasegregation-
ist and extremely conservative position accredited to Beauregard

Rytewin, he was billed successfully as a "Conservative Candidate," especially when compared with Promisom. Money began to flow into the Republican camp in some substantial amounts and in really substantial amounts into the organizations led by Democrats in behalf of Futrell. The outward evidence of this was plenty. Tarvania's cars started sporting bumper stickers in a ratio of about ten to one favoring Futrell over Promisom. The situation was serious and a number of Promisom's fieldmen were called into emergency session.

With the completion of the primaries, the Democratic candidate for governor should have been finished with politics except for a few perfunctory speeches, since the outcome of general elections had long since become routine. In 1960, however, Madison Promisom had to start all over, raising money, organizing, and putting pressure on state employees to actively support the Democratic Party. Since all state employees and anybody having any kind of political ambitions are registered Democratic, the task would not appear to be too difficult, but Republicans took unfair advantage of these time-honored methods of extortion used by the Democratic Party in Tarvania.

Probably the most obvious blunder in the eyes of the public was a series of letters issued by state employee associations in which it was made clear that employees who failed to contribute financially and energetically to the Democratic Party in 1960 would be in danger of losing their jobs. Of course it wasn't stated that bluntly, but the letters made it obvious that state employees owed a strict loyalty to the Democratic Party and that a close record would be kept of contributions. Regrettably, some meetings were called in various state-owned places during regular working hours, and the Republicans took advantage of this to the extent of causing some of the uncommitted public to feel that state services are purely adjuncts to the Democratic Party, which is a blatant falsehood. Nevertheless, it had its effect in creating doubts as to the virtue of the Democratic Party leadership.

Optimo Futrell made a particularly astute move at this point in advocating a Civil Service status for all state employees below the policy-making level. This had a direct appeal to state employees who have always been subject to political factionalism within the Democratic Party, and at the same time made a favorable impression on the public, which, though unfamiliar with state employment intricacies, has a suspicion that political loyalty is often placed above competence in Tarvania.

Yet not everything went to the advantage of the Republican Party. We were fortunate in catching Optimo Futrell in an early statement which indicated that his program for education would be even more costly than that of Madison Promisom, who was under attack as a spendthrift. Although Futrell corrected his earlier mistake, we hammered at it throughout the campaign, and it was effective in casting doubt upon the ability of the Republican candidate. As representative of a party long out of office, the problem of attacking the Democratic Party was pretty simple for Futrell. Though we had had good government in Tarvania for sixty years, there are a number of statistical indices which show that Tarvania's progress is not as real as our Democratic claims. By the constant reiteration of public officials, such as Governor Investus Bragery, not only had the United States as a whole come to think of Tarvania as the most progressive of the Southern States, but many of our own people thought the same thing. The Republicans had contradictory facts and, if they had used enough skill in presenting them, it could have been extremely embarrassing. Fortunately, they were short of capable spokesmen and for the most part failed to get across the message of government inefficiency that they might have successfully portrayed.

One salutary effect of the Republican challenge was the immediate response of the Democratic candidates for Council of State. In Tarvania we elect all kinds of officials, including the Superintendent of Public Instruction and others who would normally be appointed by the governor in other states. Each of these became aware that his job was in jeopardy and hit the campaign trail with a zeal unknown for many years. Their big pitch was that the Democratic candidates had a combined experience in running Tarvania of over a century, and it would be foolhardy for the public to advance untried Republicans in preference to the experienced talent being offered by the Democratic Party.

Somehow the Republicans had anticipated this move long before we decided upon it and had issued a brochure, which reached nearly half a million homes in Tarvania, expounding the virtues of the Republican candidates. I read one of these things and, while it did not actually tell any lies, it certainly painted the Republican candidates in an extremely favorable light, far beyond that which they deserved.

All in all it was going to be one tremendous campaign, and I was looking forward to it with the zeal of a bird dog when he is put in the car trunk on the first day of the season.

Most of the South and all of Tarvania get a lot more excited about the primaries than about the general elections. They are "tantamount to election," as freshly graduated reporters put it. Indeed, for most places, it's all over but the formality of the general election. In Jefferson County we have to go through the whole damn thing again with the Republicans.

While Promisom, Taycare, Rytewin, and Lee were running

a razzle-dazzle race for the governorship, everybody in Jefferson County was also concerned with the outcome of the Amchase-Ponticorn primary. Amchase had his political future at stake and Judge Ponticorn had his political past on the same block. Family connections were sought out as never happens except at election time. Folks became kissin'-cousins who barely acknowledge the existence of one another throughout the rest of the year. Friendships were strained to the breaking point. I was working on lawyer Combes. We were never particularly close, but I guess we could be called friends.

"Leon," I said, "I hope you are giving this Amchase-Ponticorn race a lot of thought before you use your influence one way or the other. Now I'm not gonna try to tell a man as smart as you how to vote, but, and I say this as a friend, I think it's in your best interests to support Judge Ponticorn. I know young Amchase has a lot more years ahead of him than the old Judge. If you want to think in a purely selfish way, however, you'll have to vote for the Judge. Anything you do to help young Amchase is just building up your own competition, and it takes more than just being a good lawyer to make a good living in Jeffersonville."

"You know I put principle above personal consideration," said Combes, properly indignant.

That was a bit of exaggeration, I thought, but now that the real point had been made I was ready to give him some lofty principles by which to vote.

"I know that, Leon, but you can't ignore the fact that an old man like Judge Ponticorn can put in the right word for you here and there and do more good than Amchase would ever do. You know you younger lawyers pretty near have to come up on the coattails of the older ones," I said, just to be sure the point wasn't missed. "More important than that, though, is the record of service Judge Ponticorn has given to this county and to this community. Though he may be a little senile, you know very well when you send him down to the General Assembly that things will be done for the best interests of Jefferson County. I know that no selfish interest would affect your vote for either man, but I'd think that with your high ideals of good government you'd want to back a man whom you're sure of."

"I'll think about it, Mr. Bill," said Combes. A few days later I heard he was quietly supporting Judge Ponticorn.

Opulant and Queems were up to their famous methods. Grandin Opulant was openly favoring Judge Ponticorn and Sharster Queems was helping Sylvester Amchase. There's nothing unusual about the fact that the partnership should be supporting both candidates, but I was distressed to see Queems on Amchase's side. Queems was a winner more often than Opulant.

In order to maintain a picture of real sincerity in their support of the candidates, Opulant and Queems became unfriendly, at least as far as the public was concerned. In many elections they could agree as to who the winner should be, or could be, and would get together and damn near nominate the man. In this case it wasn't clear which one would win, and they were playing both sides of the fence. This took a lot of skill because it was pretty well known that they didn't really disagree on anything. While the purpose may not have been clear to everybody, it was so obvious as to be ridiculous. If Amchase won the nomination, and of course the election, he would owe it to Queems and would be beholden to him for favors requested, and it was certain there would be favors requested. If Judge Ponticorn won, he too was sure to win the general election and Grandin Opulant would be in a position to ask for special consideration. Heads, O&Q won the election; tails, they won it anyway.

I had to admire the spirit they were showing in the race.

There was actually no doubt in anybody's mind where Grandin Opulant stood with reference to the Judge. At the same time, there was no doubt in anybody's mind where Sharster Queems stood and that he strongly favored Sylvester Amchase.

Young Amchase was doing everything possible to win the nomination. He not only remembered every past favor he had done for anybody, but was generously promising future favors. He made appeals to the school teachers, the State Highway Patrol, the Farm Extension Service, the Prison employees, and to anybody else to whom he could possibly promise anything within reason.

Judge Ponticorn was working equally hard at his own candidacy. I'll bet he and Susan covered every passable road in Jefferson County during the campaign. It wasn't easy for the old Judge to jump out of that car and shake hands with anything that looked like it could vote. He couldn't remember half the names, but it wasn't long before he knew the prospect's grandfather, or grandmother, or some kin, and it took a pretty cold man not to feel that Judge Ponticorn had been a protector of the family for several generations. Susan Ponticorn was doing all the driving and got to look pretty near as haggard as the old Judge. She also learned a lot about Jefferson County that she never knew, and never would have known if it hadn't been for the campaign. She told me about one of the biggest shocks she got out on the the campaign trail.

"Mr. Bill, did you know that there are literally hundreds of children not going to school in Jefferson County?" asked Susan.

"Sure I know it, young lady, but there's not much point in talking about it. We've got truancy laws; they just aren't enforced," I said.

"Well, why aren't they enforced?" asked Susan in righteous outrage.

"I guess we just never got around to it, honey," I said lamely.

"It's a very good thing that the Republicans aren't alert enough to take advantage of the situation," said Susan.

I thought the same thing, but had no comment.

"What's really distressing is the malformed children for whom we are doing nothing," said Susan. "I've seen children in those hills who were so badly retarded, mentally as well as physically, they couldn't gain anything by going to school and there's no place else to put them. Those poor melonheads! They're so pitiful I could cry every time I look at one," said Susan.

"Yeah, I know," I said, "and one of these days we'll get around to doing something about it. You've got to remember that, despite all our claims of glory, Tarvania is a very poor state and we are having a hard enough time educating those who are able and want to go to school without spending too much money on the lazy or unfortunate."

"It's a pretty poor state of affairs when we can have one of the highest state employee payrolls in the United States and not be taking care of these unfortunate children," said Susan.

I didn't care to defend the position of our government at this point.

While it is quite true that there is a good deal of similarity between our Democratic primary in Tarvania and a general election elsewhere in the United States, there is an essential difference. That is, the campaign in a primary is more or less a private affair. Rarely indeed do you find opposing Democratic candidates using public invective against their opponents. Newspaper advertisements and radio broadcasts tend merely to brag about a candidate rather than to detail his opponent's faults. Rarely is serious fault revealed because there's the danger of its being used by Republican demagogues.

On May 28 the choice was to be made, and, like any other magic date, it finally came to pass. The candidates had done everything possible to get support, and now it was pretty much a matter of hauling in the votes that wouldn't come on their own power.

It was a bad day for young Sylvester Amchase, but to his credit he was quick to come to the Judge and offer congratulations. He realized that he was young enough to overcome the onus of defeat, particularly when he went down under the prestige of a man like Judge Ponticorn. Sylvester Amchase would come back another day to win elections for the Democratic Party of Tarvania.

I guess I'd never seen Judge Ponticorn as happy in victory as he was in this one. Along about 8:30, when it was pretty clear that his lead of three hundred votes would hold fast, the Judge came by Bunker's headquarters for what will probably be the most unlikely celebration in the history of Tarvania politics.

Because the Judge had no special downtown headquarters of his own, all his friends came into Bunker's place to drink a little whiskey and gloat over the results. It just ain't right to celebrate a victory in the household of the enemy, but there we were and right among us was Horatio Bunker himself. You'd never have guessed that he was to be the opponent of the Judge in the coming general election. He joined right in as if those supporting Judge Ponticorn would also be his supporters, which was obviously impossible.

Only Susan Ponticorn seemed to recognize the paradox and, despite the exaltation of victory, she wore a worried look for fear Bunker was gathering information that would destroy the Judge in the general election. Maybe it was her State Department training, but she went over the room with a careful eye and a determination to find the hidden microphone which she knew existed, despite my insistence that the place was clean. Bunker got quite a laugh out of the situation.

"Miss Ponticorn," he said, "please accept my word that any information gathered here tonight will not be used in the coming campaign. You know, we Republican politicians are men of great honor and we shall use only those issues that can be legitimately brought against your good father."

"Mr. Bunker," said Susan, "I am confident of only one thing with reference to your conduct in the coming election, and that is that you'll do anything you need to do to win and hurt anybody you have to hurt to accomplish your end."

"Miss Ponticorn, I have observed your work in the past primary election, and at this time I should be very pleased to hire you, at fifty per cent more than your present salary, to serve as my campaign manager during the coming election. Any actuarial figures will show that the probability of my surviving for a long period of time is great and that your father, regardless of his good health, must necessarily depart from this world and thereby leave you without a source of income. This I could well provide, assuming that you went about your duties in the same careful way you have demonstrated while working for your father," said Bunker.

If you've ever seen a small fox terrier chase a neighbor's sheep dog off the property, you have a picture of Susan Ponticorn going after Horatio Bunker. She just about chased him out of his own premises. Something must have happened, though, before it was all over, because she was laughing with him before we killed the last bottle of bourbon.

The time to leave Bunker's employ had arrived. I'm no purist, but I wasn't gonna work forever for a man and not give him value for payment.

"Mr. Bunker, I first want to thank you for having me work

in headquarters for you. I've done the job you told me to, and I've enjoyed it. Now the general election is before us. I am a Democrat, I intend to vote for Judge Ponticorn, and it is time for us to part company. As friends, I hope," I said.

"Mr. Bill, you speak honestly, which I will not say of most of your Party leadership," said Bunker. "Before you terminate your employment, I am due one further service. I intend to win this election, as you know. Is it impossible?" he asked.

"No, Mr. Bunker, anything is possible in Jefferson County. Harry Truman couldn't win in '48, but he did. I'd say the odds were three-to-one against him. I'd say the odds are one hundred-to-one against your winning," I said.

"This optimism for my cause overwhelms me. Suppose you detail why I can't do it," said Bunker.

"Usually it's the little things that decide close elections. In your case you have a lot of big things that will defeat you, without mentioning the incidentals," I said.

"Granted that Jefferson County is usually Democratic, I understand that Republicans won in 1928 and 1952; why not in 1960?" he asked.

"True, they win every generation. That alone is enough to insure that Republicans stay out another twenty years. We Democrats get complacent. We stay in office election after election. Some of our officeholders get useless, maybe even corrupt. Our organization gets sloppy because victory comes too often, too easily. Meanwhile the Republicans regain their strength with each new generation of innocent children. They give their best for a big presidential election, and by hanging on coattails, and by working like demons, they carry the county. Only eight years ago we were beat, and defeat is still fresh in our minds. The Democratic Party is capable of winning this county any time, and it is certain we will take no chances this year," I said.

"You believe that the Party can be militant and effective when most of its members are completely out of step with Paul Butler, Chairman of the Democratic National Committee, and the Democratic candidate for President?" asked Bunker.

"Son, it's a long way from Jeffersonville to Washington. It's equally far from Tarvania City, although not in mileage. Democrats in Tarvania want control of the state and every county and, when the chips are down, we will win here and cuss the National Democratic Party in the same breath. I want nothing from the Democratic political control of Tarvania," I said in my virtuous voice. "I'm a working Democrat because I believe that our Party is right, most of the time. I do not intend to forsake it just because a bunch of left-wingers have gotten control of it nationally, for the moment," I said. I thought the time from 1932 to date might be considered a long moment. I added, "And if it weren't for little loyal men such as I the Democratic Party would never come back to the ideals of Thomas Jefferson. No, I am not going to desert when the Party needs me most." A pretty effective statement, I thought.

"Well, you would have been a loyalist at the time of the Revolution. I can hear you now, 'King George is our King, and by our King, I'm for the King, though my King be a miserable King,' " said Bunker.

"The right-wing youngsters may have to leave the Democratic Party, but I guess I'm too old to change. Of course, I'd be a lot more likely to do so if we had something better to go to," I said.

"Does not the Republican Party on the national level better suit you than the Democrats?" asked Bunker.

"Possibly, but there's not enough difference between the two to cause me, or many Southern Democrats, to change. The horse may be lame, but I'm not gonna switch to a blind one when the other side of the river is so close," I answered.

"Proceed to other reasons, stubborn old man," said Bunker in the best of humor.

"All right, Yankee, you're asking for it," I replied, slightly nettled but nowhere near ready to admit defeat by showing anger. "I'm not prepared to say that I wouldn't vote for a Northerner, but I would damn well prefer a local man, and so would the rest of Jefferson County."

"You mean the Civil War and Reconstruction days are still an active political issue here?" asked Bunker.

"First, accept one piece of advice. The 'War' is referred to in the South as the 'War for Southern Independence.' If you can't get that out without smiling, refer to it as the 'War Between the States.' It's only called the 'Civil War' by Yankees," I stated with pleasure. I had finally caught Bunker way off base.

"A point well expressed, Mr. Anchor, and one I shall not forget. Now tell me how strong the feeling is against Republicans on that issue, somewhat passé though it may be," said Bunker.

"Here in Jefferson County you are at the dividing line. Some of our people fought for the Union, and that's the reason a lot of counties have Republican strength to this day. The majority of our people suffered for the Confederacy, however. Tarvania lost more men than any other Southern state, and the abuses of the carpetbaggers were as bad here as anywhere in the South," I told him.

"That was nearly one hundred years ago. Few indeed are those who can remember the Reconstruction era," said Bunker.

"That's true, but a lot of us old codgers can remember what our fathers and grandfathers said. They knew firsthand, and they said 'Never vote a Republican ticket' so that it wasn't forgotten. Today the second-hand memories are in fewer minds and I can not pass on the horrors of the War and the years that followed with the vehemence of those who knew them," I said.

It was quite true. When I had talked to meetings of young people in recent years about the terrible things the Yankee Republicans had done to us, they didn't get excited. Maybe the state textbooks are getting too objective, although all I have ever seen stuck to the Party line and the rightness of the Confederacy. They'd better keep telling the story our way or there'd be a quick replacement of the Superintendent of Public Instruction.

What has really happened is that the direct family impact has been forgotten. It's hard to love somebody you've never known; it's hard to hate something you've never seen.

"Horatio, the reason for hating Republicans has been forgotten by our younger people. They are Democrats mostly because their folks are Democrats," I said, disliking to admit the obvious truth.

"Maybe the time has come when there is enough of importance to cause a change," said Horatio.

"Maybe so," I said, "but you aren't the man to make 'em change. If Republicanism is to amount to anything in Tarvania, it will have to be from the beliefs of our own people, not of foreigners. Maybe you didn't know that we have more native-born citizens than any other state in the Union."

"And have more cases of aggravated assault per capita, as well," added Bunker. "Possibly a foreigner can lead the children from the wilderness."

"Granting that remote possibility, it will be foreigners who can learn to act like us," I said.

"A few changes appear to be in order to make me a successful politician," said Bunker with obvious interest.

"I'm not gonna give aid to the enemy," I said, "but I'll mention just a few things that are wrong with you."

I had no trouble here. Bunker was dressed wrong, talked wrong, acted rich, and was too damn direct, just to name a few.

"Now to return to the subject, sir, from which you have clearly departed. My employment should end promptly. Is there anything I can do between now and the end of the week?" I asked.

"Yes, Mr. Anchor, sign this contract, if you please," said Bunker. He left the office without a further word.

It read as follows:

"I, William S. Anchor, do agree to remain in the employ of Horatio Bunker subject to the following conditions until the close of business, November 8, 1960:

"I shall keep an office, supplied by Horatio Bunker, open between the hours of 10:00 A.M. and 6:00 P.M., weekdays, except Wednesday.

"I shall offer no advice on voting except when asked for it, and that to be given in such manner as I see fit.

"I shall receive a salary of $80.00 per week, paid weekly, and shall be free to terminate this contract at my option.

"I shall advise candidate Bunker as to his political conduct, but in no way shall I be held liable for poor advice, which I may give to said candidate for the purpose of defeating him.

"I shall be permitted to show this document to anybody at any time to demonstrate my intentions and the foolishness of Horatio Bunker."

There was room for both our signatures. The sly one had outwitted himself at last. He thought that I would appreciate past favors enough to help him in his ridiculous effort to be elected as Representative of Jefferson County, and this would be a face-saving device for me to fall into the trap.

I signed the document with malice aforethought. This instrument would be the one with which to repay Horatio Bunker for the repeated humiliations suffered at his hands. I would not fail to use it at the proper time. Never give one an even break.

12

BECAUSE

I had agreed to continue on with Bunker, I gave him advice on how to win, with confidence that he wouldn't take it.

What happened was astounding. First thing I knew, the Bentley, chauffeur and all, was secreted in the garage behind Bunker's big house. In its place was a two-door black Ford, about 1948 vintage, which is an especially popular model in Jefferson County. Some of our good citizens put extra springs under the rear, soup up the engine, and haul illegal liquor in cars of this type. These machines fetch a premium price and, though the wreckage is great, there always seems to be an additional supply.

Bunker's Ford even had the extra springs which made it sit up in back as if it had been goosed. When heavily loaded with half-gallon jars the car returns to a normal level. This one was not normal in another way. Across each side in bold script was painted "Bunker for Legislature."

Bunker's Ivy League suits were replaced by Cohen's concept of what the Jeffersonville business executive should wear. They weren't a lot different from the best of Boston, but they made Horatio look like a Jeffersonville lawyer, instead of a Yankee.

He was following instructions to the letter. Voters expect a candidate to be an attorney, and he looked the part.

Other changes were less obvious to others, but I could tell the man was trying to completely change his personality. He talked to everybody, showing an interest in their problems and gradually picking up a talking knowledge of rabbit hunting, oak lumber grading rules, and the best slop for a hog. Even his language was undergoing a change. I heard him use "I reckon," "y'all," and "ground peas" in the same conversation. Of course, he couldn't completely conceal his Yankee accent, but lawyers talk funny anyhow to most people. He passed for a native a good deal of the time.

The biggest change was in his attitude. I had told him he must be really interested in people's problems if he wanted their support. If he wasn't interested, he had become the greatest actor in Tarvania politics, and we've had a few good ones, just to recall old Bob Roynalls.

Bunker got so he could talk about how pollution was ruining the fish in Yatawba River just as if he cared one way or the other. One time he went fishing, for authenticity.

He started referring to the Country Club crowd as if they were terribly inferior to the working people. My advice, "Don't fool with those who wear white shirts and neckties; they don't vote in volume," had taken hold.

I might still be highly suspicious of his integrity, but I was coming to admit that Horatio Bunker was making a hell of an effective candidate.

The hypocritical bastard even joined a church. He claimed to be a Congregationalist up North, the "Church of the Pilgrims," he called it. Of course there is no such church in Jefferson County. We have the high-toned Baptists, usually identified by being members of the First Baptist Church; the middle-class

Baptists, normally attending the Elm Street Baptist Church or the North Jeffersonville Baptist Church; and the rural and working-class Baptists, who support the thirty-one other Baptist churches in the county. Of these, three are composed of wild-eyed Baptists, usually associated with the Free Will Baptists.

Numerically, religiously, and politically second are the Methodists. Important prestigewise, if not prolific, are the Episcopalians. The Presbyterians are numerous and rank high in per capita income. Lutherans are a small solid contingent in Jeffersonville. The Seventh Day Adventists, who are more devout than most, are a sizable group and good people, except they somehow think that Saturday is Sunday. The Church of God is active and well-housed. Jehovah's Witnesses have their Kingdom Hall, and even the Catholics have just built a small church.

Unrepresented by edifices, but still part of the religious community of Jefferson County, are the Moravians, Jews, Christian Scientists, and one Congregationalist, named Bunker.

One day there was one less Congregationalist and one more Presbyterian. I suppose Bunker didn't want to be too obvious in getting into the accepted pattern of political success, which would mean Baptist or Methodist.

Politics and religion may not mix anywhere else, but they are completely intertwined in Tarvania. Rare indeed is the successful politician who is not also a prominent layman in some church. It is a matter of fact that you always introduce an otherwise unnoteworthy candidate as a "fine Christian gentleman."

Bunker had joined the church with scarcely a hint from me. I think he had observed Boston politics enough to know that being a Catholic was a prerequisite there. Being a Protestant, and an active one, is required in our state.

Maybe his Christian affiliation was not without its effect. For one thing, he stopped paying biweekly calls to the home of Miss

Betty Ray Cline. More likely, he was just too busy. In any case, since the campaign had begun as a full-time job, Horatio Bunker's Bentley was no longer seen in front of Betty Ray's home. Either disinclination or physical exhaustion had turned him into a righteous man. A little too righteous to believe, in fact.

Bunker seldom took a drink, but he came in after a rally one night and, without a comment to me, opened the bottom file drawer (nobody ever bothers bottom file drawers) and pulled from it a full fifth of Scotch. Its whereabouts had regrettably been unknown to me.

He poured half a tumbler full, added equal tap water, and consumed the entire amount without so much as offering me a smell.

"Mr. Bill," he said, "please overcome your scruples and join with me this one time in unrestrained libation."

I've never had such scruples, but appreciated the thought.

The liquor made us both more informal than was usual—not that our relationship was strained at other times, just business-like. Neither Bunker nor I talked about personal matters. With a noticeable amount of J. Walker inside us, we both got notice-ably less reserved.

The inevitable subject of women came up, and while I may be no potential rapist, my memory and intentions are not pure, I am proud to say. Our little waitress friend, Betty Ray Cline, came under discussion. Although no lurid details came out of the talk, to my disappointment, one statement of Bunker's stands out in my memory.

"She may not be a pillar of morality, but at least she is not so professional as to be capable of pretending a previous life of virtue," he said.

Horatio didn't forsake Miss Cline on my advice. It was accepted practice for unattached men in Jefferson County to have improper relationships with unattached females. It would be more damaging politically not to have such a properly clandestine situation at his age. A few queer ones have lived in Jeffersonville, but they have long since departed for New York, or Hollywood, or some other God-forsaken place. It was even said of two governors in my time that they had affairs with female assistants while in that highest office. They later got elected to other public offices.

Horatio Bunker now devoted no time to females. His life as a candidate became ever more busy. There came a time when I thought the ceaseless search for votes was killing him. I don't know why I cared, but I thought it time to tell him the facts of life.

"Horatio, I can't help but admire your determination to win the election and I'm flattered by the way you have used my suggestions in conducting your campaign, but you can't win no matter what you do," I said.

"Really, Mr. Bill," said Bunker, clearly indicating that my opinion upon this occasion was not worth considering.

"If you were a Democrat, I'd admit you might someday be governor, but trying to make any political headway as a Republican is a waste of time, and that doesn't exclude the election as Representative for Jefferson County," I said, provoking him into listening.

"You mean that the system of free elections for which our forefathers and our contemporaries have paid with their lives has been in vain?" asked Bunker.

"Democracy is very much alive in this state, sir," I said. "It's just conducted with a capital 'D,' and that means we want no Republican in office."

"Surely you wouldn't want to be classified with democracy

in the Communist style: one party right, wrong, or indifferent," said Bunker.

"You have read the Election Laws of Tarvania and noted that the Democratic Party is seldom, if ever, mentioned and certainly enjoys no special privileges," I said righteously.

"Yet you maintain that it is nearly impossible to get elected unless you are a Democrat," said Bunker.

"Ignore for the moment that we control all state jobs, and they are worth four votes per job. Just look at the Election Laws. First, look at the way we've set up districts." I got out some maps of political subdivisions in Tarvania. "Congressional districts are so well gerrymandered that, even though about a third of the state votes Republican, it is highly improbable that one should get elected. Hooking enough strong Democratic counties to close counties ensures victory for our Congressional candidates. Naturally we wind up with some weird districts, some of 'em meandering around the state like a disjointed snake. Despite our care to exclude the possibility of a Republican Congressman, a fellow named Cary Plunder Jones got in with Eisenhower in '52 and we haven't gotten rid of him yet. I think his middle name has appealed to the female voter, but we'll dispose of him by redistricting before the 1962 elections. Here's a district of which we are particularly proud." I pointed to the Seventeenth Solicitorial District. "We believe it is the only noncontiguous political district in the United States. As you can see, if any of the counties adjacent to the Seventeenth were to replace a county in it, we could easily have a Republican district."

Bunker had a chart showing normal Republican voting strength in Tarvania counties. He compared the shape of the districts with the voting record, speechless for once.

"Speaking of the judiciary, we have another little gimmick to ensure the election of Superior Court Judges. They serve only in their own districts after election, so each district nominates its particular candidate in the primary," I told him.

"There's nothing objectionable about that," said Bunker.

"However," I added, "for the General Election we vote for District Judges by the state as a whole. Since we are overwhelmingly Democratic statewide, we are certain to elect only Democrats, no matter how popular a Republican might be within his own district."

"It's like having Georgia electing officials for Vermont. There would be no Republican elected in Vermont," said Bunker.

"That's about right," I laughed.

"What would happen if the Republicans should take over control one time?" he asked.

"We would be caught in our own trap and it would be hell," I said. Bunker had had enough for one lesson.

Carrying on a winning campaign requires a multiheaded workhorse. Bunker's background had prepared him to assume direction of an organization where instructions were carried out. He soon found out you issue few instructions to precinct leaders, especially Republicans.

We Democrats have some control over our workers because most of them have a member of the family working for the state. The Republicans are an ornery, independent breed to begin with. When you have no patronage with which to apply pressure, I don't know how you would keep them in line.

"Inspire them, Horatio, inspire them" was all I could recommend. "Of course Republicans are loyal despite our best efforts to show 'em the political truth, but it must be remembered that they have suffered many defeats and few victories. Their spirit is somewhat dampened, if not crushed. The problem that you have is to get all the Republican votes and work for enough Democratic votes to carry the county."

"How would I go about this inspirational effort?" asked Bunker.

"It would be my suggestion that you should first visit every precinct chairman in the county and spend enough time with each to get to know him and to let him know you. They do better working for some known Republican than for somebody with whom they are personally unfamiliar. The party faithful will vote for you anyway, but if the total Republican vote is to be brought to the polls, they need to feel that their effort is appreciated and that there is a chance for victory," I told him.

It didn't take Horatio Bunker long to get into the mechanics. He found out quickly that most of the precinct chairmen didn't really know the boundaries of their precincts, and soon thereafter I was hard at work making maps of each precinct. He had me put an over-all map of the county on one wall of headquarters, and the operation began to take on a look of political efficiency. I might add that I made an extra map for my Democratic friends, since they are no better informed about precinct boundaries than Republicans.

Soon thereafter Republican Precinct Chairmen started dropping by headquarters when they were in town. Some of them wanted a copy of the Election Laws, others wanted literature and buttons, and they all started demanding lists of the registered voters. This brought about another major task for me in copying the books. It is impossible to know who needs to be registered if you don't know who's already been registered. Horatio Bunker was obviously doing quite a sales job in convincing the precinct leaders to make a house-to-house survey of each precinct so that all the unregistered voters could be spotted.

He had also done quite a selling job on his own behalf, in that the men who came by were anxious to find out a lot more about their candidate and showed a good deal of interest in winning this election.

During all these proceedings I was in an extremely uncomfortable position because it went thoroughly against my grain to assist Republican workers, but I could hardly fail to give reasonable co-operation to Bunker since I had accepted employment on my own terms. I thought repeatedly about quitting the job and exposing the contract we had made, which would be right embarrassing to him, now that the campaign was really under way. Somehow, day after day went by, and I never did anything except think about quitting. Maybe I enjoyed being in the office, or maybe I was just tired of being an unpaid party worker.

Without any prodding from me, Bunker had learned some other techniques. When he found some precinct chairmen to be relatively weak, he set up separate campaign managers for his own candidacy. This was the proper procedure, because he didn't alienate the duly elected chairmen but at the same time got somebody in the precinct who would really work in his interest. The other candidates on the county ticket didn't much like his procedure, but they couldn't help but see the necessity of it if the ticket was going to win. It wasn't long before they were trying to do the same thing. I'm not sure whether they wanted to win as much as they wanted to do as well in the election as this foreigner in their midst.

Bunker was too smart to fall for one trick that has defeated Republicans in Jefferson County on many occasions. We call it "trading off," and essentially what it amounts to is the promise that we will support their best candidate if he in turn will privately support the rest of the Democratic ticket. We usually wind up beating the whole crowd without any difficulty when a Republican falls for the scheme. Word always gets out, and the Republican team ceases to be a team and becomes a bunch of individual candidates fighting among themselves.

I had a chance to hear Horatio Bunker's technique when one of the precinct chairmen came in to visit with him.

"I'm awfully glad you came in, John, because I was real anxious to see you and I'm sorry I missed you when I went out to your home," said Bunker. "Slippery Rock Precinct is as hard to get to as it is to carry Republican. That road leading out there is about the worst I've ever seen in the state of Tarvania. You would think that every living soul in your box would vote Republican just in hopes of a change."

"I'm mighty glad to meet you, Mr. Bunker. I've heard a lot about you and I hear that you're running a real race. I've waited thirty years to carry Slippery Rock Precinct, and by God I believe we can do it this time," said John McBee.

"Nobody calls me 'Mr. Bunker,' " said Horatio. "I'm always 'Horatio' to Republicans like yourself. I want to tell you that I'm going to do everything in my power to help you carry Slippery Rock, and after you do carry it, you can count on me to help you in any other way I can, when I am down in Tarvania City."

"Well, Horatio, we are ready to do our part. We are mighty hungry for victory and we will get behind you all the way. We'll need a little money out there, though, because our folks are about as poor as you'll find anywhere and most of 'em haven't got enough money to pay for gasoline to run their cars," said John McBee.

"I know that, John, and we're rounding up some money to help out. We won't have enough to go around to do the kind of job we ought to do everywhere, but we are certainly keeping

Slippery Rock in mind. When we've got our registration books opened up here, we will have a good idea of how much money to spend where. We're sorta running a little contest to see who can get the most new folks registered, Republican, of course," said Bunker.

"Well, if you've got one of those maps I've been hearing about and a list of the registered voters, it would help us a lot," said McBee. "I'm not much on map reading, in fact, on any kind of reading, myself, but I've got a daughter who was trained to be a school teacher and we'll be able to use the material to do some good. She'd be a school teacher if she weren't a Republican."

"That's what I like to hear, John," said Bunker. "I know Slippery Rock is mighty tough to carry our way, but I've got a lot of faith in you because they say once you make up your mind to do something, you're a hard man to stop. In fact, I've been bragging around town that if the Republicans carry Slippery Rock we will carry every office in the county. Maybe I'm sticking my neck out too far, but we are counting mighty heavily on you."

"We'll do our best, Horatio, and we want you to come out and talk to our people sometime real soon. We can get the women folks to fix up some eatings, and I'll get a couple of guitars to the schoolhouse and we'll have a real rally. We haven't had one out in Slippery Rock for four or five elections. Actually, I think we are carrying the box, but we are getting votes stolen from us. Old man Pritchard is our judge out there and he's mighty nigh blind. He's a good honest man, but I think they're slipping ballots in and he can't see 'em. I don't like to recommend another judge, but if he could be replaced somehow, it might help a lot," said McBee.

"I talked with Mr. Pritchard when I was out looking for you," said Bunker, "and I could tell he was having trouble with his eyes. I think I've got him where he's willing to be replaced as judge and I think he'd be just as happy if you recommended his boy to serve as judge for the precinct. I'm not encouraging the use of liquor to win this election, but if it should come to pass that a few mason jars are handed around election day, it might be a good job for the old man. Lord knows you need an honest man handling liquor."

"Good idea," said John McBee. "Don't you forget about my daughter and the road after we get our crowd elected."

"I won't," said Bunker, "and be sure to come by every time you come to town."

It was right revolting to see Horatio Bunker "con" old man John McBee into working for the Republican Party. He had given him hope of immediate reward in money and hope of future reward in a road and a job for his daughter. If it takes a scheming operator to make a good politician, Horatio Bunker was developing all the characteristics. I had to admire him.

13

BUNKER
had no sooner come into headquarters after an afternoon of campaigning than he asked the question that I had been expecting.

"Mr. Bill, what about the Negro vote?"

"Aw, it's just about like the white vote except a greater percentage of it is subject to direct negotiation," I answered.

"Meaning that most of it can be bought?" asked Bunker.

"That oversimplifies it, yet sums it up pretty succinctly," I said.

I had noticed that Horatio referred to our colored brethren as Negroes, rather than niggers. It was probably the current trend and he was likely doing the right thing. Like most Southern children, I was raised side-by-side with nigger kids. They were my companions and they were my friends and they'd remained that way all my life, although I wasn't close to any of the younger ones. I don't suppose they like it any more being called "hey, you, nigger, gimme a hand over here." I notice the young ones look at me with extreme distaste. It's about time I changed my ways. Of course I've called old Jim Howard a "nigger" all his life and I know damn well he'd be mighty suspicious if I called him anything else. We didn't have any integration problem back in the old days. Niggers didn't go to school at all, and not many white children finished more than a few grades.

"The Negro vote looks mighty important to me. They account for about sixteen per cent of the population and I suspect they account for that much of the total vote," said Bunker.

"That's about right, Horatio, but they won't vote that many of the total. We've let 'em register and vote in Jefferson County since 'way back in the twenties, but not many of 'em are really interested enough to bother. I wouldn't say they would account for more than ten per cent of the total vote at the most. Of course, that could conceivably swing an election one way or the other in a close race. In your case, I wouldn't bother worrying about 'em," I said.

"Assuming that I did need them to win, how would I go about getting them?" asked Bunker.

It was a difficult question to answer. You'd think that the Southern nigger would automatically vote Republican in appreciation for what Abraham Lincoln did. In recent years Eisenhower had done more for Civil Rights than anybody since Lincoln. But I knew they would vote Democratic in Tarvania and I knew why. Both major political parties advocate welfare programs of one kind or another, but the Northern Democrats have been more generous than the Republican leadership. Any welfare program amounts to taking from the rich and giving to the poor, and damn few niggers south of the Mason-Dixon line are rich. Most are very poor. They'd be crazy to bite the hand that feeds them, and I would guess that they'll vote for Kennedy over Nixon regardless of what their preachers tell 'em to do.

"Horatio, the majority of the nigger vote in Jefferson County tends to vote Democratic because they wisely realize that this is the party for the little man. However, the majority can be reduced by two methods. One of these is to promise them some jobs that they wouldn't otherwise expect to get. Of course you, as a member of the General Assembly, would not be in a position to make appointments, but Republican County Commissioners could very well put a few darkies on the county payroll," I said.

"That's about the same thing as buying their vote," said Bunker. "What's the other method of getting them with you?"

"Buy 'em," I said.

I went on to explain how it was done in the big cities, where key Negro leaders controlled blocs of votes in Mecklenton, Greensedge, and Brightburl. They even went so far as to print ballots showing how the average Negro should vote so that there would be no mistakes.

"In Jeffersonville we are less well-organized, and you pretty near have to go to 'em individually and line 'em up. Use the absentee ballot as much as possible so that the work can be done casually rather than trying to concentrate it all on election day. All a registered voter has to do, in Tarvania, to vote absentee is to say that he expects to be out of town on election day. Then he merely applies to the Chairman of the County Board of Elections for an absentee ballot. One of our men is looking over his shoulder, or actually writing it out to be sure it's done properly. Part of the cash is paid on the spot with a promise that there will be a little extra on election day. Although damn few niggers would try, it's possible they could vote in person on election day and thus void their own absentee ballots. Republicans are notorious for attempting to change good Democratic absentees.

"Of course we don't get 'em all before the election and it's a major chore hauling 'em to the polls and getting 'em voted right.

Once delivered to the polling place, the nigger is turned over to a Democratic marker, who proceeds to mark his ballot in the proper fashion. Of course the Republicans are doing the same thing, and a real smart nigger can get paid off by both sides on election day. He can vote absentee one way and in person the other way."

I'll never forget Lester Johnson working on old Jim Howard one election. Despite Jim Howard's being one of my best friends and one of the best niggers that ever lived, he's always kinda leaned Republican. Lester Johnson was using every trick in the book to get Jim Howard on our side. When he finally got old Jim to the polling place at Stony Creek, several of us markers heard Lester say, "Right this way, Mr. Howard, right this way." No white man ever called a nigger "Mister" a few years ago. After old Jim had left the polling place, we really kidded Lester about using the formal title. Lester felt pretty strong about winning elections. As he put it, "I'd have kissed Old Jim's black butt if I'd had to, to get his vote."

"I was exaggerating about the nigger vote always being for sale, Horatio. They are usually for sale because the nigger has no reason to expect anything good from either candidate, Democrat or Republican. There's not a helluva lot of reason why the average nigger shouldn't sell his vote. Five dollars on a cold day in November can be mighty important when you're needing coal in the stove. What every nigger wants is for somebody to pay him a little attention after election. They'll even settle for less than that. If they can trust you, they will more than likely support you. From what I hear coming out of Opulant & Company, the nigger help thinks pretty well of ya. You should get your share," I said.

"Would it help if I sort of quietly showed that I wasn't opposed to integration?" asked Horatio.

"'Twould ruin ya for sure," I said. "Niggers wouldn't believe you, and every white person who ever considered voting for you would be aware of what they already suspect, namely, that you are another damnyankee trying to force integration down our throats."

"At least half the white people in the South are preparing for integration, and are not really upset because it's coming," said Bunker.

"I know that, and you know that, and so do a lot of other folks with a grain of sense, but even the sensible people down here are emotional as hell about integration. They may realize they have to put up with it, but they sure ain't gonna be for anybody who supports it publicly. Privately, either," I added.

"What's really behind the opposition towards integration of the schools?" asked Horatio.

"Not so much here in Jefferson County, but down east the niggers live like pigs. Even when they can afford better, they live in shanties and won't take a bath unless they're caught in the rain. A great many of 'em have social diseases, to put it most politely, and you can't blame the mother of some immaculate little white girl for not wanting her shoulder-to-shoulder with nigger children. Meanwhile the white fathers feel that school integration will promptly lead to horizontal integration, and they don't want to be grandfather to some taffy-colored infants. I admit that it indicates some lack of confidence in the virtue of their offspring, but that's the way they feel and no federal court order is gonna change it," I said.

Horatio Bunker had his own opinions. "I'm prone to agree with you that even hinting that integration wouldn't be terrible would amount to political suicide, but I have a different idea as to why the majority of the white population is opposed to sharing public facilities. About the only thing some white people have between them and being the lowest human creatures in the community is the Negro population. Any conversation about their being opposed to horizontal integration isn't borne out by the evidence. There's hardly a Negro in Jeffersonville who doesn't have some European ancestry."

I can remember back to when I was about fifteen years old and held hands in the hayloft with Bertha Howard. She was Old Jim's younger sister and maybe a little dark, but certainly not unattractive. I'm not sure I ever convinced Emmy Lou that I was not the father of one of Bertha's numerous illegitimate children. I sure felt bad when her oldest boy got killed fighting over on Guadalcanal.

Thinking about the niggers in Jefferson County caused me to want to defend our way of life. I had to tell Bunker of some of the advantages of being a Negro in the South.

"Yeah, I know, if you've ever been a nigger on Saturday night, you'd never want to be a white man again," mimicked Horatio.

I wasn't going to discuss the point, but it was no compliment to white leadership and the Christian ideal we profess to realize that one out of every twelve Tarvania babies is born out of wedlock, and that the vast majority of these are nigger young'uns. That fact had caused legislation to be proposed on repeated occasions to sterilize unwed mothers who were drawing heavily on welfare funds. There was no sense in worrying Bunker with such matters, since he wouldn't be in the General Assembly anyway.

"Until these damnyankees started messing with Southern customs, Southern niggers enjoyed more legal privileges than any white men anywhere on earth," I said.

"You wouldn't know it by the road gangs," said Horatio.

"There are a lot more dark boys swinging weed-cutters than there are white ones."

I didn't bother to explain to Horatio that they got in trouble with the law more than white boys, but I did tell him about the way the courts operated.

"Here we have four sets of punishments and they sure do favor the darkies. Take murder for example.

"If a white man willfully kills another white man, he usually gets life imprisonment, which is about the worst punishment you can get.

"If a nigger kills a white man, we put him in the gas chamber with dispatch, so that his punishment is brief, as well as cheap.

"Now if a white man kills a nigger, it's usually in self-defense, but even if it weren't, the white man would be morally obligated to support the nigger's family one way or another. Jefferson County niggers have notoriously large families.

"Now, if a nigger kills a nigger it's usually some spontaneous brawl over a nigger woman. He's usually sentenced for ten to fifteen years but actually spends only two or three years on the roads and thereafter is free to lead a normal, happy life.

"In addition to the actual sentences imposed, the white man is always looked upon with a great deal of suspicion if he ever gets out of jail after committing murder. The Negro, on the other hand, is accepted back into the community and all is forgiven."

"Old man," said Horatio, "you'd like to bring slavery back, wouldn't you?"

"My grandpappy damn near died of dysentery during the first Battle of Manassas," I said, "and I'd hate to think he had altogether suffered in vain."

It was raining hard on Wednesday afternoon. The stores are

closed then, and downtown Jeffersonville is as deserted as at midnight. Old Judge Ponticorn had come into town to buy an overcoat, forgetful that it was Wednesday.

"I've got to get out among the people this time, come fair weather or foul," he said.

He had dropped by Bunker's headquarters to get out of the rain and pick up any information I would reveal about his opponent's progress.

"The boy sure is seeing the people, Judge. Of course he may be losing more votes than he's winning with that Yankee accent," I said.

"Time was when the thought of electing a Yankee in Jefferson County would have been the acme of impossibility. And as for old-time Republicans, what fun it was to wave the bloody rag!"

The Judge was referring to standard Democratic campaign techniques. A Republican could usually be laid low by reference to the indignities we had suffered after the Union victory. We got to talking old times.

"Reminiscing is the privilege and the joy of life of old men," said the Judge.

"Times are different, all right, Judge. It's hard to believe that a whippersnapper Yankee Republican could be giving you a run for your money in Jefferson County. What's worse is that I'm halfway helping the bastard," I said.

"Forget it, Bill. Nobody is worried about you. You're just doing a job, and I didn't see any Democrat do handsprings to help you when you needed it. It's not folks like you that worry me. It's young folks like my girl Susan. They've forgotten what our people went through after The War."

The Judge and the others of our generation always refer to the contest of 1861-1865 as "The War." Other conflicts, such as the 1918 and 1941 wars, are specified.

"And their attitude about niggers is puzzling," continued the Judge. "You would believe they want to integrate everything from the schoolrooms to the bedrooms."

"Oh, it isn't that bad," I said. "The young people are just confused by all the high-sounding talk. They'll grow out of it," I said with damn little conviction.

"It isn't just the Negro question," said the Judge. "Folks are putting up with a state income tax, withholding tax, legal liquor, compulsory auto liability insurance, and Lord knows how many more Yankee practices. The whole pattern seems to be changing much too fast."

"The moving finger having written, moves on," I misquoted.

"When we last celebrated Lee's birthday, there were only a dozen people out to hear Grandin Opulant, and he made a good speech. I can remember when the whole town turned out. Remember when we tarred and feathered Fetcher Guggencrow when he got drunk and painted the soldier on the Confederate Monument blue?"

That was before World War I, and a lot of things had changed, including Judge Ponticorn. Lost were his hopes of being Federal Judge. Meanwhile, Fetcher Guggencrow, who wanted to be an artist, wound up a bootlegger. Maybe even his old friend, namely me, William Anchor, has changed.

The old days were good days. On the Fourth, all Jefferson County turned up downtown for the parade, the ladies besting one another in finery, the men seeking to prove their worth as marching soldiers, musicians, or alcohol consumers. The kids played, contested, fought, and regurgitated. The picnic by the Yatawba was a contest with flies and dogs, and one helluva lotta fun.

Senator Clyde Calhoun was a master of the old school. He died with his political boots on in Washington in 1954. He was the last who wore formal clothes at all times. Nobody who ever saw him could forget that living example of the Glory of the South. While his colleagues in the Senate wore normal business suits, Old Clyde was decked out with a swallow-tailed coat, a stiff collar, and a white carnation. His grey-white hair was luxuriant and swept back with the authority of a race horse leading the pack down the home stretch.

Senator Calhoun made the speech. Although it was not exactly new to me even then, I best remember it when Justice Ponticorn, long before he was a Judge, introduced the distinguished visitor. Ponticorn was just raising his political head, yet his verbiage was already established.

"Friends of Jefferson County, indeed it is not only a beautiful day, which is most appropriate for the glory of the Fourth of July, but a day we shall all treasure until we pass to the farther shore and, who knows, shall remember for eternity? (His voice always rose at the end of a sentence, question or not.) Today we remember the sacrifices of our forefathers: their successes, as when they gathered at King's Mountain, and their failures, as when they fell back to British guns at Guilford.

"These things we remember with reverence. We remember most today the men who fell long ago for liberty. At the same time we forget not our more immediate forebears who fought, who bled, who died and, if you will, live forever in our hearts. True sons of the revolution against the tyranny of George the Third, these, our men, fought against the guns and conscripts of Yankee invaders. We lessen not the memory of the courage of those who fought under Robert E. Lee when we also remember the brave men, and their courageous women, who pitted their adamant bodies and unyielding spirits against the paid mercenaries and cruel commanders of the armies of Cornwallis.

"Of all men of Jefferson County, my honor is greatest this day, for it is my pleasant task to introduce the most respected man in Carolina, a man whose father bled at Gettysburg, a man whose ancestors pointed their muskets at the war-skilled red-coats, a man descended from those who fought by fisticuff and axes the savages who once roamed this land upon which we now repast. I present to you the man who began his life as a simple farm boy, just like most of us. The man who earned his way through school the hard way. The man who fought for Democracy as he charged up San Juan Hill, its slopes blazing with Spanish guns. The man who returned to his home and was sent, by the grateful citizens of our neighboring state, to uphold the rights of the people against the Yankees in our nation's Capital. This is the man whom all Southern states have come to love and admire. The man who has been sent to represent the people in the august halls of the United States Senate. How long, oh how long, has it been since we have been so favored as we have in such a Democrat, such an American, as Senator Clyde Calhoun of Carolina?"

Senator Calhoun always made an inspiring speech, much of it the same from one year to the next. Part of it pleasantly haunts my memory:

"My friends of Tarvania, it has been my happy privilege to represent the South in the great Congress Halls of the United States for lo these many years. I have recently made a great survey of the great state of Tarvania. I have been down in that great eastern section of Tarvania, that great farming section of Tarvania. And down in eastern Tarvania I see the people of eastern Tarvania going about their daily tasks. And I believe that the people of eastern Tarvania are a happy people.

"From there I go to the great Piedmont section of Tarvania. I hear the hum of machinery; I see the great manufacturing plants turning out great quantities of goods to be shipped to all portions of the world; and I see the people of Piedmont Tarvania going about their daily tasks, and I believe that the people of Piedmont Tarvania are a happy people.

"From there I go into the great mountainous sections of Tarvania. That great western section of Tarvania. I see the advancements and improvements being made there in the dairying industry and I see the advancements and improvements being made there in the other industries and I see the people of western Tarvania going about their daily tasks and I believe that the people of western Tarvania are a happy people.

"As the poet has so ably sung, 'My country 'tis of thee, sweet land of liberty, of thee I sing. Long may our land be bright with freedom's holy light. Protect us by thy might, Great God our King.' "

The good Senator would bow graciously and the applause was prolonged and sincere. Boys looked up, and some would emulate him all their lives. Older men would thank God they lived in America and that there were men like Senator Calhoun. The women would be more deeply moved, and some would even cry.

Gone is the youthful Ponticorn who was "going places," gone is Senator Calhoun, and gone are the speeches that made us proud of being Americans. What happened to our respect for those who died in our behalf? Where went the righteousness of the cause of our country?

Today we don't celebrate the Fourth, except that most plants close down, unless business is too good to close. Oh yes, we do have boat races and auto races on the Fourth.

Judge Ponticorn has become an anachronism, and I am an old man who remembers how the fireworks flared, and we were proud to be Americans when the sun set along the Yatawba River on the Fourth of July.

14

WHEN
you knew Grandin Opulant you also nearly knew his
son, usually called Gran III. I often wondered if the next generation would be Gran IV and the chain would add links like English royalty.

Like his greying father, Gran III is tall, handsome, impeccable, and will probably grow the same distinguished moustache in years to come. His bearing is proper and his manner
pleasant, and with a Triniton education supplemented by some
world travel, and two years of reserve officer service on the
Enterprise, he has a cosmopolitan touch that puts him a notch
above Jeffersonville's other best-family young men. He is the
only one who can express himself in languages other than
Tarvanian.

Although he is not a national golf champion, he always wins
the annual championship at the Jeffersonville Country Club. He
plays tennis well, above average poker, and is the pride of the
summer colony at Vanderbilt Hills. As a thirty-year-old bache-
lor he is more in demand than the Chairman of the Appropri-
ations Committee during the General Assembly. He is an

evasive daughter-target for every conscientious mother in upper-class Tarvania. I'd say his only fault is an abundant enthusiasm for poontang, and I, among others, am not critical of that.

Gran III is a moderate drinker but on one occasion was slightly overloaded at the wrong time and place. Preacher Melton told me about it.

"Mr. Bill," he told me, "I've been fighting liquor all my life."

"And have every intention of continuing the hopeless battle," I added. Everybody loved Preacher Melton, yet couldn't resist kidding him about his devotion to ending the scourge of alcohol. He took it seriously, even when he was invited to cocktail capitals, like Vanderbilt Hills.

"Of this matter I have made a study and have found that our detestable liquor stores carry thirty-two brands of whiskey beginning with 'Old.' These include Old Crow, Old Grandad, Old Forester, Old General, and Old Fitzgerald, to name just a few."

"Throughout my life of sin I have not really known any great whiskey except Craven County Corn, and it is never very old," I answered. "You have tested these poisons to complete your knowledge, I trust?"

"That has not been necessary," said the good preacher. "They are all equally evil, although those bearing the label '100 Proof' are the worst."

"Most interesting," I replied.

"I shouldn't have been eavesdropping, and it wasn't intentional," continued Preacher Melton, "but I was up at the Magnolia in Vanderbilt Hills for Sunday dinner when I overheard Gran III on the telephone. You know I have been trying to get that fine young man to swear off whiskey for life, even though he is reasonably moderate in his wrongdoing. Anyway, I was shocked to hear him openly planning an orgy with a brand named 'Old Poontang.'

"Monday I dropped by the liquor store in Mecklenton, the same one I have been visiting in behalf of the manager, who has promised to give up his loathsome trade. I inquired about 'Old Poontang,' and the clerks and customers broke out in sustained raucous laughter," said Preacher Melton.

By this time I was laughing at the preacher myself. Apparently the seminary had established very virtuous habits, but I couldn't laugh at the good man without an explanation.

"Preacher, people weren't laughing at you, just at your ignorance in this instance. Old poontang is not a liquor but a rather informal method of courting. It would probably fall in the same general category as heavy necking, if you are familiar with that subject," I said. I wasn't about to tell him the whole truth.

"In that case I shall ask young Opulant to give up old poontang along with alcoholic beverages."

Aside from his collection of golf trophies, Gran III valued his number of feminine conquests, although to his credit he mentioned neither names nor numbers. It has been said that every additional small black dot on the right door of his white Jaguar convertible marked an accomplishment. Damned if I understand how a young man can do anything more familiar than carry on a shouted conversation in those little sports cars.

When Susan Ponticorn came back to Jeffersonville it was natural that Gran III should eye this pretty parcel with joy and hope. He went after such objectives with dash and determination, and it was generally assumed that mission was accomplished when the prospect stopped being his constant companion in the flashing Jaguar. Off he and Susan went to Pinehurst, to Myrtle Beach, and to Vanderbilt Hills. Susan's short-cropped hair was still being buffeted after four months of maximum courtship. Whenever another girl would take her place, gossip gave him another seduction, but Susan kept reappearing in the favored right-hand seat, indicating a very slow conquest or a lot of side attractions beyond a mighty shapely figure.

Susan Ponticorn and Gran III had a lot in common, aside from both wanting the Judge to beat Horatio Bunker. Well suited by age and education, above average in ability and energy, these two would make the prime young family of Jeffersonville. The old biddies, who constantly relayed their gossip to me, already had 'em married. It seems that a woman just can't stand for a man to be free. If she can't get him, or her daughter or kin can't get him, she wants some woman to get him.

"Oh, young Opulant will give up his wild-oatish ways once he's married to Susan. She's just the woman for him. I just can't wait for the announcement. Don't forget, Mr. Bill, I told you first."

Fifteen loose-jawed females told me the same story. I began repeating it myself. Indeed, I couldn't imagine a finer couple. Susan wouldn't have any more trouble controlling Gran III than Emmy Lou had with me. All I could do after the marriage day was to talk about the good old days, and I had to be mighty careful when I did that.

Susan confided in me on the subject, which made me right proud.

"Gran III is a mighty fine young man, Mr. Bill. I know he is one of the prime catches of Tarvania and I'm not getting any younger," added Susan.

I laughed in disbelief. I could remember Susan before she could carry a doll.

"An awful lot of advantages go with Gran III. He's the kind of man who could go anywhere, especially with a woman nudging him a little," I said, sounding more like a matchmaker than one of the bothersome females.

"I agree," said Susan, "but he doesn't want to go anywhere. He's content with a little bit of business in insurance, a little bit of real estate trading, a little bit of golf, tennis, and cocktail parties. He'll be on half a dozen boards of directors, run innumerable fund-raising drives, and be appointed to countless boards, commissions, and agencies. Assuming of course that the Republicans don't take over the state," laughed Susan.

"Gran III may lack specific ambitions, but that is merely a lack of final convictions. When he thinks something is sufficiently important, when he knows where he's going, he'll get there," I said.

"I just want a man who has a place to go even if he won't get there, like your protégé, Mr. Bunker, though no sane woman could put up with the rest of him," she added.

"That's the price you pay. Get a nice sweet boy like your State Department friends, or get a horse's rump like Bunker with enough gall to overturn society. Gran III falls as close as you'll get to the perfect compromise," I said.

"I'm not sure I'm ready to compromise, yet," said Susan.

Despite her election activity, Susan Ponticorn continued subject to the courtship of Gran III, although no progress was evident except that, as winter approached, the white Jaguar was driven with its canvas top mounted. While Susan wasn't capitulating biologically or matrimonially, Gran III was more and more eager to win her hand, which proves that it pays for a girl to be chaste. Regardless of the affirmative advice of her relatives, acquaintances, and her own good judgment, Susan remained aloof to Grandin's proposals, even when they became most honorable.

15

ALTHOUGH
I've been in and out of campaign headquarters all my life, I can't recall ever having been in one marked "Republican" until the unfortunate events of 1960. Horatio Bunker's was like the others.

He had rented a store with about a sixteen-foot front with glass facing the street, separated in the center by a glass door. Taped to the inside of the window were large reproductions of Nixon and Lodge on one side and of Optimo Futrell, the Republican candidate for governor, and Bunker, of course, on the other. All these pictures further reduced the inadequate lighting, so that the long interior was like one of the tunnels the Southeastern Railway goes through on the route to Knoxville. Once you got accustomed to the half-darkness it was right restful, having a conspiratorial atmosphere. This was appropriate for political activities, especially Republican, since they border on subversive at best.

Along the walls were seats provided by the Webb Funeral Home. They will provide seating for nearly anything, each seat being labeled with the name of the free-lending establishment. Direct advertising is frowned upon in the funeral business in Jeffersonville.

Scattered around the room were an assortment of well-used tables covered with assorted Republican propaganda. Towards the rear was the biggest table, which also served as my desk. While it was adequate in size, it was by no means sturdy, each leg enjoying freedom of independent motion. Every time the carriage of my typewriter moved, the entire outfit swayed noticeably, being held upright only by long habit. A telephone completed the working tools of our trade.

In the very rear, a section was partitioned off, presumably to serve as a stock room when the store was used for commercial purposes. Part of this was my private boudoir consisting of a bathroom without bath, a couple of crates for a dresser, and my cot. Bunker had rigged two ropes over the bed so that I could navigate to and from the wheel chair easily, supporting myself like a trapeze artist. A plywood panel shielded the clandestine quarters, and I got to like the hideaway. No Heliotrope yapping at me, and an agreeable collection of newspapers, magazines, and assorted trash made the place just right. It even had an inconspicuous back door if I should take it in mind to sneak in a lady for the night.

The center of attraction of the Bunker headquarters was a large black stove, somewhat antique and in the style of a well-rounded beer barrel. It was a consumer of coal and was kept going round the clock whether it was cold outside or not. It had a flat top and provided the heat for coffee. It was soon apparent that Bunker's best attraction and most costly campaign item would be coffee and paper cups. He and I had our own porcelain cups. We carefully labeled each in fear of contamination.

I was drinking the stuff one chill evening when Bunker came

up with the damnedest scheme conceived since the last Chinese dynasty.

"It is a chilly night and I think I shall now write and acquire a wife. My home is spacious and it needs to be filled, even if my body did not need warmth in the winters to come," said Bunker.

There could be no sensible comment to this statement, so I awaited more.

"I seek your assistance, Mr. Bill, firstly because this matter should be handled in confidence and I know you will tell no one," he said.

The appeal to my high sense of honor was effective. "So long as you are planning no mass rape or other major crime, I will not reveal your questionable activities," I said, curious about his next devious step.

"I had a long conversation with the lady who handles the Alumnae affairs at the Southeast University for Women. She keeps track of most of the graduates, and I am going to use her to locate prospects for this project. The reason for your help is to get out the correspondence. It's not that I don't trust my secretary at the plant, but in a thing of this nature, her feminine instinct for gossip would likely outweigh her businesslike habits," said Bunker.

"Let's get on with the plot," I said, putting some paper in the typewriter.

"Miss Celia Longstreet, comma, Alumnae Office, comma, Southeast University for Women, comma, Greensedge, comma, Tarvania, period. Dear Miss Longstreet, colon. Paragraph. Pursuant to our conversation heretofore, comma, below follow the requirements that I consider essential to our program, period. It is understood that your fee shall be $25.00 per prospect, comma, with an additional fee of $50.00 if an invitation to a social affair is provided, period. In no case shall your name be used in negotiations, comma, and any information received by me shall be held in confidence, period. Please direct mail to me in care of Mr. William Anchor, comma, 627 Main Street, comma, Jeffersonville, comma, Tarvania, period. Paragraph."

Already I could see that I would be deeply involved in a plot that would be undercover and likely dishonest in one way or another.

"We consider the following essential, colon," Bunker continued. "Age, comma, between twenty-two and twenty-eight, period. Weight, comma, one hundred ten to one hundred thirty, period. Height, comma, five three to five nine, period. Education, comma, BA or BS, parenthesis, majors in mathematics, comma, physics, comma, chemistry, comma, and physical education excluded, end parenthesis, comma, B-average in scholastic attainment, period. Residence, comma, Tarvania or immediately neighboring state, period. Financial status, comma, net worth twenty-five thousand or unearned income of two thousand annually, period. Paragraph."

"You forgot whether you want your prospect white, comma, Negro, comma, or Chinese, period," I added.

"Never mind the humor; let's continue," said Bunker.

"Social status and reputation must be above average, period."

"Here's where I'm going to really restrict the field," laughed Bunker.

"Paragraph. Marital status, comma, widowed with at least one child, period. Paragraph. Very truly yours, comma. Unquote. Show my name and I'll sign it," concluded Bunker.

I didn't have much to say, but I knew that anybody educated at the Harvard Business School was overtrained way beyond his peak. Of all the damn fool methods of selecting a wife, this was the worst. A normal man would be better off throwing a dart at a random page in a telephone directory.

"Save a lot of time this way," said Bunker, as if guessing my thoughts.

He signed the letter and left the office.

On a Sunday afternoon the last week in July Horatio Bunker went to Tarvania City to ferret out the voting record of Judge Ponticorn. There also went Susan Ponticorn. One went to prove that the old man had voted against the best interests of the people; the other went to recall a record of devotion to public duty.

I would have known little of what happened at Tarvania City had it not been for the report of my sometimes friend, sometimes opponent, Enebra Sellers. He owes his happiness and loyalty to the liquor interests. I have no quarrel with him as a lobbyist or with the product he represents, but only with his infuriating fence-straddling in Democratic primaries. The old grafter will never stand up for a candidate unless he is absolutely certain he has picked a winner. Normally, he waits until the returns are in and then convinces the winners that he has supported them from the beginning.

Despite his sneaky ways, you get kind of tolerant of somebody you have put up with for decades, so I was glad to see Enebra when he was through Jeffersonville in September. He had aged a lot since I was last in Tarvania City. Enebra Sellers has the flabby figure and florid face of a heavy drinker, and he's been told for thirty years that he wouldn't live to be counted in the next census. He's somewhere in his seventies, and I have to admit he is still getting around under his own power, which is more than I can say.

For the length of a normal lifetime Sellers has been the protective lobbyist for liquor makers. His job is to see that no legislation passes in Tarvania that might be detrimental to the liquor industry, which is no small task since three-quarters of the General Assembly are elected on a promise to outlaw liquor throughout the state.

The tools of his trade are a suite in the Sir Johnson in Tarvania City, a generous expense account, and a virtually unlimited supply of bourbon. With these he keeps those who are for legal liquor happy with their position, and sways the uncertain to think more benignly of liquor when they get to Tarvania City away from the clamor of the drys. One sure way to build a feeling of kinship is that every state Representative and every state Senator who ever takes a drink finds at least two pints of good whiskey every week in the top drawer of his dresser at the hotel. Unless the statesmen actually refuse the stuff, he has them hooked for the session. It's damn hard to get really determined to outlaw legal liquor when you're drinking the product every evening.

There is more to it than dispensing bottles, however, and Enebra is rightly credited with being the dean of Tarvania City lobbyists. He invites friends up to his suite, tells good, risqué jokes, and can be trusted not to repeat anything said under the influence. He drinks with his guests, but never gets even slightly drunk, although professing the outstanding quality and high alcoholic content of the product pouring into the bloodstream. But even this does not account for his unblemished success in controlling the forces of abstinence.

His room is not his headquarters, nor is the rotunda in the Capitol, where other lobbyists harass members of the Legislature. Instead, he practically lives in the lobby of the Sir Johnson, where no one walks by without a friendly word from Enebra Sellers. It's a good walk from the Capitol to the Sir Johnson, and there is somehow always a nice, soft chair near Enebra Sellers. There are no chairs near the elevators.

Enebra is always glad to discuss your problems. Although he

almost never expresses an opinion, he has the ability to make a man feel that he is doing the best thing for his county and his state, even though the best thing might have been the opposite the previous day.

In a spirit of mutual confidence, he somehow brings the subject around to the simple fact that your favorite project is doomed if revenues from the legal sale of liquor are cut off. Even the most ardent dry gets the feeling that the Baptist Church and Enebra Sellers are really working as partners before the session of the General Assembly is finished. Anyway, the innumerable bills to call for a state-wide vote to outlaw liquor never get out of committee.

By the efforts of Enebra Sellers, Tarvania has had local option for a quarter of a century, and every year that goes by another town or county opens ABC stores. Naturally, Jefferson County won't convenience those who take an occasional drink, so we have to go twenty-five miles or pay the bootlegger's profit for red liquor. Probably Enebra Sellers was now in Jeffersonville to work towards correcting this situation.

In accomplishing his nefarious mission in life, Enebra rarely leaves the Sir Johnson, and they say he never sees sunlight while the General Assembly is in session. There is good reason for this, because through the lobby walks every politician of consequence in Tarvania, in or out of season. Rare is the salesman or other regular Sir Johnson guest who is not known to Enebra Sellers. From his observation post in the lobby, each newcomer is a curiosity; the occasional tourist and hordes of conventioneers are readily identified and speedily dismissed as of no consequence by the able lobbyist.

When Susan Ponticorn checked in late Sunday afternoon, Enebra Sellers had to search his memory to place her. Eight years had passed since she was a student at Southeast University for Women, but liquor hadn't dulled Enebra's catalogue of names and faces. He recalled as if yesterday the pride of Judge Ponticorn when he showed off his bright young daughter at dances sponsored by the United Daughters of the Confederacy.

Enebra Sellers started to greet the young woman; then, on second thought, fell back into his seat. It occurred to him that a young single woman might be checking into a relatively distant hotel for no good reason. There would be time later to identify himself. There was no possibility of her remembering a fat old man who looked like a lot of other fat old men. Besides, one of the women behind the desk had served him well in many ways and might not take kindly to his interest in the young woman. And Susan Ponticorn did look ripe. Her lightweight summer suit still looked fresh, despite the wrinkles set by driving. Indeed, they enhanced a well-rounded figure. Enebra Sellers would have had a third thought a few years before.

Enebra Sellers held his place and wondered for the umpteenth time why everybody had to wait for an elevator, even when the Sir Johnson was nearly empty. He never complained, because the elevator service had made possible a life of comfort for one aging lobbyist. Scarcely had Susan headed upwards when an unknown young man strode into the lobby.

"Reservation for Horatio Bunker" could be easily heard by Enebra Sellers.

"Probably three or four days."

"Hot in Tarvania this time of year" was all that Enebra Sellers could hear. He wondered why the young man was complaining. Bunker had obviously just gotten out of an air-cooled vehicle. Everybody else in Tarvania City was in shirtsleeves and wet with sweat. Sellers evaluated the man as somebody whose name he knew or somebody who might be worth knowing.

The new guest was no newcomer to money, as indicated by

the expensive and quiet clothes. Sellers himself used the same type; he was comfortable in any crowd. Bunker's tailoring was Yankee, however, and his speech had the clear accent of a Harvard lawyer. Maybe he was from Mecklenton, thought Sellers. The old lobbyist usually classified strangers on first sight.

That name, "Bunker," wondered Sellers. He moved from his seat and shared the elevator with the newcomer. Once in his own room Sellers quickly spotted Bunker's name as the Republican candidate from Jefferson County. No wonder Susan was meeting him a long way from home. She ought to have her pretty rump kicked for messing around with her father's opponent.

Enebra Sellers told me that his usually correct assumption about the conduct of people at the Sir Johnson Hotel did not turn out with Horatio Bunker and Susan Ponticorn.

The hotel dining room was nearly empty Sunday night when Enebra entered, adequately fortified with a bit of five-year-old, eighty-six-proof. Susan was seated alone and struggling with a desire for chicken with dumplings in preference to the low calorie special of the day. Horatio Bunker caught her eye as he walked in, and Susan started. Enebra knew there was no pre-arranged rendezvous between these two.

"Good evening, Miss Ponticorn. I hadn't expected the pleasure of seeing you this day or at this place," said Bunker.

"Nor did I expect to see you, Mr. Bunker," said Susan.

So ended the dialogue of the two young people from Jeffersonville. Enebra Sellers was disappointed.

By the next afternoon he learned from "Green Ink" Goodfellow, Secretary of State, that Bunker and Miss Ponticorn were disturbing the normally relaxed summer atmosphere of the Capitol by their search through old House and Senate Journals. More interesting was the fact that they were necessarily constantly together in the cramped record rooms. The temperature may have been high, but the atmosphere was icy. Polite, brusque exchanges deteriorated into cold silence on the part of Susan. Of course Horatio Bunker was undoubtedly his usual unpleasant, cheerful self, apparently undisturbed by antagonism. I hoped someday to see him lose his temper and hoped somebody antagonized him who could maul hell out of him.

Enebra Sellers' report of the next evening was more interesting. The Tavern in the hotel was limited to the sale of wine and beer in accordance with Tarvania City law. There Enebra often found his acquaintances and more often than not invited them up to his suite for a libation of more potency, much to the distress of the Tavern manager.

A table and most of the length of the bar were already occupied by local tipplers, exchanging highly opinionated prognostications of baseball and political developments. Bunker picked a table and was merely watching the bubbles rise in his beer glass when Susan entered. She looked as if she needed a long cool drink badly but hesitated when she saw only men in the Tavern. Bunker gestured for her to join him. She perked up by ignoring him and pranced into the Tavern.

Single girls in barrooms mean the same thing all over the world, and two young men went into action. The more aggressive of the pair accepted a five-dollar bet that he could pick up Susan Ponticorn, at least to the extent of buying her a drink. She was a respectable-looking girl, but a few beers had made him confident.

Striking up a conversation with an unwilling woman is as difficult as terminating one with a willing one. The young man was not discouraged easily, and soon the entire taproom was watching the verbal assault, some silently cheering and others frowning at the proceedings.

Horatio Bunker walked to the table and uttered one short sentence: "The young lady wants you to leave."

The young man got out a "What the hell business . . . " before noticing Bunker's angered eyes and clenching hands. Bunker was close to blowing up, and the beer drinker didn't need a red flag to back off. Bunker returned to his seat, and Susan quickly left the Tavern.

Enebra Sellers regretted he hadn't been the hero, but now that the moment was past he thought a little common courtesy was in order. He might not live to see it, but this wild Republican might someday be a political force in Tarvania. Enebra didn't fraternize much with members of the minority party, but tried to keep on good terms with them when not being observed by his Democratic friends. Regrettably, Republicans were all pledged to outlaw legal liquor, even though they would usually drink any amount of any kind they could get.

Bunker was polite but reserved. He finally agreed to accept a drink in Sellers' suite, provided the favor could be returned another evening. Bunker had a few phone calls to make and would be available within the hour.

Enebra found Susan alone in the lobby, introduced himself, and was soon telling her of some of the more pleasant moments he had known with her father. Carefully mentioning that others would be present, he asked her to his suite. Sellers' lady-friend behind the desk was also invited. Enebra's part in this little drama was to be an observer rather than a protagonist, and he always took care not to offend, by exclusion, the lady behind the desk, who was in truth the unpaid confederate of the liquor lobby.

Enebra told me it was mixing up adverbs to say that Susan manfully thanked Bunker for his conduct in the Tavern. He then proposed an agreement that would benefit them all. Instead of sitting far apart in uncommunicative and mutual dislike, Enebra offered a resolution to the effect that politics and political personalities be excluded from the conversation. Bunker readily agreed, and Susan finally threw up her hands in a gesture that all was hopeless and laughed for the first time in Tarvania City.

"That leaves the topic of religion, unless Mr. Bunker is inclined towards Freud," she said.

Enebra Sellers took the lead with his favorite subject, the desirability of legal liquor in Tarvania, which of course is as political as you can get, but one in which there could be harmony of opinion. Everybody present was at least getting more relaxed under its influence.

The views differed. Sellers maintained that liquor was available anyway, so that by making it legal it could be controlled. In addition, it provided funds for rehabilitating unfortunates who succumbed to alcoholism and provided substantial revenues for public schools.

Susan repeated her father's views without conviction. Judge Ponticorn believed that liquor should be outlawed as a detrimental opiate and uncontrollable release for the masses. The few who could handle liquor were of adequate financial status to get it illegally. Susan had difficulty in reconciling an advocate of violation of the law with a statesman and judge.

Horatio Bunker wouldn't take the subject seriously. He piously advocated prohibition on the grounds that it was the official position of the platform of the Republican Party of Tarvania, which nobody had read or was likely to read. He further noted that the religious leaders advocated prohibition. He also pointed out that a sizable portion of Jefferson County was engaged in liquor, and the economic welfare and moral welfare of the people would be impaired if ABC stores were permitted. He put it this way:

"The greatest people in America are farmers, and their most profitable product in Jefferson County is corn. Who would deprive our farmers of income?

"Small independent merchants are the backbone of the nation. Those who sell sugar, and much of it is used in corn whiskey, should not be exterminated.

"The artisan must have his markets. Metal workers, who fabricate boilers, tanks, and tubes, should not be outlawed. Neither should our auto mechanics, who carefully maintain souped-up vehicles for illegal transport.

"Our local government officials also benefit to the degree that the sheriff's department would not have high caliber men were it not for the supplementary pay provided by our moonshiners for overlooking the location of stills.

"Sir, this is excellent bourbon," added Bunker as he gulped with gusto.

"You are a hypocrite," said Susan without anger or enthusiasm.

The lady behind the desk believed in quotas for individuals. Years of observation at the Sir Johnson had led her to the conviction that, beyond a pint per night, drinkers destroyed more hotel property than the hotel made in profit through the sale of set-ups.

The foursome moved to the dining room, where Enebra and his good lady were soon ignored. Susan apparently forgot all about her father's ideals as she launched into the extreme liberal positions so often advocated by intellectual young women. Bunker maintained the conservative positions pretty much in line with those of Judge Ponticorn. They were still arguing heatedly in the lobby when Sellers could no longer stay awake.

All that transpired between Bunker and Susan during late July in Tarvania City will never be known. Enebra Sellers gave me a few possibilities.

As the week wore on, Susan and Bunker spent more and more time arguing with each other and were less and less interested in having other parties present.

"You would think," Enebra said, "that they would have enough of each other's company sweating in the records room without carrying on the battle all night as well. I'll bet if they ever got around to friendly activity it would be a memorable event." Enebra has an uncouth mind.

16

I MUST

have been more convincing than I thought possible when I told Bunker to "see the people." The antique campaign car bearing "Horatio Bunker for Representative" was being reported from places seldom seen by politicians or even salesmen.

Rocky Creek runs through some of the most rugged land east of the Rockies, and in Rocky Creek precinct live some of the most rugged citizens on earth. Old man Jupes heads up the clan, and about the only thing that can be said in his favor is that he has been highly reproductive. Even this doubtful virtue is offset by his homicidal tendencies. Twice indicted for murder, twice acquitted, and four times guilty of murder, he takes great delight in showing visitors the grave of his most important victim.

It seems that old man Jupes and his brother-in-law were in disagreement about the exact location of a line separating their property. Brother-in-law York was lawing Jupes for the foot of land, even though the cost of the lawsuit far exceeded the value of the rocks and nearly vertical land involved. Jupes's deer rifle settled the dispute. When he was brought to trial, Jupes had a passel of offspring equal to a platoon testifying in his behalf.

They have various names, having been conceived both "inside and outside the fence," as they say in the mountains. Most appeared as character witnesses, although about all they could say in truth was that old man Jupes had been to church a few times. Others swore to a story that proved Jupes was visiting his sister in Knoxville at the time of the murder. Of course Jupes has probably never been out of the county, and the state prosecution couldn't locate the sister in Knoxville, or anywhere else. The fact that the corpus delicti couldn't be found caused the jury to acquit Jupes once again. I never talked to a juryman who wasn't dead sure he was guilty. "The evidence just wasn't there, that's all," they would say, "and York was more of an asset to society dead than alive," they would add in justification.

Most people coming to the Rocky Creek area are there to fish on the Jupes Branch, wherein fine trout do dwell. The Jupes method of collecting tribute is unique. Each morning during the fishing season roofing nails are spread on the entrance road. The uninitiated uses his spare and punctures a second tire before coming to terms with old man Jupes. Bunker learned beforehand of the standard routine.

As the victim regards his flat tire, an old man appears on the scene from nowhere. The scene is a single-lane, unpaved trail which allows vehicle passing only in dry weather. Mountain bush conceals both side directions. No sign of a house or building is evident, which makes a lost quantity of roofing nails highly improbable.

The old man is bent with age, alcohol, and fornication. His eyes are red-rimmed blue and watery, yet alive with good evil spirits.

"Howdy, stranger," says Jupes.

"Hello," says the victim, "some damn fool has spread nails on this road."

"That's peculiar," says Jupes. "Never heard of it happening before, and I live right over the ridge."

"Don't know anyone who could fix it do you, old-timer?" the victim asks.

"My boy, Jake, is pretty handy with tools. He ought to be coming along here sometime soon. But let me warn you he's as contrary as a rattlesnake. You'll have to sweet talk him into helping you."

About that time Jake comes lurching down the trail in a rolling piece of junk that was once a Studebaker pickup truck. Jake proves to be unfriendly and unhelpful.

"Don't believe I care to fix yore flat, stranger," says Jake.

The victim earnestly solicits help, offering great remuneration in desperation. Old man Jupes joins the victim in pleas for help.

"Well, for five dollars, I'll do it," says Jake.

By this time the victim is delighted to be robbed. With complete tire repair equipment from the back of the pickup, Jake dispatches the job with surprising efficiency. Old man Jupes tells the victim that he'll have the roofing nails removed by mid-afternoon. All possible customers will have arrived by then. So goes the collection of tribute for fishing on the Jupes Branch.

Horatio Bunker's invasion of Rocky Creek Precinct would have followed the usual pattern except that the campaigner had done some preliminary research. He knew that Rocky Creek voted from 167 to 173 votes if old man Jupes got interested in the election. Otherwise it voted half that. If nothing were done to tamper with the box, it would vote straight Republican, except for two Democratic votes represented by Smokey Bowen and his wife. He is Game Warden and appointed by the state, so there had better be two Democratic ballots.

In a close election, Rocky Creek has been known to go heavily Democratic. Old man Jupes deals from a negative position as a Republican. They don't pay him anything, naturally, but we Democrats must pay him to switch the vote. If he were naturally Democratic, we wouldn't have to buy him, and since the Republicans have no funds to speak of, old man Jupes would never enjoy any revenue if he were a Democrat.

Bunker did his duty by puncturing the left front tire of his old Ford. When old man Jupes made his appearance, his usual cordial manner changed. This man was a lawyer, obviously, and the patriarch of Rocky Creek had had ample opportunity to know every lawyer for counties around.

The sign proclaiming "Bunker for Representative" on the side of the Ford indicated the political season had begun, but old man Jupes knew not the name or party affiliation, putting him in a position of dealing with an unstacked deck, which he didn't like. Another thing that disturbed him was that this Ford was clearly a liquor-carrying conversion, and it was rump-heavy, indicating a load aboard. If there was one thing that old man Jupes wasn't going to have, it was liquor coming into his own back yard. He is an exporter, not an importer.

Instead of the usual niceties, old man Jupes simply asked, "Whatcha doin' here?"

Horatio Bunker was not unprepared. "Heard that spring crops were very poor here, and a few of the friends of Mr. Amos Jupes sent me up with some vittles to help out. Do you know where I can find him?"

Old man Jupes never had a friend in his life, and he and the clan were no worse off than usual in the summer of 1960. In fact, fishermen were numerous. The transparency of the lie did not create contempt, but admiration for the stranger.

"And who might you be, friend?" asked Jupes in his most cordial manner.

"I am a businessman in Jeffersonville running on the Republican ticket for Representative. My name is Horatio Bunker, but that's not the reason I'm here. Just assigned to do the transporting, and here I am stuck with a flat," said Bunker.

"Well, I'm Amos Jupes, so you've found your man," said old man Jupes. "Don't worry about the flat. My boy Jake will be along and fix it in a minute."

Sure enough along came Jake in the Studebaker pickup. He was a little surprised by the old man's curt order to fix the flat, but was a little too stupid, or too smart, to question the order.

Soon Bunker was at the family headquarters and the loot from the Ford was being unloaded. A disproportionate amount of sugar was included in the haul, conveniently packaged in half-gallon fruit jars. Other items included flour, chewing tobacco, and 30-30 rifle cartridges. This unexpected bonanza brought out the hospitality of old man Jupes. Out came the white liquor and orders to "set another place, Ma."

The Jupes homestead is poor in material goods but rich in fecundity. While the old house is about to collapse, new life is everywhere. Dogs, cats, pigs, and chickens share facilities in equal freedom with the human occupants. Some of the human life is pitiful. Old man Jupes's third wife is a daughter by his first wife, making for an extremely complex family relationship. Some of the offspring show the results; they are pathetic little creatures deformed in one way or another. They fortunately seldom reach maturity.

Bunker entered the Jupes residence with a firm step and a timorous heart. The house was without interior light, and dark after coming from out-of-doors. Once his eyes adjusted, he could see that it was wallpapered with newspapers, not for artistry but for winter wind protection. Except for one large shaky table, the furniture mostly consisted of beds, cots, and bunks. These also served as chairs when the family was awake.

"Made it myself," bragged Jupes as he shook a half-gallon fruit jar of clear liquid. He held high the jar to show the bead. A large amount of small bubbles is supposed to assure fine quality. Without further formality, an assorted collection of unwashed jam and peanut butter jars were filled three-quarters full. The younger members of the family enjoyed the same privileges as the rest when old man Jupes became the perfect host.

They waited for Bunker to take the first gulp. I've been there, and the thought of his misery gave me pleasure. Jupes's white liquor would taste like gin or vodka if it didn't taste more like a mixture of zinc and rotten corn. It smells more like the smoke from a paper pulp plant. Getting down the first mouthful is like trying to drink undiluted ammonia, and damn nigh as lethal. After the first swallow, it gets better. Even though your stomach's on fire, you are partially numbed.

Jupes's private stock was not watered down, so that a glassful exceeded in potency a full pint of commercial liquor. Old man Jupes was mindful that if Bunker became insensible a few dollars wouldn't be missed from his pocket. Bunker had come prepared, however, and was previously fortified with a heavily buttered sandwich. And he didn't object to thefts of his constantly refilled glass. Lesser family members didn't get seconds, unless they were stolen.

When dinner reached the table, several of the clan were no longer interested in food, because of either illness or prostration. Bunker made the table and acted as if he thought Mrs. Jupes a great cook, which was excellent hypocrisy if the usual food was served.

Visualize assorted pieces of pork cooked in its own grease.

Add potatoes floating in pork grease. Add black-eyed peas soaking up pork grease. Finally, pass the biscuits and sop up pork grease for a spread. You have a meal to remember.

Meanwhile, some of the Jupeses vented their naturally sweet dispositions. Two or three fights were running all the time, restrained only by old man Jupes's reach with his walking stick. He broke the skin on one girl's head, but with blood running down around one ear she went on eating and yelling.

How Bunker fell into the graces of the belligerent Jupes I'll never know. He should have been badly mauled at least. As it turned out, he walked back to his car, immaculate in attire and in good political shape with the Rocky Creek voters.

Bunker was exhausted Saturday afternoon and had to appear at a rally in Treetown that night. He was so tired of campaigning that any other subject was a relief. Somehow it turned to Susan Ponticorn. He was interested in everything I would tell him about her early life in Jeffersonville. The little incidents, like the time she knocked down Chief Tate with her bicycle, kept him amused, and I was glad to take his mind away from his hopeless battle.

"I suppose she has changed a great deal, having been in a cosmopolitan atmosphere for a half-dozen years," said Bunker.

"Some, of course, although she was about the same when she got out of college. She may appear a little more sophisticated, but I suspect she is still the little girl waiting for Mr. Ideal to come along," I said.

"And who would that be?" he asked.

"It might be you except for a few minor faults, most of which are that the things she holds most high are contemptible to you," I said.

"Public welfare, for example," laughed Bunker. "She wants every stray cat and illegitimate mother to live like royalty at public expense. I say let not the rest of us lose the fruits of our labor in their comfortable support."

"Never mind the orating," I said. "If it weren't for a few people like Susan this would be a damn poor world to live in."

"Probably so," said Bunker," but I doubt if she'll ever find her ideal. They don't grow many that way. As much as she's traveled, she ought to know it, or has she been married and already proved that the ideal doesn't exist?"

"No, Horatio, Susan is probably one of the few twenty-five-year-old virgins alive in Tarvania," I said.

"I doubt that," he said cynically.

One of the most difficult things for an amateur in politics to learn is that he must rise above principle. This is especially hard for a man who has entered politics for the primary purpose of improving the government. He is plagued with idealism and suffers under the unrealistic illusion that a man should present himself to the people as a champion of better things at a lower tax cost.

Horatio Bunker had planned his campaign in such ignorance. For example, he maintained that the judicial system needed radical reform. Of course it does need reform in Tarvania, but reform would involve the loss of a livelihood by a great many JP's and local judges, to say nothing of the great injury done to the members of the legal profession defending drunken driving and other misdemeanors. As it now stands, a man can be fined anything from five dollars to a hundred dollars for the same violation from one location to another, even within the confines of a given county.

Again I was guilty of giving aid to the enemy by telling Horatio the story of Moss Trilliman, who had served in the General Assembly repeatedly and with practically no opposition.

One of the major problems of the electorate in Jefferson County has always been the matter of the foxes and the rabbits. About half the hunters in the county own rabbit hounds and maintain these beasts throughout the year in order to shoot rabbits for a few days in the fall and winter. Considering the cost of feeding the hounds, the ammunition and other equipment involved, rabbits should bring about $212.00 per pound. Of course the big reward is that they provide a conversation piece throughout the rest of the year.

Less numerous, but vocally as well represented, are the fox hunters. The cost of fox per pound is even higher because there are fewer foxes, although this is irrelevant to the case in point.

Rabbit hunters want free use of fox traps because foxes are hard on rabbits. Fox hunters want restriction of fox traps because fox traps are hard on foxes.

Moss Trilliman used to agree with both delegations, who would go all the way to Tarvania City to plead their cause. As Moss put it, "The fox hunters are my friends." Also, "The rabbit hunters are my friends. I am for my friends and, therefore, when the subject comes up for a vote, I always manage to be in the Capitol's rest room taking care of chores that can not be delayed."

Horatio Bunker was particularly unrealistic with reference to the liquor question.

"Bill Anchor," he said, "you drink liquor, I drink liquor, and more than half the people in Jefferson County drink liquor. The most logical thing in the world is to get legal stores into this county and we could realize between eighteen and twenty thousand dollars worth of tax revenue for the school system. As it is now, we drink liquor and our neighboring counties get the revenue from its sale."

"Horatio, are you implying that the good Democratic sheriff

in this county permits the sale of illegal liquor?" I asked in grieved tones.

"You old goat, as you well know, it's a rare service station on the highway that doesn't sell beer and about half of them sell hard liquor. You can buy it at the golf club, the Moose Hall, the Elks Club, the American Legion Hut, the V.F.W. Club, and quite probably at the Women's Christian Temperance Union, if they had a club house."

"Assuming that there is a fraction of truth in what you're saying, let me assure you that anybody who comes out for legal liquor in Jefferson County is politically dead. In your case, you are probably dead already so it won't make any difference, so go ahead and support a referendum."

"Okay, Mr. Bill, tell me the story and I'll make my own conclusions," said Horatio.

"It is as politically essential to be for the prohibition of liquor in Jefferson County as it is to be for the preservation of the memory of our great Confederate dead. A substantial portion of our economy is based on the production and distribution of white liquor. In the sheriff's department, persons might be considered underpaid if it were not for their ability to overlook certain productive facilities. But the big thing is the intense feeling of our church-goers that liquor is evil. As for myself, I intend to vote dry, and for dry candidates, as long as I can stagger to the polls."

Horatio had other problems with his conscience. The State Power Company owns a lot of land in Jefferson County and enjoys preferential treatment with reference to land valuation and taxation thereof. The Southeast Railway also has certain advantages of this nature. Bunker wanted to do away with this preferential treatment. Opulant & Company, enjoying the political sagacity of Opulant and Queems, has special tax considerations, particularly with reference to the value of inventory. This would get Bunker right in his own back pocket if he tried to equalize things.

"Horatio, I know that you would be willing to pay fair taxes for Opulant & Company, and you will probably have to anyway, now that you're the President and O&Q are no longer in direct control. The reason that you won't be able to make an issue of it in this campaign is that these monied outfits support the key men of both political parties. Let me assure you that your Republican friends running for County Commissioner will not be willing to sacrifice important political contributions just for the sake of reducing the taxes for an unorganized individual. If you did attempt to go about it alone, you would merely alienate your own party support in the elections."

"When does a man stop compromising?" asked Horatio.

"After the election, my son. When down in Tarvania City making the laws for the people of Tarvania, you do what you think is right on most issues, sell out on a few major ones in order to get through some local legislation, and do the best you can to make a record that will keep you in office in the future. I'll tell you one reason I have been a member of the Democratic Party all my life. It hasn't always done the best thing on little things, but when it comes to the big things, I'll stick with the record of my Party."

"Mr. Bill, you need to be brought up-to-date. The record of the Democratic Party in Tarvania is a disgrace. Take education, for example. Your ridiculous platform claims that we are unsurpassed in education among all the states of the Union. The truth of the matter is that we rate right at the bottom in every major category. The rate of illiteracy is one of the worst, the rate of truancy is one of the worst, the rate of illegitimacy is one of the worst, the rate of crime is one of the worst," and he caught his breath.

"You're just dealing with facts, like a damn accountant. Anybody can see that our roads are good. Anybody listening to our leading politicians can be proud of Tarvania. I believe it and so does the rest of the state, the rest of the country, and, indeed, everybody except a few bookworms interested in statistics," I said.

"Mr. Anchor, you wouldn't change if I proved that we have the most inefficient government in the United States, and I pretty near can. You'd still vote Democratic," said Bunker.

"Right," I said.

Getting elected requires swinging a lot of votes, and even though I'm too old to change, a lot of Democrats in Jefferson County would vote Republican if the right man with the right ideas should come along. Some of the ideas can be made public; others must be withheld because of their first-appearance unpopularity.

When the state withholding income tax was passed, and we needed it to get to the small taxpayers who weren't worth chasing down individually, the man who introduced the legislation won on a campaign to clean up the sewerage disposal in the Cowpasture River. The river is still the same and must remain the same until the Lowland Paper plant figures out a way of disposing of waste without going broke.

Hypocrisy, compromise, and deception are a necessary part of getting elected. I've often wondered how a good man kept what he said separated from what he believed. The worst Senator we ever had was Barethread, and his fault was that he not only rose above his original beliefs but got to believing what he had been saying. He introduced some of the stupidest bills ever seen by the state. I'll never forget the time he wanted to provide a pension for dogs left behind by Confederate widows, but that's another story.

The fall campaign hadn't been open a week when Sharster Queems came by to pay his respects. It was by appointment, so Horatio Bunker was on hand. Queems seemed a little disturbed at my presence, and Bunker told him that anything said before me would be kept confidential. Horatio was guilty of assumacy, because I had made no such commitment. He was using his regular technique of relying on my integrity, and I was waiting on the propitious time to prove that an illusion.

"Regardless of what's gone on in the past, Bunker," said Sharster, "I want you to know that I am with you all the way in this campaign. I don't readily commit my support to anybody, but when I do, I am ready to go all-out, win or lose."

Horatio Bunker expressed his appreciation without suspicion and also without animation.

"Actions speak louder than words, Bunker," continued Queems. "I've got five hundred dollars here, and I want you to spend it as you see fit to promote your candidacy."

It was characteristic of Sharster Queems to deal in cash. A good many of his operations were hip-pocket affairs and didn't have to go through any books. Of course he kept books for his real estate business and other regular businesses with which he was connected. The Treasury Department checked these religiously, but it is mighty hard to check on cash income and outgo from a roll of bills stashed in Sharster's pocket.

"Just accept this as a gift, my boy, and there is no need to declare it as a contribution to your campaign," said Queems, leaving no doubt as to his desire to leave no tracks for curious tax people.

It was here that Bunker would make a decision with which

he would live throughout his political life. One of the big problems for an honest politician in Tarvania, and I guess the rest of the country, is when to accept contributions. Every contribution bears a price tag. I've seen major legislation influenced in the General Assembly by so little a thing as a supper given to a legislator by a lobbyist. Of course the lobbyist didn't imply that there was any payment due for the relatively small cost of the dinner, but when his pet legislation came up for a vote, the legislator didn't forget that he had been a guest for a five- or six-dollar meal tab. Men in business are accustomed to paying their debts, and when you owe a man a favor you pay him back, even if you didn't ask for the favor in the first place.

There were no strings attached to Sharster Queems's donation to the cause. Bunker would be under no obligation ever to do a favor for Queems. The giver would say that he made a contribution to good government, and the candidate could reasonably take it in the same spirit. It just doesn't work that way in politics. Although Bunker was no professional at running for election, he immediately sensed the implications.

"Queems, your offer represents the only donation that has been proffered towards my campaign. There is no doubt that my effort to get elected is going to cost some money. The rent on this office space will be $400.00 alone, and Mr. Anchor's salary will be a considerable expenditure. I have brochures to buy, telephone pole posters, and a good deal of traveling expense. I would like to buy some radio and possibly even some television time. All of these things will add up to a total of four or five thousand dollars. It is not proper that a candidate be required to pay this out of his personal resources. Incidentally, my income isn't too great since we reset the salaries of executive personnel at Opulant & Company," said Bunker.

"I thought you overdid that a bit, myself," said Queems, "but since I was no longer active in the management, I could hardly protest."

"Nonetheless," continued Bunker, "I would prefer not to accept any donation of over ten dollars. If I get in a real bind, I'll call on you for more." If Bunker got in a real bind, Queems wouldn't be available for a further contribution, I thought.

"Frankly, Bunker, I'm right disappointed that you won't take this money. I'm not asking for anything in return except that you win the election and do a good job when you are in Tarvania City. I've had enough experience with you to know that you aren't bought easily, and this is not enough money to pay the price for your supporting some legislation I might favor."

"I'm glad you see it my way, Mr. Queems," said Bunker. "I'm thankful for your support and I'm glad that you do not want to obligate me in any way. While you would not have me feel obligated, unfortunately a large sum of money would cause me to reflect very favorably on anything that you wanted if I should be elected. Therefore, I don't feel that I should accept it if I am going to attempt to represent the entire people of Jefferson County."

"I see, I see," said Queems slowly.

Sharster Queems had backed a lot of political horses in his day, and this was the first one who had refused to accept the oats that could enable him to trot. I smiled and kept silent.

Queems talked with me quite a while just as if it were old times. He even offered to let me in on a land purchase that would prove mighty profitable if the proposed by-pass cut through the acreage. One thing I'll have to say for Queems, he never gives up. If he couldn't get to Horatio Bunker directly, he was glad to work with somebody who he thought might have some influence with him. Having no scruples in this matter, and knowing full well that I couldn't influence Bunker to any significant degree, I promptly took advantage of the offer made by Queems. Altogether, it was a great day for democracy and a good day for the fortunes of William Anchor.

Horatio Bunker not only used to full advantage the tricks of political success he gleaned from me, but he thought up a lot of his own.

Over in the western part of Jefferson County there is a section known as Chicken Head, likely named for the average intelligence quotient of its inhabitants. Among those people, most of whom do their part to contribute to a low rate of literacy and high rate of crime, is a family of people named Bunker. Except for an occasional appearance in court, they are not often seen in Jeffersonville, spending the rest of their time in unsuccessful farming, cutting cord wood, and reproducing their kind. Even though they always vote Democratic, I must say that it is fortunate there is a good deal of homicide and high infant mortality up Chicken Head way.

At any rate, Horatio Bunker was not above seeking the vote of the Bunker tribe. He had spent some time around Chicken Head and left word for the aging matriarch to visit him when she came to Jeffersonville. Like most farm families, they made their monthly tour to the city on a Saturday morning, and the esteemed Mrs. Bunker came into Bunker's headquarters with cane in hand and ferocity in voice. No human or beast could have much control over the Bunkers unless there was a good deal of threat in every move of leadership.

"My dear Mrs. Bunker," said Horatio, bowing as if before the Queen of Greece. "I am honored indeed by your condescending to visit me, and I hope that you do not take my invitation as an evidence of impertinence."

Old Mrs. Bunker scowled and snarled, but I knew she was pleased by Horatio's courtly performance. With all the finesse of a headwaiter at a high-priced New York hotel, Bunker seated the old lady and congratulated her on her spryness despite her reputed years.

"Young man, hit don't make nary bit o' difference to me, your fancy talk. You hain't gittin' our folks to vote Republican in this here comin' election," said the old woman with sparkling eyes.

"Probably so, probably so," said Horatio sadly, "but I could hardly consider my campaign complete unless I sought out the votes of those who bear my name. I know that the good Bunkers of Jefferson County are traditionally loyal to the Democratic Party, and I could hardly ask that the bonds of forgotten family ties be stronger than loyalty to conviction."

"Ya gotta lotta spunk and idgication fur a Bunker, son. Whar the divil do we have any common forebearers?" asked the old woman.

Bunker suddenly got very authoritative on family history.

"I'm glad you asked that question, Mrs. Bunker, because it was my father's hobby to trace our ancestry back to England. He found that our family had its origin to the south of London in the County of Nottingham and that Bunkers who now live throughout the civilized world all originated from that small area and from the family whose most illustrious member was the famous Earl of Bunker. While I can not give you the exact relationship we have one to the other, I do know that some of the Bunkers sailed from religious persecution to the shores of New England. Others escaped the vicious British yoke and the debtors' prison, innocent though they were, under the command of General Oglethorpe. These Bunkers settled along our southeast shores of the United States, and from these colonists, it is my understanding, the Bunkers who live right here today in Jefferson County are descendants. Of course, a lot of strange blood has been added to the Bunker line. Some of it is good and some of it bad, but on the whole I would say that the Bunkers are a respected family, though few in number, wherever they live, north or south in this great Nation."

Old Mrs. Bunker rose to the occasion, and a new dignity was in her voice.

"Can't say that any of us Bunkers here in Jefferson County are particularly outstanding in recent times, but I can brag on 'em in ever war that's come along. We fit at Kings Mountain and we fit at Gettysburg, and our boys went and fit in ever one of them foreign wars. So many got kilt, I guess the weaklin's are what we got left. But don't git it in mind that that applies to me."

"No, Mrs. Bunker, you're reputed to be a woman of strong will and noble character, holding together a family that has seen better times. Though I can not hope for your support in this effort I am making for election, I am proud indeed that I have met one of the truly great ladies of the Bunker family."

"'Twould be quite a shock to our neighbors to have a Bunker sent to represent Jefferson County," said the old lady thoughtfully. "Of course, we ain't really no kin, but them ignorant folks out in Chicken Head wouldn't know no difference. And a lady has the right to change her mind," said Mrs. Bunker archly. She turned on me as if noticing me for the first time. I was surprised that she recognized me, for it had been twenty years since we had met.

"Hullo, Will Anchor, I see you got yoreself busted up in some damn foolishness. 'Pon my word but it's good to see you still alive."

"Thank you, ma'am," I said. "I swear you look as good as you ever did," I said gallantly.

"Damn lie, Will Anchor, but it's good to hear a flatterin' lie once in a time." Mrs. Bunker painfully rose to her feet and left the office with dignity.

I thought how much better the world would be with more people like old Mrs. Bunker. I knew she had her faults, but she wasn't weak on character—except in one respect, I remembered with relish, and that was over half a century ago. My mind went back to the days when I was cutting bark up Chicken Head way.

Watching Horatio Bunker lean back in his chair and smile made me resent him more than ever. This damn foreigner had somehow related himself to the Bunkers with nothing more than a name. He then compromised them, and he hadn't backed away for one second in his snobbish, superior attitude towards anybody in Jefferson County. He had just made Mrs. Bunker, and probably the whole damn tribe, vote for him in the coming election. They're a real tribey bunch and would probably vote the straight Republican ticket if our boys didn't get busy and teach 'em how to split the ballot up in Chicken Head. Kinfolk vote together in Jefferson County, and the Lord help us if one of their leaders ever starts voting Republican.

Horatio Bunker used some other stunts that could well be emulated by Democrats. Every so often somebody would come up to him and say, "Bunker, I've never voted for many Republicans and I'm not going to vote for the Republican ticket this time. But I believe you are better able to represent Jefferson County than old Judge Ponticorn, and I'm going to vote for you in this election."

Instead of gushing out thanks, which would be a normal politician's reaction to such an unsolicited token of support, Bunker took it as his due reward for being a superior candidate. He went further, and I was fearful it would be effective.

"Mr. Bedford," he would say, "I appreciate your support and I'll do my best to live up to your expectations. But you know,

this is a tough election, especially for a Republican and especially for a Northerner. If you would do me one favor, it might
be the difference between winning and losing."

"What's that?" would ask the suspicious victim.

"I want you to get me just one vote, other than your own,
that I would not otherwise get. That doesn't include your wife's,
who always votes with you, nor any Republican, nor any Democrat who has already indicated he would support me. What I
want you to do is get me one vote that I would not otherwise
have gotten except for your efforts."

The victim would agree, since it was a possible task and he
felt he would be doing all that Bunker had asked of him. He did
not realize, but Bunker did, that a very few votes could decide
the election, and that one vote switched meant two votes in
terms of victory or defeat. At the rate he was pulling the stunt,
it could very easily enable him to win on November 8th.

Marcus, Bunker's silent chauffeur, took an unusual role in
helping his boss with the election. You could see he didn't much
like driving the old car that was Bunker's rolling advertising
billboard in place of the beautiful Bentley, but he never complained, or said much else for that matter. He often accompa-
nied Bunker out into the ridges of Jefferson County and took a
few notes while Bunker was talking to the electorate. He never
said anything and rarely smiled. Antagonistic citizens felt they
had to listen to Bunker for fear his companion might be a hired
gangster. Chicago gangland tactics are well known in Jefferson
County, and Chicago and Boston are within a few miles of each
other in the minds of most Tarvanians.

All Marcus was doing was getting the name and address of
the prospect. These he would bring back to headquarters and I
would peck out a form letter which Bunker had dictated.

"Dear Mr. —————————: I was mighty pleased to get the

chance to meet with you and talk to you about the ————— problem. I want to assure you that if I am sent as Representative of Jefferson County, whether or not you vote Republican, I am going to do my best to see that something is done about the situation you described. Sincerely yours, Horatio Bunker." The ————— I filled in with pigs, milk prices, secondary roads, gasoline tax rebate forms, or any other fool thing Bunker had been talking about.

I was delighted when Marcus made a mistake and had me write one old lady about the gasoline tax. I knew for a fact that she made her husband keep a horse and buggy and had taken a dislike to motorized transportation from the time the automobile had been invented. She would a darned sight rather have had the gasoline tax quadrupled than reduced.

I dutifully mailed the letter, then told Horatio the circumstances after the deed had been committed.

Bunker let out with one of his occasional spontaneous laughs.

"I thought I had that old lady pretty well lined up," he said. "I'll have to go out and work her over again, and it's going to take some pretty tall talking to straighten out the mess you've made." He laughed again.

I didn't put it past him not only to regain her vote but to gather a few more while he was at it.

I told Bunker of one vote-getting method that he wisely ignored.

There is one place a politician can go and secure votes that has no equal. It is better than county fairs, home-comings, baseball games, or church picnics. That is, attending funerals. Nobody is sure whether or not the deceased was or wasn't a friend of the person paying the final respects. A politician doesn't have to say anything except to occasionally mutter what a fine old man, or woman, was he, or she, who lies in state. Mostly family and close friends of the deceased are about all that are at the scene, and they tend to think well of friends of the beloved deceased.

Judge Ponticorn was a master at the method. He knows most everybody in the county, and when he shows up at a funeral there's no suspicion that he might have had a very casual acquaintance with the deceased. In his case, another advantage was that he wouldn't have the man up before him at the bar for some misdemeanor. Nobody can think real hard of somebody who is paying his final respects to the dead, even though he might have hardly known the dead.

Had Horatio Bunker tried this stunt, he would probably have lost more votes for hypocrisy than he would have won for devotion to the beloved deceased. I still say it is a nice, quiet, pleasant way of gathering up votes.

17

JUST
before the fall campaign got real hot, the Jeffersonville *Democratic Bugle* slapped Horatio Bunker on the wrist. He had been out making a few statements regarding the inefficiency of the state government of Tarvania. In particular, he had attacked our esteemed Governor, saying that Investus Bragery talked a lot more about efficient government than he did about it. The Jeffersonville *Democratic Bugle* didn't mention Bunker's name specifically, but it stated in effect that Northern newcomers should know a lot more about Tarvania before they were critical of its form of government.

This caused Bunker to write a pretty pithy letter to the editor. I have to give credit to Effer Vestal for publishing it. Of course, news is pretty scarce in Jeffersonville, and they'll publish most anything that doesn't slander one of their subscribers or advertisers.

I can remember most of the contents:

"It has been said by our governor and by many of our leading politicians that Tarvania is progressive in every way. It is obvious in this campaign that it is certainly not progressive in education. There are also other areas of governmental endeavor that need drastic renovation to bring about any semblance of order.

"Here we call to the attention of the public that there are over one-hundred-ten administrative agencies in the state of Tarvania. They overlap, conflict, and confuse. They hire thousands of people whose primary task is competing with each other to do nothing in various areas of government.

"Of course, the superfluous agencies in themselves are bad enough, but many of these have a dozen or more important institutions or subsidiary agencies under their supervision. Confusion of authority and blockades to action are fantastic. Appointments are made in every conceivable manner, with the Governor having a hand in most of them. No attempt is ever made at consolidation or establishing clear lines of function. The only remedy for an agency seems to be the creation of another agency.

"In addition to all this, there are more than two dozen examining and licensing boards. Why the taxpayer should be concerned with the function of air-conditioning installations and various other forms of private business enterprise remains a mystery to all but the so-called businessman Governor of the state of Tarvania.

"It is interesting to note that more than a dozen agencies are concerned with cultural and historical matters. All of these cost money. In addition to these, there are another dozen agencies dealing with the conservation and development of resources. The roster of these agencies is amusing, including some with important-sounding titles such as 'Committee to Promote Plans for the Celebration of the Landing of Early Settlers in Tarvania.'

"It is interesting to note that, aside from appointing full-time personnel, the governor has the responsibility of appointing over five hundred people, most of whom draw per diem or other compensation. No effort has been made by this governor, and doubtless the trend will continue, to reduce the number of unnecessary overlapping government agencies.

"We think we can defend our contention that Tarvania's administration is inefficient."

The letter to the editor caused quite a stir and was published in several other newspapers across the state. Tarvania has long lived in a governmental lethargy brought about by complacency and a belief in the righteousness of the Democratic Party. It occurred to me, as I read and heard of this blast, that the time might have come when we Democrats should pay a little more attention to the business of running the government. If we continued to fail to do so, it wouldn't be long before somebody else took our place, and there's nobody on the horizon but the damn Republicans.

By September it was evident that something very unusual was happening in Tarvania politics. Since 1900 the complete victory of the Democratic Party had been assured. No serious challenge had ever been made to its authority. Something was wrong this year. Republicans all over Tarvania had come to life. The scent of a possible victory was in their noses, and they were ready to follow that scent to the limit of their ability.

Fortunately, their ability wasn't too great, though they had made some obvious strides in recent years. Their big vote for Eisenhower in 1956 had brought new life to the Party, and the fact that they were carrying one Congressional District with disturbing regularity gave them cause for hope.

New faces were seen in their state organization, and many of the counties acquired new leadership. A good part of it was young businessmen who had the ability to get a job done. Of course, they still had a fair share of old patronage boys. These mostly consisted of Republican County Chairmen who managed to keep control of a County Executive Committee for the single purpose of providing their families and friends with federal jobs whenever the Republicans took over the national administration. These political parasites did little more than call themselves Republicans to assure that each county convention re-established them as County Chairmen. In most counties nobody bothered to contest their grasp.

By 1960 most of the counties of the state had competent men in control, and these represented a real danger to our present and future well-being. The worst part of the transformation of the character of the Republican Party was that its new leaders were more concerned with good government than with acquiring jobs for themselves and their supporters. They made good use of the Democratic record to show that there could be improvement.

In contrast, a large part of our Party had fallen into hands that were something less than idealistic. The Democratic County Chairmen were too often overly concerned with state jobs. Of course they rounded up some kind of a ticket, but it was more or less an accident if they got good men. Most of our Party strength is in young lawyers. For their first few years after passing the State Bar examinations they tend to spend their time in public office in order to establish their name in the community for private practice. No lawyer in his right mind in Tarvania would join the Republican Party, because we control all but one of the solicitors, most of the General Assembly, and practically every type of work that the state hands out to the legal profession. We have excluded all but loyal Democrats from serving in the capacity of Judges by the simple method of electing them from the state as a whole, even if they serve only a small area.

As I say, things had changed a little bit in 1960. The Republicans flared up in a very aggressive fashion. At the Republican National Convention in Chicago, they managed to get their candidate for governor as one of the men nominating Richard Nixon for the presidency. This immediately established the name of Optimo Futrell throughout Tarvania. After the convention, not only did the regular Republican organization spring into action, but the off-brand, pro-Futrell organizations came into being. They consisted of Democrats who were dissatisfied with the Party, for one reason or another.

Democratic leadership quickly recognized that the campaign might be lost if it centered entirely upon Madison Promisom, our candidate for governor. Although Promisom was an able organizer, he was somewhat lacking in legislative experience. He had served only one term in the General Assembly, and that had been half a dozen years ago and not marked by any outstanding accomplishment. He made a series of political blunders early in the campaign. For one thing, he denied being at a meeting with Kennedy in Tarvania City shortly before the Democratic National Convention in Los Angeles. He later admitted that the meeting took place and then dodged the accusation of a direct falsehood by saying that he had thought the question applied to Senator John F. Kennedy, while he had actually met with another Kennedy. Of course his action in Los Angeles was regarded by many loyal Democrats as gross treachery. Although Promisom was able to carry only part of the Democratic delegation with him in support of Kennedy, he broke the back of the opposition to liberalism and Catholicism in the South.

Soon after returning to Tarvania, Promisom saw that he might have a little trouble with the Republicans, and he promptly set up Democratic headquarters and reactivated his campaign. Normally, the whole show is over by the time the primaries are completed, but Madison Promisom is no man to take chances.

Then followed some statements he would have loved to retract. I would gladly have choked him to keep him from making them, because I can imagine nothing that could have helped the Republican Party more. In one speech he stated that Tarvania no more needed a Republican Party than a mechanized farm needed a plug mule. The Republicans quickly rephrased this so that it appeared that Promisom had said that anybody who voted Republican was a plug mule. This steamed the Republicans into fine fettle and stiffened the backs of many a Democrat who had been voting Republican nationally but sticking with the Democratic Party on the state and local levels.

Promisom came out with another choice remark when he appealed to an eastern Tarvania audience to get out the full Democratic strength in order to offset the votes of the more backward parts of the state. Of course this remark was construed by the Republicans to include all of Tarvania except the far east.

Madison really pulled a choice one out of the madhouse when he charged High Peak with being the worst Republican town in the state. While it might have been true that High Peak and Greenbrook County did vote nationally with the Republican ticket, they had been a source of sizable majorities for the Democratic state and local candidates throughout the years. Promisom even indicated that the High Peak area was hopeless. The High Peak *Interpreter* picked up the story, and even though it was a pro-Promisom newspaper, it was obvious not only that the paper resented the remark but that everybody who was on the fence in the county would go Republican all the way in 1960.

Meanwhile, Republican candidate Futrell had made one

choice blunder himself. He had been appealing to the people of Tarvania as a conservative candidate and painting Madison Promisom as a wild-eyed liberal. This line was selling pretty well until somebody reviewed his remarks on an increase in pay for teachers. He had promised a 50% increase, and this exceeded the amount promised by Promisom, who was being labeled as the reckless spender. Optimo Futrell had his troubles explaining this away, and it made an important issue for our side during the entire campaign.

The Republicans were hammering hard on Promisom, so we decided to bolster the candidate for governor with the rest of the slate for state offices. Normally nobody ever pays any attention to anybody besides the governor. As it became obvious that Promisom needed all the help he could get in this campaign, we started playing up the virtues of our entire ticket. These included everything from Lieutenant Governor to State Auditor, with a few Judges thrown in for good measure.

And our ticket had the experience. Nearly a century of service on the state level was represented by the old-timers, including such men as our Secretary of State, our candidate for State Treasurer, and our perpetually elected Commissioner of Agriculture. Our Democratic candidate for Lieutenant Governor, a prominent tobacco manufacturer, was played up as a lieutenant governor had never been played up before. His record was conservative, and if he had been running for Governor instead of Promisom, we wouldn't have been in all this trouble.

At the same time that we preached the virtues of the Democratic ticket of our state, we were demonstrating that the Republican counterparts were inexperienced and probably incompetent. Unfortunately, Republican leadership had anticipated this move, and they had prepared a brochure featuring their entire state ticket. While none of their candidates were really outstanding, their biographical sketches looked pretty good on paper. By sheer circumstance, their candidate for Lieutenant Governor had served four times in the General Assembly, which considerably weakened our charges of inexperience.

Although the Republican slate was not ideal, it didn't compare too unfavorably with ours. Then the Republicans pulled another stunt that weakened our position. Town by town visits had been pretty much discontinued due to the general use of radio and television as a means of presenting candidates. The Republicans didn't have enough money to use public media, so they reverted to the old technique of hand-to-hand contact. The whole ticket started out on a gypsy tour of Tarvania, using personal cars for transportation and an antiquated flat-bed truck for a public platform. They mounted heavy-duty loud-speakers on the truck bed, and you could hear them a mile away when they got up to cuss out Democrats and praise their own questionable virtues. They carried this travesty all over the state of Tarvania, picking up congressional and local candidates as they went and sometimes forming a motorcade of a hundred or more cars as they proceeded through the towns of Tarvania. Altogether they probably saw about three hundred thousand people in what we called a "four-thousand-mile political farce."

In addition to carrying on an active campaign, the Republican Party made the most vitriolic attacks on the Democratic Party in Tarvania that we have ever seen. They accused us of buying votes, coercing state employees into contributing to Democratic campaign chests, corruption of the Highway Department, and general political chicanery. They made accusations so fast that we had trouble finding time to deny them. The worst part of it was that some of the accusations were true.

We decided to bring the big guns into Tarvania, and they came in droves. Senator Kennedy visited five cities himself, and in his wake came vice-presidential candidate Lyndon Johnson, House Majority Leader Sam Rayburn, ex-president Harry Truman, Kennedy's brothers, mother, and sisters, Adlai Stevenson, and a host of other Democratic leaders from throughout the United States.

At the same time the Republican National Committee saw hopes of victory in Tarvania. They sent Tricky Dick in twice, Cabot Lodge twice, and practically anybody else who had ever been, or might ever be, somebody in the Republican Party. About the only one they missed was Eisenhower himself, and thank God for that, as that man had been a plague on our lives for eight long years. Indeed, Tarvania became a real political battleground in 1960. Nobody really knew what would happen. Republicans couldn't quite believe they had a chance of winning, because they hadn't won for so long. Democrats were not quite sure of victory, because they were aware that their organization had become soft after years of easy victories.

Then there was the religious issue. While the Republican organization stood by Nixon's position that religion should not be mentioned in the campaign, they knew very well they didn't have to mention it. Good Baptists and other Protestant leaders were deeply concerned with having a Catholic in the White House. You know, in 1928 Herbert Hoover beat Al Smith in Tarvania over the same subject. Back then they talked about prohibition, which the Democratic candidate was proposing to repeal. Underneath the public debate was the fear in heavily Protestant Tarvania of having a national political connection with the Vatican. I even had doubts myself about the advisability of putting a Catholic in the White House, but I'm proud to say my loyalty to the Democratic Party always outweighed any other considerations.

In an effort to offset the anti-Catholic feeling, the leadership both in Tarvania and out of the state spent most of the time disclaiming the insertion of religion into the campaign. Actually, we were the only ones inserting it, although we constantly complained that the Republicans were responsible for this violation of the sanctity of religion. All in all, it was to be the hottest political campaign in the memory of man in Tarvania. I was getting pretty damned old and this might be my last election, but I sure would enjoy beating those nigger-loving Republicans one more time.

Horatio came in and struck without warning.

"You old goat," he opened, "I don't believe you could win an election yourself if your life depended upon it."

Appropriately nettled, I replied without thinking, and probably gave the best advice you can give a politician.

"I'd first get my own house in order. You sure won't win without getting your Republicans working for you," I said.

"Won't they be for me anyway?" he asked.

"In a fashion, yes. Sure they'll vote for you, even if you were a yellow dog."

"You're getting too close to evaluating my character," Horatio chuckled.

"Let me illustrate," I said. "In 1956 you had a fine old gentleman named Grover Grobbins running against Green Ink Goodfellow, who has been in office since I was a child. Your Mr. Grobbins didn't run a very active campaign, but when the votes were counted, three hundred thousand citizens had voted for him. Indeed, he captured more than a third of the vote."

"So?" asked Horatio.

"The remarkable thing was that he had died several months before the election and nobody took note of the tragedy. Our Secretary of State has since been greatly distressed that a third of the voters prefer a dead man to him."

"Amusing," said Bunker, "and your point is made. Could he have gotten more votes had he been alive?"

"Yes, another one hundred thousand Republicans didn't vote at all. Had Grobbins stirred around, he could have made it a close race. That would have been difficult for a state-wide election without a live candidate and a tremendous organization, but it can be accomplished in Jefferson County," I said.

"How can I get out all the Republican vote?" asked Bunker.

It wasn't long before I was informed that he was out every day visiting another precinct. He was checking out the Republican judges to be certain they were competent and relatively unbribable and getting them replaced when they were not. He was getting each Republican precinct chairman steamed up to the degree that each one thought that victory or defeat hung on the results from that precinct.

"Grass roots politics" is a casual phrase used by lecturers speaking to knife-and-fork clubs. They usually don't know that it means to get one good man or woman in a precinct really working for a candidate. Once such a person is ready to go, it is a matter of finding out who is registered how. Families usually vote together, so the next step is to see that a complete household gets registered, if one member is right. Those registered in the wrong party are intentionally ignored, but those who are newcomers or just too damn shiftless to register get the treatment. A good worker can nail these down for at least the current election. Most people feel some kind of obligation to anybody who takes an interest in them.

The churches operate that way in our county, and it takes a right skillful atheist to keep out of the Baptist Church; that is, if the Methodists haven't gotten him first. I'm not very religious, but I claim to be a Baptist just to keep the damn do-gooders from worrying hell out of me.

Horatio went out and got missionaries. If he couldn't get an aggressive precinct chairman, he got some other misguided soul to champion his cause. The name of the game is to get every last mildly sympathetic person on the registration books and then get ready to drag 'em to the polls on election day. Horatio had complete copies made of the registration books and, as election day approached, every registered Republican was tagged to be telephoned or picked up by a Republican worker. Even baby sitters were lined up in advance so that no one could escape on account of young'uns.

Then, too, the good absentee ballot plays a big part in Jefferson County elections. It is the choicest bit of political rascality known in America. The law sounds fair enough, but in practice we vote a lot of dying, dead, and deported people.

Applications for absentees are supposed to be submitted by the individual voter, except that members of the family can apply for a bedridden relative. Those living out-of-state can apply by mail. Between the entombed citizens and those who have lived in Detroit or Cleveland most of their lives, we can muster about a thousand absentee votes in Jefferson County. Last year we voted more people in one Tarvania county than there are people. Of course the Federal Census-takers were Republicans in 1960 and they didn't count everybody.

The good old absentee has saved many a deserving Democrat from political extinction. There is an evil movement afoot to get rid of it, even among some loyal Democrats. This damnfoolishness would not only cost us a half-dozen counties but would take half the fun out of campaigning. Thank goodness we still have it this year.

18

A LETTER

arrived postmarked "Greensedge," with the return address, "Tarvania University for Women." I was so damn curious I started steaming it over the coffeepot. I knew it would contain a reply to Bunker's request for a wife prospectus.

Mercifully, Bunker let me read the contents.

"Dear Mr. Bunker: Pursuant to our contract, I am pleased to report that three excellent prospects seem to be available, although I am prepared to submit only one at this time. My recommendation is to take immediate action with reference to this prospect.

"Name, Mrs. Virginia Burlcone Stevens, widow by auto accident two years ago, one child, a boy age 6, daughter of Chatham Burlcone of Burlcone Textile Corporation, financial strength unknown but extremely high. Subject woman a leader in civic activities, prominent supporter of Tarvania Symphony, and of excellent reputation. Marital relations thought good despite tendency for excessive golf by late husband.

"The father of Mrs. Stevens is interested in re-establishing normal family life for daughter, and has been in market for proper suitor. Contacted him as Trustee for University on another matter and described you in glowing terms. Expect invitation to meet with him for business proposition on Saturday, September 24th. He will probably mention staying over for large party that evening, which is the real reason for his contacting you.

"Am certain he has already run a Dun & Bradstreet on you; if it stands up well, you will be under terrific pressure. Chatham Burlcone handles most of the promotions for the Burlcone interests and he has a record of success.

"Enclosed find invoice for $75.00. Very truly yours, Miss Celia Longstreet, B.A., Ph.D." Thus ended the romantic missive.

"Your friend at the University is a sentimental soul. I'm surprised she didn't give family actuarial figures and the prospect's Rh Factor," I said.

"Aged cynic, she is probably more interested in playing cupid than you are in sabotaging the Republican Party," said Bunker. "I wondered why Burlcone called for a conference for merger and made it sound too good to refuse to see him. Come this Saturday, I go to Greensedge to seek a bride."

Horatio Bunker came in the next afternoon pretty agitated, after spending hours over in the mill section.

"I wonder why people feel that anybody running for office is bound to have an ulterior motive? Half the people I talked to today wanted to know what I was going to get out of it, if elected," said Bunker.

"You've discovered something as new as the Yatawba River, which was here before the River Jordan flowed in Israel. I can't remember when the public wasn't convinced that anybody running for public office had a hidden profit or some kind of graft in the background. Of course, a great many politicians do have a real angle. Everybody working down at the courthouse has a

208

pretty good income and very little work. About half the lawyers in the General Assembly will profit indirectly by their public service. But I've been at it a long time, and for the most part people seeking public office gain absolutely nothing that you could evaluate in dollars. Why Kennedy and Nixon should be fighting a death battle for the presidency is a mystery. Either one who wins will be subject to considerable abuse, an end to any private happiness, and, very likely, a much shortened life-span."

"Why the suspicion that every politician is in the game for questionable reasons?" asked Bunker.

"Simply because a great many voters can not understand any other reason for subjecting yourself to public slander and a lot of hard work for very little published salary. They think there's a hidden motive and, of course, in a lot of cases there is. You remember we had a few doctors in Tarvania dispensing drugs to addicts, and the entire profession was given credit for illicit conduct. In business, competitors don't make a state-wide broadcast of questionable tactics, and they just never reach the public eye. But make a slip in the political arena, and you are permanently labeled as a full-time thief."

For the thousandth time I thought it amazing that we could get so many good men to run for so many poor-paying offices. When people start running down the United States, they would do well to think of the amount of effort and time good men and women put into politics with no hope of reward. I might add that I am one of that good number.

Another thing that's good for me to see after a lifetime of politics is the interest that the voters have in elections, rather than the apathy for which they are given credit. It may be true that nearly half the eligibles don't vote, but the half that do vote

are mighty interested in the outcome and fight tooth and toenail
as if it were a matter of everlasting importance whether a man
like Judge Ponticorn or a man like Horatio Bunker won a relatively insignificant seat to a relatively insignificant legislative
body.

Anybody who needs his faith restored in the vitality of the
American system should come to Tarvania during an election.
Horatio Bunker was in good company when he got into the
political game, because by and large all the men who fight their
battles in front of the public are the best of our society. Those
who sit back on their haunches and bitch about things are doing
very little except listening to the sound of their own voices.

"Make that the least of your worries, Horatio," I said. "When
the average voter thinks you're making a noble effort to save
your country, something will have happened to the whole
American way of thought and we will probably go Communist
or some damn thing. As long as they think you're half crooked,
you're fitting into the traditional pattern and it has worked
pretty well for a long, long time."

Bunker got a further taste of the attitude of the public towards politicians when he was sought for a television interview.
Up until recently the public media of Tarvania have always
been pretty friendly towards politicians, and when one had a
press, radio, or television interview it was a cordial affair. Acquaintances who have been to Congress tell me that any time
you speak to a reporter in Washington you're about to get yourself in hot water. Every question is loaded, and no matter how
it's answered, it is designed to embarrass the victim. It is not so
in our part of the country, where we don't have the big city
competition among newspapers. There is rarely more than one
serving any city. Interviews are soft-soapish and designed to

flatter the politician. But now that we are getting more than one television station in a city, the questions tend to be sharper. It creates viewer interest, they say.

Horatio Bunker's TV appearance was the product of a Yankee broadcaster who was trying to bring big city ideas into Tarvania. For several weeks he had been inviting politicians to appear on his program, and I guess because he was seeking oddities he made a special effort to get Bunker to the studio. The interviewer had his guns primed, and Bunker was to be the bird. Often subjects are given a list of questions that they can expect to be asked, and they usually have the right to veto any objectionable queries. In this case Bunker was either unaware of the danger, or just didn't care, because he went into the program without any advance warning as to what he would have to face.

The program began with the usual introductory questions, providing the audience with a knowledge of Bunker's background and the office that he was seeking. Then the interviewer threw in a question that more or less reflected a lot of public feeling about candidates for public office, and the implication was that Bunker had some hidden profit motive in seeking election. I can remember the exchange almost word for word.

"Mr. Bunker, as a relative newcomer to Tarvania and one from the Northern part of the country, you realize that your chances of election are not exceptional at this time, and the fact that you are a member of the normally minority party is a further disadvantage. In view of these handicaps, there must be a considerable reward for you to devote the time and effort you have evidenced in this campaign. Without questioning your motivation in any way, I wonder if it would be proper to ask what you seek, if you should win victory?"

"I seek the opportunity to serve the people of my adopted

state," said Bunker clearly and with a threat in his voice.

"I think that could be said of the great majority of our political aspirants, and I am sure that it applies in your case. If we could be more specific, I think the people would be interested in what side benefits might accrue to you as an individual?"

Horatio Bunker chuckled before continuing. "Sir, I think possibly the challenge of doing the highly difficult, and maybe impossible, is the reward that I have already received as a candidate for the House of Representatives from Jefferson County. I'm told that it is not considered likely that anybody but a long-time resident of the county could possibly be elected to this office. I am given to understand that in no case would a Yankee be elected by the public. I have reason to believe that the active manager of a business is an unlikely candidate, especially when there appears to be an opportunity for him to assume further direction of people's affairs beyond that which he already exerts in the conduct of his business. There are other factors, but these things alone make my election extremely difficult, though I hardly think impossible. As evidence of the validity of this statement I want to call to your attention the fact that the opposing camp is devoting an unusual amount of time and money to ensure its victory and my defeat. I don't feel that they have accomplished their purpose at this stage of the game.

"Possibly in your business as a broadcaster you do not understand this kind of challenge, but I'm sure if you were engaged as a salesman, you would know the challenge of selling an account generally considered impossible. If you were a hunter, you could not resist the hunting of bears in the rugged mountains of western Tarvania. If you were one of our good ministers of the Gospel, it would be easy to understand this challenge, although it would sometimes appear that the forces of evil had permanent dominance over those of good. The challenge of a difficult political victory is equally appealing to those who understand such a challenge."

The interviewer flushed because somehow the tables had been turned on him for the moment. He unwisely pushed on.

"Mr. Bunker, you can say with absolute candor that a victory in this election would not provide you with any business or personal benefits?" came the question.

"This I have not said, sir. I have already told you that the individual benefit would be tremendous in accomplishing victory over what appears to you to be insuperable odds. Likewise, I am confident that my business would benefit by my election. But not my business in particular, because it is just one of many small businesses that need favorable legislation to grow and prosper. I might add that when business is good in Tarvania the people as a whole are well off because of the chain reaction. Lest there be confusion, let me explain that in our business every additional five thousand dollars in sales volume means the employment of another worker. He in turn provides for a family, and the expenditures of this family provide income for the farmer, the clothier, the house builder, and the television broadcaster."

"Then in effect you are an apostle for business interest?" said the interviewer.

"In a sense this is quite true. I do not concur with the general public view that government and labor unions are the prime cause for the development of the economic prosperity of this country. On the contrary, I believe that the brains and efforts and sacrifices made by management, particularly small and developing business management, such as has been in all businesses at one time or the other, are the prime factor in moving forward our economy. As our economy moves forward, likewise does our ability to educate, provide leisure, and give the average man an opportunity for thoughtful and philosophical contemplation that he would otherwise never have."

The interviewer had begun to lose interest in trying to prove that Bunker was motivated by some definable personal gain. He had taken a dislike to the man, which I might say was not unusual for Bunker to create. He delved into a subject which no Tarvania politician cares to discuss.

"Mr. Bunker, you were raised in the North and from the Northern states has come most of the impetus for integrating Southern schools. Of course we are aware that the Supreme Court decision of 1954 was the turning point, but it is generally felt that that decision was brought about by continual pressure from Northern liberals. You quite probably were educated in integrated schools yourself. I think our viewers would be interested in knowing what your views are on this subject." The interviewer smiled benignly.

"I'm glad you asked that question, sir," started Bunker.

It has been my observation over the years that whenever a person under questioning doesn't want to answer a question he begins his evasive tactics with that phrase. It serves to imply to the listener that the candidate has forthright views on the subject and is about to make a very frank declaration of principle. The opposite is usually the case, and Bunker was just taking time to select his words carefully before he continued.

"You have indicated the possibility of my having gone to school with mixed races. Your supposition is correct and, therefore, I think that I probably have a better knowledge of the results of integration than some of my good friends who have not had the same experience."

Now Bunker wanted the interviewer to press further, and this the man was reluctant to do, but he had no choice since it had come this far. He went all the way.

"Do you or do you not favor integration?" asked the TV man.
"At the present time my position on integration is that I am opposed to it in Jefferson County. Let me explain that the role of a political leader, even though I might not qualify for that description, should be the forwarding of programs he considers to the best interest of the people he represents, provided they are in reasonable accordance with the best interests of the state and nation. If he is to be effective in his work, he should be willing to stick his neck out for some causes that are not always the most popular, even though they might be to the ultimate best interest of all concerned. Now in the matter of school integration of whites and Negroes, I find myself not in a position of leadership but in a position of following the will of the people. In a highly emotional political-sociological issue, such as this, it is practically impossible to exercise any influence over the public, at least for the short term. Therefore, a person aspiring to represent the people should in this case actually know the majority wishes of the people he is elected to represent. Certainly, in the case of Jefferson County, the people want the schools to remain segregated, although I doubt if they would resort to violence if the law should require integration in the very near future. I am reminded of one of my acquaintances in Jeffersonville who is vociferous on the subject. Indeed, he assumes leadership in some kind of a patriotic council, the object of which is to resist integration by every means possible. In talking to this friend I have no quarrel with his extremely conservative position, although I think it is highly unrealistic in the face of the trend of the times. He maintains that we should resist by force the integration of our schools in Jefferson County. I have offered to follow him into battle in the matter, but I am distressed to find that he doesn't even own a rifle, much less intend to lead the county in a secessionist movement. While these things are relative to

your question, it could be answered most briefly by saying that, while integration is not desirable for Jefferson County at this time, I would favor it rather than let our public schools close, which appears to be the other alternative. Perhaps there are other alternatives, and I would comment on them if you would suggest them," said Bunker.

"No, Mr. Bunker, you have expressed your views adequately." He hadn't finished his working over of Bunker, and posed the next question.

"There have been repeated bills before the General Assembly providing for the sterilization of mothers who are repeated offenders with regard to illegitimacy. Especially those mothers who are seeking public funds by which to raise these unfortunate children. Would you care to comment on this subject?" asked the interviewer.

Horatio Bunker raised his eyes to the ceiling. If he answered in favor of sterilization, he would be offending the sacred institution of motherhood and several religious groups. If he answered negatively and came up with no logical proposal to solve the problem, and no such proposal exists, he would label himself as inadequate to make constructive decisions.

"That is a question that has given me a great deal of concern. It is one properly posed at this time. I regret that it is the one area in which I am relatively unfamiliar. Indeed, I, in this case, would yield to the judgment of my opponent, the Honorable Judge Ponticorn, who, through years of experience on the bench facing this situation repeatedly, should be able to give the proper approach to the problem. I greatly regret that I have not heard a single expression of his views on the subject and that his voting record shows that he was absent when the bill came to vote in the General Assembly upon his last election to that body. I want you to know, and I want you listeners to know, that when the bill does come before the General Assembly and I am in a position to vote on it, I shall not evade my responsibility, and it will be clear to all as to how I feel about the sterilization of mothers who are bringing the great expense and responsibility of illegitimacy to our great state."

"Our time is up and we greatly appreciate your being with us," said the interviewer. Both men stared straight ahead as the television camera faded them out.

It is my opinion that Horatio Bunker had somehow learned in a very short period of time what a great many politicians never learn over a lifetime. Under no condition does a successful politician oppose God, the Flag of the United States of America, or Motherhood.

Bunker's attack upon Judge Ponticorn's record of being absent on an important vote in a former General Assembly brought about a number of reactions, not the least of which was the entrance of Susan Ponticorn. She pranced into the office the next morning like a Cherokee doing a war dance. If she hadn't bounced in such a feminine way she could have been a warrior.

"How could you, Horatio Bunker!" she stated, not asked. "Papa is just furious and I'm afraid he's had a stroke," she nearly shouted.

"Elderly gentlemen should not engage in political contests. Why don't you suggest that he withdraw?" asked Bunker.

"You, you," she stammered for the proper expletive, "contemptible bastard," said Susan, and burst into tears as she departed.

"Have I transgressed the limits of legitimate issues?" asked Bunker, mostly of himself.

"No," I answered. "I'll be glad to tell you when you've overstepped the bounds. As long as you talk about his voting record you are within honorable political limits."

"I don't like to hurt any one unnecessarily," said Bunker.

I recalled he hadn't been so merciful with Opulant and Queems and some of the employees at Opulant & Company. Or was that necessary? I wondered.

I was in the office early Monday morning after Bunker's week-end sojourn in Greensedge for his round of romance. While in Massachusetts the Lodges may speak only to the Lowells, in Tarvania the Burlcones speak only to other Burlcones.

True to his despicable nature, Bunker made me wait until late in the evening before turning up at headquarters.

"Surprised to find you still up, Mr. Bill. You must be feeling a lot better these days," said Bunker.

"Never mind the amenities. What happened with the Burlcones?" I asked.

"All I asked you to do was handle the correspondence. You aren't obligated to follow through to the nuptial bed, although I am flattered by your obvious interest in my welfare," said Bunker.

"I'm just plain curious," I admitted.

"The Burlcones are delightful people. They have a beautiful home, attractive friends, and a charming daughter, Mrs. Virginia Burlcone Stevens, you will recall," said Bunker.

"Never mind the frills; just give me the facts," I said, irritably.

"I am afraid you will be disappointed in that the young lady and I restrained our passion, at least for the week end. There was some amusing byplay, however. Chatham Burlcone is a thorough man and had enough research done on me to write a major biography. He even knew I couldn't make the first team in lacrosse. In any case, he had stamped his 'OK for formal inspection' by the time we reached the family mansion," smiled Bunker.

"What about the Stevens woman herself?" I urged him on.

"Well, the rest of the family only took a look of polite curiosity. The old man apparently is regularly bringing in approved prospects. It seems that the young widow is hard to please, and what's more, she can afford to be choosy. She's got everything you could ask for, and is gracious enough not to make a display of it. She makes you draw her out and it's all good. For your special interest, she is properly and adequately proportioned in the best tradition of long-legged American beauty."

"Sail on, sail on, oh ship of state," I said with glee.

"The only thing that bothered me was that she would be more than adequate as a wife. I feel she would not only run Belmont, the children, and the society of Jeffersonville, but Horatio Bunker as well."

"Nobody would run you, you stubborn egotist," I said.

"And good reason I have for thinking well of myself. Virginia Stevens was interested enough to tell me how she had always wanted to live in a small town where she could become an individual in her own right rather than just another Burlcone, as she so modestly described their dynasty."

"So you've found yourself a mate?" I asked.

"Not quite a consummated romance, but well on its way, I'd say," replied Bunker. "The only thing that marred the proceedings was that we got on the subject of Susan Ponticorn as the only person we knew in common. It seems that they were sorority sisters at the University. We pretty well agreed that her liberal ideas were a throwback from some unknown ancestor of the Reformation. We must have talked about her quite a bit, because Virginia accused me of something other than a casual attitude towards Susan."

"And this you denied?" I asked.

"On the contrary," said Bunker, "I told Virginia Burlcone Stevens that I considered Miss Ponticorn an excellent catch for any man, including me. I believe this piqued her competitive instincts, which was the purpose of the comment."

"I trust, and hope, that you and I have different departments in eternal damnation," I said, and laughed at his connivance.

19

AS

the campaign wore on I noticed that Bunker was devoting less time to attacking the record of Judge Ponticorn and more to giving the Democratic "machine" all forms of oratorical hell. I wondered if the image of Susan Ponticorn was changing his method of seeking victory.

One day in early October I knew the answer. It was late in the afternoon when Susan came by the office. She obviously had come by for my advice, since it was technically past the official hours for my labor on Bunker's pay roll. She must have known that he was there, with that ramshackle Ford out front.

"Oh, I thought you would be out campaigning, and no doubt telling lies about my father," she said bitingly. The words were bitter, but her tone of voice was humble, almost beseeching.

"Not tonight, Miss Ponticorn," said Bunker. "Old man Anchor and I were just discussing evil versus virtue. Come on in; I won't be here long." His voice was kindly.

"The young fool is still a Republican, but the forces of evil will not triumph," I said.

Bunker outlined a special mailing to school principals for the following day. He had things organized into form letters. I merely had to take care of getting them individually addressed and typed up for his signature. It had become pretty routine by now. Susan sat down in silence. While Bunker signed some of the outgoing propaganda, I stole a glance at Susan.

She was looking at Bunker's profile with an expression more of adoration than of dislike. Her hands were clasped around her middle as if she were holding something dear close to her body. Her eyes were not the clear and sparkling ones of the little girl I had liked so long but those of a woman in love. They were a little misty, and if they sparkled, it was in a submissive way. Susan's posture and expression stiffened when Bunker turned away from his desk.

"How goes the campaign of my worthy opponent?" he asked, not with interest in the answer, but with interest in Susan Ponticorn.

They traded uncomplimentary remarks about each other for several minutes, but what was said in words was denied by their softness of speech.

"I hope we can speak under different circumstances after the campaign, Miss Ponticorn," said Bunker.

"That would be most difficult, Mr. Bunker," said Susan as he left.

Horatio Bunker proved that he was getting really interested in Virginia Burlcone Stevens when he accepted a football week-end invitation during the midst of the campaign. He had been going without a rest period for months when he accepted an invitation from Chatham Burlcone to join them and their daughter for the Tarvania versus Tidewater football game. It was really no contest between the two teams, because Tidewater used relative amateurs compared with those making up the Tarvania squad. Relaxation was not the reason for Bunker's prompt acceptance.

I had to make a few unpleasant remarks concerning the avarice of Bunker. It is not just that I am romantic by nature, but I could hardly stand this fellow being so successful as to captivate one of the most important heiresses in the financial structure of Tarvania. I had nothing against the young lady in question, but I did want to create as much doubt in his mind as possible.

"You may hit the bird, Horatio, but all you'll get is a handful of feathers," I said. I had heard the girl was on the slender side, dressed elegantly to make up deficiencies.

"Mr. Bill, the crudeness of your thoughts continues to amaze and astound me," said Bunker. "While I am not prepared to deny that the accouterments enhance the face and figure of Mrs. Stevens, I will defend with ardor my contention that hidden 'neath the finery are well-rounded appendages and other accessories which would compare favorably with those of the most beautiful of women. Furthermore, this wonderful person is functional as well as delightful to behold. Her son is an example of a six-year-old boy who will make a fine tackle and doubtless will be recruited for the Tarvania first-string line within some twelve years," said Bunker.

Desperate to break up what appeared to be another perfect maneuver by Bunker, I jumped completely out of character in asking him if he really loved Mrs. Stevens.

"Mr. Bill, I've been down that road one time, and it was a good road. Now I am not willing to chance having another such wonderful route end at a precipice. It is better now to seek a good partner than to attempt to recapture that which belongs to youth. What you preach, you do not practice. I can not imagine you as another Ponce de Leon in a search for that which can not happen. I understand that you were one of the first men to go all the way through Deadman's Gorge back when Lake

Jones wasn't even Lake Jones. Did you ever want to do it again?"

I had to admit that some things are best only once. I was a little more sympathetic with Bunker's position after that conversation. I could readily understand that from his point of view it was just as well to marry a beautiful rich woman as anybody else.

I could hardly wait for his return from a two-day treatment by the Burlcones. I was not too proud to ask questions the first time he came by headquarters.

"Mr. Bill, all is well with the world. Chatham Burlcone has apparently investigated our operations at Opulant & Company and found them to his liking. He left me with the clear understanding that he had always hoped to have a son-in-law who would be competent to take over the management of the entire Burlcone organization," said Bunker.

"There's not much to a man who wears low-cut shoes and waist britches," I said, remembering what my father had to say about anybody who lived in town.

"As for Virginia Stevens, and we are now on a first-name basis, she is interested not only in bearing issue from a possible partnership but also in actively assisting my political career, although I must admit she was not too pleased at my choice of political parties. She felt that we might not live long enough to be rewarded with the occupancy of the governor's mansion. For a man seeking a seat in the back row of the General Assembly, I certainly have moved into a very high league in a very short time," said Bunker thoughtfully.

"Well, if that's what you want, the Burlcones can deliver. With enough money, the public will be convinced that you are the guardian angel of all oppressed and all things good. Of course, their public relations employees will edit all your speeches so that there can be no slip-ups. It has been said that they have been instrumental in the election of several governors. I am quite sure that you would be the proper clay in their hands, even though you start out with a considerable partisan liability," I said in my most sarcastic tone of voice.

"Not all you say is false, old man," said Bunker. "There are some things about this apparently ideal opportunity that do not appeal to me. For example, there was a strong implication that Greensedge would be a much more suitable home for me than Jeffersonville. Despite the faults of this little town, and weird characters like yourself, I am coming to feel that this is my home. I have little inclination to leave Jefferson County."

There was nothing in my contract with Horatio Bunker to cause me to go by headquarters on Sunday morning. It was three Sundays before election day, and at this point the campaign was wide open. Bunker's friends had gotten to coming by headquarters for a few moments before church just to review the situation and compare notes on the effort for next week. I don't know why I was opening headquarters for their convenience except that I like to have a cup of my own coffee before church. Heliotrope is a pretty good cook in most ways, but she just won't put coffee in coffee.

Bowen Brown, the Republican County Chairman, was complaining bitterly about what had gone on the day before. Stateston is the only other town of any size in Jefferson County, and he had spent the entire Saturday running interference for Bunker. Saturday is a mighty good day for campaigning in most Tarvania towns. Most of the plant workers, as well as the farm people, come to town and, if the weather is halfway decent, they've got enough time on a Saturday to listen to a candidate. In fact, they have too much time, and that's why Bowen Brown was helping Bunker to see as many people as possible.

"That fool candidate of yours wore my legs out yesterday. I'm going to send him a bill for a new pair of shoes, if we ever get through this damn campaign." Bowen turned up the sole of his left shoe, and it had a hole about the size of the one Adlai Stevenson displayed in his 1956 campaign.

"He really had me moving. We shook hands with 631 people by actual count."

"Why were you brought into the act?" I asked.

"Oh, Bunker had it all figured out so he could see more people if I were along. He had me trained like an organ-grinder's monkey," continued Bowen. "Whenever I knew the name of a passer-by, I introduced him to Bunker. When I didn't know the name, I was supposed to act like I did and just say, 'I'd like to introduce you to Horatio Bunker; he's running for Representative on the Republican ticket,' and then Bunker would introduce himself again and the stranger would usually give his name. But that was just part of the routine."

Bunker had developed a special skill in the art of campaigning—listening to other people's gripes. Often as not their problems had nothing whatsoever to do with the candidacy under discussion, but if a campaigner can listen with enough sympathy and act like he might be able to do something to solve the problem, he can win a vote. A real good campaigner can listen to the problems brought about by a drought and leave the impression that, if he is elected, he will somehow bring rain. The trouble with being a good listener is that it inspires the speaker so that he wants to go into infinite detail, which is not only boring but time-consuming. Bunker was using Bowen Brown to save time.

"If I said it once, I said it 631 times: 'I hate to rush you, Mr. Bunker, but we're going to be late.' Bunker would reply, with marked irritation: 'Let's be a little late. This man is a lot more important than anything else we have to do today. The others can wait a few minutes.' If the conversation wasn't concluded in another thirty seconds, I was supposed to say, 'There are quite a few people waiting, Horatio; we've just got to get to them.' Bunker would reluctantly answer, 'Okay, well, we'll move on. Glad to have met you, sir, and I hope that you can support me on November 8th.' He acted like he was leaving his mother to go off to war."

Pretty good campaigning, I thought. One of the big tricks of winning an election is to see as many people as possible, and Bunker certainly was doing this. It was exactly the same thing every other candidate in the close contest was doing. You don't win elections with advertising, television, and radio. What they do is remind the people who know you, or of you, that you are in a campaign and not to forget you on election day. What you have to do is get to the people so they will feel that they really know you.

Kennedy and Nixon were doing it on a grand scale. They had started shortly after the National Conventions and were at their fighting peak a month before they should have been. It was fortunate that they were both young enough to take it, because what they were doing would have killed older men. There is no telling how many hundreds of thousands of people they were seeing a day, and don't think that doesn't mean votes. They did it every way possible. Huge rallies were scheduled at auditoriums; they spoke from the backs of trains and the backs of trucks and the stairs of aircraft.

The number of hands shaken by Kennedy and Nixon compares with the figures in the national debt. At every stop there was a reception, and besides that, they would go around and shake hands with everybody in a wheel chair and anything else that could move. Children are a particular object of hand-shaking, not because they can vote, but because it makes a tremendous impression on their parents and gives the candidate a human touch that is mighty valuable for the perfect image, come election day.

We have segregated audiences pretty much in Tarvania, but a big-shot candidate will walk over and be as friendly with the darkies as he is with the white folks. This doesn't cause any resentment on the part of our people, because they expect it of a big-time politician and would think something was wrong if he didn't go through the act.

In the state and Congressional campaigns, things are pretty much the same way, except the crowds don't turn out in any big volume. The candidate comes into a town scheduled for a luncheon, or some other meeting, at which he gives a talk to his friends. This doesn't win any votes in itself, but it gets the friends a little closer to the candidate and they get a little more steamed up about his virtues. The real work is done on the streets. A candidate goes into the stores, shakes hands with the proprietor, and meets the clerks. He catches every passer-by who is loafing on Main Street. Even the Republican candidate, Optimo Futrell, would drop by the police station and fire station to shake hands with the Democratic employees. It never hurts to have a man know you in an election, even if he isn't going to vote for you.

What made the ordeal so great for the state-wide candidates was the travel involved. Campaigns are never organized geographically. You would think that things would be scheduled so that a candidate could work an area and then leave it for the rest of the campaign. In practice, a candidate will be at a county fair at one place in the eastern part of the state, and the next morning he will have a dedication of some damn thing in the far western part. That afternoon he may be in central Tarvania for a luncheon and have to be back in the western or far-eastern part of the state by nightfall. It is not uncommon for a candidate to cover two thousand miles a week right in his own state. Optimo Futrell claimed to have made sixty-two stops in one week, and I guess he was about telling the truth.

For a candidate running inside a county, you would think it would be a lot easier. It is just as bad and maybe worse, because he is going into places that big-time candidates skip. The back roads and the little stores, the little settlement seven miles up on a twisting dirt road, are all a part of his campaign effort.

In a close election, winning or losing may be decided by that one extra handshake before darkness. Bunker was playing it to the hilt. He was someplace in the south hills and had been hopping fences all day to shake hands with farmers and wood-cutters. He claimed he caught himself soliciting the vote of a goat when it was getting too dark to see and he was too tired to tell what he was doing. That's what it takes to win a close election, and it's hard to figure what keeps a good campaigner going down to the last hour. One thing is that, if he pulls that extra vote, it may make the difference. The other is a matter of pride. Even if he is destined to lose the election, he doesn't want to have to admit that it was not close. As nothing but a Republican, Bunker would be lucky to get within three or four hundred votes of victory. That would be nothing to be ashamed of in Jefferson County. The way he was going at it, and if he kept the pace up, he might even win. It bothered me because it is as certain as the fact that a Tarvania sheriff will take a liquor bribe that Bill Anchor would be blamed if Bunker won this election.

Bunker was missing one major area of operation for a Tarvania politician. He wasn't involved in church affairs up to his ears, and I've rarely heard of a good politician in our state not being involved in church affairs up to his ears. Few of them are preachers, but they can make a pretty good little talk that will suit most any service. They don't even hesitate to bring the Lord into a political speech, in a nice way, of course. An awful lot of rural Tarvania's society is centered at the church. They have picnics and home-comings and rallies, most of which are only slightly flavored with religion. A politician points toward these affairs. He not only gives the impression that he is closely allied to the good work of the church, but also has an opportunity to meet an awful lot of people. In this phase of politicking, you have an advantage as a Baptist and, to a lesser degree, as a Methodist. It just doesn't look right if you are from an alien church and turn up at many affairs outside your own denomination. That's being a little bit too obvious, you might say.

I've often wondered if politicians as a group have any religion. I know for a fact that they are generally bad about cursing, drinking, and violating the Seventh Commandment. All this should make them the biggest hypocrites on earth, and yet I think they have some kind of a religion of their own. A man just can't devote the major part of his life to public service without being inspired by something besides his immediate personal prestige. The rewards just don't equal the cost of time, money, and effort.

It was getting close to eleven o'clock now. I wondered if I were going to church for religious inspiration or just to see some friends that I knew turned up every Sunday. Bowen Brown left me with a remark that made me know I wasn't the only one with mixed motives on Sunday mornings.

"Hope old man Silas Grant is at church this morning," said Bowen. "He is mighty hard to get money out of most of the time, but he's easiest when he has been softened up by Preacher Melton. Somehow Preacher Melton can make old man Grant feel stingy, and I want to get to him when he's in the mood to change his ways. It don't last for more than a few minutes after church."

Bowen Brown and I closed the office door and headed for worship.

One of the issues that Bunker was using to advantage was new.

Everybody was used to the Republicans fussing about reapportionment, the absentee ballot, and a bunch of other fool partisan state-wide issues that didn't switch many votes. Bunker had had some experience with electrical and heating contractors that sent him off in another direction, and it was proving to be pretty effective. I heard him on the radio attacking the professional people.

"Friends of Jefferson County: In my campaign for Representative from this good county, I have been repeatedly asked why we can't get more dentists and doctors in Jeffersonville. I want to tell all of you the reason, and it's also a reason that you should support candidates of the Republican Party to serve you in the General Assembly.

"Down in Tarvania City there are literally dozens of agencies authorized by the General Assembly for the so-called protection of the public. The way they work is to form a Board, appointed by the governor in most cases, and that Board decides who can practice air-conditioning, electrical work, veterinary medicine, or dentistry.

"I'm not going to say that it is bad to set high standards in medicine, law, or any service organization. But I am going to say that these agencies are using their power to form monopolies in each profession.

"Oh, it's good if professional standards are high. But unnecessarily high standards are a great deal more expensive to the consumer. The way it is now, for example, you have to have six to eight years of college to practice dentistry. That costs a lot of a man's time and a lot of money and it greatly restricts the number of high school graduates who can seek to be dentists.

"I don't contend that the dentists we have are not of unusually high quality, but I say that the prices they charge are commensurate with their caliber.

"This leaves the average person with the choice of finding one of the scarce dentists and paying the price he asks, or having no dental work done at all. And the same thing applies to electrical contracting and dozens of other fields of special skill. About half the homes of Jefferson County are wired by rank amateurs because top-flight electrical contractors are beyond the pocketbook of the average working man in this county.

"In setting high standards, these various professions have created a virtual monopoly in Tarvania, and it's gotten beyond the point of doing more for the people than it's taking away from them.

"What I propose to do when elected by you to the General Assembly of this state is to put a lot more people on these licensing Boards other than people who are already established in the various professions. In other words, we should have average men and women, who have no axe to grind with any particular field, serving as the majority of the membership. Oh, I know it is the prerogative of the governor to name these members, but the General Assembly can enact into law restrictions that will protect you and your pocketbook.

"What we need in this state is recognition of people of lower competency. You all know that we rate our restaurants A, B, or C, depending on the facilities and the degree of sanitation that is maintained. Of course, we all like to eat in Class A restaurants all the time, but there are a lot of pretty nice little eating places in Jefferson County that can't afford all the high-cost stainless steel, and other gadgets, that are required of an A restaurant. Therefore, most of us eat at B, and sometimes C, grade restaurants. They sure beat starving.

"What I would suggest to the General Assembly is that we allow varying degrees of licensing. There is no reason a man should be prohibited from wiring your house just because he wouldn't have enough know-how to wire a twenty-thousand volt electronic gluing machine. There also is no reason why you shouldn't have a dentist in your community with two years of training. Oh, he might not be able to do major surgery, but he sure could patch the holes in your teeth and pull out one that ought to come out. He could charge a price that you could afford to pay, and you wouldn't have to travel half a day to get to him.

"To bring these changes about, you can not support the Party in power. It has indicated that it believes in the 'status quo,' and every year it adds more licensing agencies to your burden. I ask for your support in this election with the promise that I will do everything in my power to give you an opportunity to have the professional help you need, at a price you can afford to pay. Thank you very much."

You've never heard such a howl as came up after Bunker started in this direction. Politicians never buck the professional people in Tarvania. One reason is that the professional people are relatively rich and can help a candidate, or can help his opponent. And they're influential, generally speaking. They see a lot of people and can influence a lot of votes.

Bunker was taking a big chance in defying them. While he wasn't getting their votes, I had to admit he was publicizing himself pretty well by the attack. Every time you came near a doctor or a dentist, or even a chiropractor, he talked about Horatio Bunker. It was in no complimentary way, you may be sure, but each professional man had to go through the whole routine of explaining why the standards of the profession must be kept at the highest possible level. Their listeners took a lot of convincing. I don't know they were all sold that Horatio Bunker was entirely wrong in his propositions.

It always amuses me when the professional people in our community fuss about unions and their trying to get closed shops for their membership. I am not condoning the unions, and I'm all for the right-to-work laws on our books, but I am equally aware that the professional people were throwing bricks from the questionable safety of glass fortresses.

20

I'VE
always believed I liked most everybody I got to know,
including niggers and Republicans. And mostly people liked
me. Yet, I had only one real friend in all my life.

Jim Howard worked for my business most of his life, just as
Heliotrope worked for Emmy Lou at home. I never called Jim
anything but "nigger" and Jim never called me anything but
"Mr. Bill." He was a few years older than I and the blackest nigger you ever saw. He looked a lot like Horatio Bunker, except
that his skin was black, his hair was short and curly, and he
smelled like a true Tarvania nigger. His build was like Bunker's,
long and skinny. But he could move his end of a five-hundred-
pound block of ice easily, while I was inviting hernia trying to
move the other end.

Old Jim had another Bunker trait, although with Jim I never
resented it. Old Jim really felt superior to me. He maybe was
just a shade smarter than I, even though he never went to school
a day in his life and couldn't write his own name, much less
read and explain the Constitution of the State of Tarvania. I
always suspected I made a blunder in getting him registered to
vote. He was one of the first in Jefferson County—back in

Harding's administration. He registered Democratic all right, but I never trusted him politically, and to this day I think the black bastard voted straight Republican. He knew about Abraham Lincoln. Jim Howard never failed to pay a debt.

We worked together like a couple of niggers until World War II came along and things slowed down in Jeffersonville. We sweated less and talked more as the big war went on, while things quieted down at Anchor Ice and Coal Company. We didn't know it yet, but we were working against the trend. The ice and coal business would never prosper after the war, and we would both be too old to start something new.

I never knew old Jim was my friend until I told him about Emmy Lou. A white man doesn't talk about white women to a nigger; much less does he discuss his wife.

The incident started when Jim got offended at me for nagging him about keeping the bills posted, which he hated to do since he had to write down a line for every ten pounds of ice. He couldn't write numbers and didn't handle a pencil with comfort.

"You're talkin' to me like Miz Anchor used to talk to you," said Jim, with hurt in his voice.

Back in the old days that was excuse enough to kill a nigger. Had I picked up the ice tongs and bashed in his skull, a Jefferson County jury would have found me guilty of nothing. I wouldn't even have had to claim self-defense.

I was dumbfounded, angry, but mostly guilty. I'd hit him with a stick plenty of times when we were both a lot younger, but I'd never hurt his hide or his feelings. I'd berated him for more than two decades, and he had laughed at me as if I were the fool instead of him.

At that moment I knew old Jim was my friend, whether or not he liked me at the moment. I told him about Emmy Lou, even though it was none of his business and not my business to tell him. Nonetheless, I didn't act in blind ignorance, for what I said to Jim I knew would never be repeated.

"Jim, you don't understand about Mrs. Anchor. She didn't mean what she said, but said it 'cause she's a woman," I said slowly.

Emmy Lou was at her worst when she was traveling with me, especially when somebody else was along. She was bad enough when we had a horse and rig. When we got the Marmon, along about the time Harding died, she became impossible. How a woman could fail to learn to drive, never associate with mechanics, and know so damn much about an automobile is a mystery she carried to her grave. You can't imagine what I put up with.

"Will, the water's overheating. You're driving much too fast. Will, the clutch won't last a week if you don't stop riding your foot upon the pedal. If you would double clutch, it would save the gears. Will, you should have put in light-weight oil for these cold mornings."

Damn but she was amazing. I told Jim about the night of the sudden cold snap in September just before he hired on at the company. People were needing coal immediately and I had burned out the front bearing of the Model T truck. It had to be replaced if we were to make deliveries, and it was Emmy Lou who stayed up all night getting the fool contraption into running condition. I didn't have to tell Jim that I loved that woman. I just described how the transmission oil leaked all over her hair while she was under that thing helping me. Emmy Lou just complained that it would take two years to get it out of her scalp and went on working.

You see, I liked Jim a lot and didn't know quite how to tell him so.

We forgot the incident when Jim bet me a dime that he could beat me in checkers. He did.

These memories came back one day in July, 1960. It was the anniversary of the day our troops struck at Normandy. Jim Howard, Jr., was killed that day, along with a lot of other boys, both white and black.

A nigger preacher can make the greatest funeral oration since Mark Antony was bragging on Julius Caesar. I was mighty honored when Jim asked me to say a few words over his boy when the army finally brought him back to Jeffersonville. White men don't usually officiate at nigger funerals in Tarvania.

Of course, Jim is gone now and that nigger wench of his, that Heliotrope, won't last much longer. If it hadn't been for old Jim, I'd have kicked her black butt out of the house when Emmy Lou died. But old Jim was my friend. If he could stand her, I could put up with her. Just barely. You see, a man doesn't have many friends in all his life. Emmy Lou was my friend and a lot more, but a man also needs a man for a friend. Old Jim was mine and I miss him.

What brought all this to mind was something that happened just a few weeks before election day. Horatio Bunker was low. Bouncing back for another try every day had left him exhausted physically, which was natural enough, only that night he was exhausted in spirit.

"I've lost the election, Mr. Bill. No matter what I do it can't be saved now. I'm ready to quit," said Bunker.

"Just what I told you the day you filed," I answered with malice. Horatio Bunker had finally met his comeuppance.

"You were right, Mr. Bill," he said slowly and with absolute despondency. The long, lean frame was partially on one chair, and his legs were dangling across two more. He looked like a cornstalk that had just been through a bad hailstorm. I guess he thought his head was turned, or that I couldn't see him in the bad light. I saw that he was crying. The big man, the man who couldn't be stopped by Opulant and Queems, or all Tarvania, had been stopped dead cold. Somehow I wasn't pleased.

Then, for the second time in my life, I started talking about Emmy Lou, saying a lot more than I had ever told old Jim. I told him things that I never expected to tell any man because they were secrets between Emmy Lou and me. I told him how she always gave me public hell and private bliss. I told him about how she kept me going, after the fire and a dozen other times when I got discouraged. I remembered how she never failed to urge me on, except the time the furniture company offered me a high-paying sales job. Even then she didn't tell me not to take it. Just that she'd miss me very much if I had to be away a lot.

As a sure sign of senility, my eyes got moist as I recalled those days not to be relived. I'm not so old as you might think, for the next moment I was telling Horatio how pretty she was. Actually she was no raving beauty, a little short and a little plump, but she had the damnedest dimples ever tied together with a smile.

Horatio started to come out of his despondency. "Bet you wish you had a dollar for every time you did," he said, and there was no mistaking his lascivious meaning. I didn't resent it.

"When it came to the appearance of concupiscence, Emmy Lou was no failure," I chuckled in retrospect.

"Your description reminds me of Susan Ponticorn," said Horatio, as if something new had suddenly been invented for the pleasure of the human male.

"There is a lot that she and Emmy Lou have in common. Except a man like me to keep them both happy for eternity," I chortled. Horatio Bunker had somehow become my friend. Events followed too quickly to ponder over this, my final fall from grace.

Horatio Bunker came to headquarters one morning, which was unusual since he normally spent the forenoon at the plant, and he still looked downright exhausted instead of his vigorous, normal self.

"Spent half the night on Turkey Ridge," he explained.

Turkey Ridge is over in the southwest corner of Jefferson County and consists of rough hills, cut-over timberland, and damn few people besides about ten families of niggers mostly named Hunter. How Bunker got involved with them got me curious. I had learned to ask for information or remain uninformed.

"Jim Hunter drives the pickup down at the plant, and he got to talking about coon hunting yesterday. I didn't even know he was talking about raccoon at first, but he got to bragging about his dogs, so I guessed that was what he was talking about. I don't think he expected an acceptance when he asked me to join him last night. It will be a long time before I join anybody else," said Bunker.

I urged him on.

"He said to meet him any time after dark at Abel's Crossroads, and there I was, twenty-two rifle, shiny new high-top boots, and the latest in hunting caps, none of which are appropriate for a coon hunt. We piled into Jim Hunter's car and headed up the Turkey Ridge road. We had quite a talk about the negligence of the Democratic Party and Jefferson County roads."

"Been up that road, Horatio," I said. "We have been promising to hard-top it for three elections. Along about two weeks before voting day we'll get some of the Highway boys to drive a few white stakes along there. I believe it will work one more time, especially if we send along a surveyor this trip."

"I doubt it this election," said Bunker with joyful malice.

"Anyway, we finally got to the Hunter place. Most of the youngsters were in bed, but the rest of the clan was up and ready for action. About five Hunters were to join the coon hunt, including Old Joe, the granddaddy rabbit of the clan, who is grey as a mouse and as old as the Courthouse."

"No dogs?" I asked.

"My God, yes; dogs and dogs and dogs, all of a breed unknown to the rest of the civilized world. They say some of them are part 'red bone,' and they look like a combination of a bird dog, a retriever, and a dachshund. They are mostly black and tan and noisy as a women's bridge tournament."

"You must have been a rare sight in that crowd, dressed like an ad in *Fortune* featuring Abercrombie and Fitch sporting clothes," I said.

Horatio laughed. "Yes, Mr. Bill, they were dressed in overalls mostly, and they ragged me a good deal about my clothes and gun before the night was over. I about tore off my pants in a thicket, and I am now covered with numerous small but painful wounds. Anyway, we headed up the ridge with dogs running around in complete confusion. I was about to drop dead trotting up that damn hill when Old Joe announced we were at location.

"We lit a fire and settled down for a while. It seems that a coon dog of ability doesn't need a human guide. He just wanders afield until he picks up a scent, and then the whole pack hits the trail after the coon. When they jumped the animal, we could hear a chorus of baying and yelping exceeding in volume a hundred-piece orchestra. Right melodious as well, when you got used to it," said Bunker.

"Those nigger dogs are good because it wasn't many years ago that they had to be good to stay alive. Coon brought a big price when you Ivy League boys were sporting fur coats before the Hoover depression. Makes pretty good eating as well," I added.

"I learned why so many Negroes make champion athletes. It's from coon hunting. My tongue was hanging out half of last night. Even Old Joe was running more than he was walking. They had treed two raccoons before I caught up with the hounds. This was humiliating, and I think they let me catch up for the final capture out of courtesy," said Bunker.

Those coon hunts are something I can remember. A raccoon is most reluctant to climb a tree and can keep out of reach of the hounds for several miles. When he's finally run up a tree, a smart coon will often drop out of a far-reaching branch onto a neighboring tree, leaving the dogs yapping up an empty tree. If the coon is truly cornered when the hunters arrive on the scene, he can be spotted by flashing a hand light into the tree. After running half the night a man can sure cuss when that coon has outwitted the dogs.

"Sitting around the fire waiting for those dogs to tree a raccoon gives a man a chance to know somebody pretty quickly. Most of the Hunters were pretty suspicious of my motives for wanting to hunt with them, which I guess is pretty normal whenever a white man enters their territory. I told them I wanted their votes, and they accepted me as a pretty standard politician, since I guess somebody goes after the Hunters every two years," said Bunker.

"I've been up to Turkey Ridge myself a few times, although I never went so far as to chase coon dogs to get their damn votes," I said.

"That's what they told me. Then we got into the gist of the business. I haven't made many campaign promises that anybody could pin me down on, but I did make one to our dark brethren on Turkey Ridge."

"I'm surprised you didn't seduce one of the nigger girls to get a vote," I said good-naturedly.

"Some of those Hunter girls are right pretty," said Bunker,

sounding more like a Georgia cracker than a Yankee. "Anyway, they got to telling me that not a single Negro is employed by the state except for schoolteaching in Negro schools or doing janitor work in some state building. They thought they ought to get a fair share of truck-driving jobs and other employment with the Highway Department. They claimed some of the girls are qualified to do stenographic work and can't get a job with the state any quicker than they can in a white man's business office."

"I guess it's about the truth, Horatio," I said, "but don't forget they pay very little in taxes and don't deserve much state employment. They will really be sick when the schools are integrated and all the Negro school teachers are replaced by white ones. You know damn well no white mother is gonna let her little darling be educated by somebody who was swinging like an ape in an African jungle a couple of generations back. It may not be right but that's the way it will probably be."

"Maybe so," said Bunker, "but I told them I would do everything I could to get them equal job opportunity for state employment when I get to Tarvania City. I know I won't be able to do much, but I won't fail to introduce a bill to give them a fair shake," said Bunker.

"Wouldn't talk about it outside of Turkey Ridge," I advised him.

"Surprisingly, a lot of Negroes, particularly the older ones, don't much want to change things," said Bunker. "Old Man Joe has got a lot of the family convinced that the Negroes were better off under the old Southern paternalism. He said nobody ever went hungry or without clothes and shelter, and the only price they had to pay was to say 'Yass, suh, white boss,' pretty regularly," said Bunker.

"Old Joe once told me that 'these young educated Negroes is

goin' to be the ruination of us rank-and-file niggers,' " I recalled. "By the way, did you ever bag yourself a coon?" I asked.

"I arrived at the tree just behind most of the Hunters," Horatio continued. "I could see the bright beads of the coon's eyes about forty feet up a black gum tree. Although guns are not acceptable, they gave me the shot, and I hit him well enough to bring him down in two shots. The dogs were mighty pleased with my work, but the Hunters laughed their woolly heads off. I wasn't sure but suspected that my raccoon shouldn't have a rat's tail."

"So you shot a possum," I chuckled.

"That's right. The night may not have identified me as the great white hunter of Jefferson County, but I'll get a majority of the votes from Turkey Ridge."

Jeffersonville was ablaze with delightful gossip, and the campaign was completely suspended for one week end. Mrs. Virginia Burlcone Stevens, son Chatham Burlcone Stevens, and governess Ivory were in Jeffersonville for a round of parties and general social activity. The retinue was staying at the only adequate facility in Jeffersonville, namely, the home of Mr. and Mrs. Grandin Opulant. Among the festivities was the annual fall affair of the Jeffersonian Cotillion Club, which is Jeffersonville's annual one-night stand of what Jeffersonville's society believe the people in Newport, Rhode Island, do every Saturday night. Of course a lot of the men's evening clothes are rented, but somehow everybody manages to turn out in something approaching evening dress. I have always believed that the whole thing was instigated by our two fashionable clothing stores, since every woman who participates feels that it is a sign of overt bankruptcy to appear in the same dress for more than one Cotillion Club affair.

Several of my lady friends gave me nonconflicting reports.

There was no doubt that Mrs. Virginia Burlcone Stevens was the belle of the ball. I heard so many repetitious descriptions of the number of pearls on her dress, the gold flecks in her hair, and something called a "French Twist" that I could recite the whole thing in my sleep. Horatio Bunker danced exactly five dances with Mrs. Stevens, including the first and last dances, but he was not alone in seeking her beautiful hand. Grandin Opulant had to ration her dances among his friends, and they said it even applied to his son Gran III.

This control of young Opulant was all to the good. Susan Ponticorn obviously resented young Opulant's unconcealed adoration of the decorated Mrs. Stevens. She was also reported as glaring at Bunker when he was dancing with the honored guest.

I got another slant on the proceedings the following day when, in my usual roll around the square, I met Susan. For some reason she was not overwhelmed by her old sorority friend, Virginia. She had some judicious remarks to make regarding the weakness of men, and particularly with reference to Gran III's fawning over Mrs. Stevens. But most of her remarks were a description of the relationship between Horatio Bunker and the lady under discussion. I can't remember whether they danced too close together or too far apart, but in any case Susan had been carefully observing their contact and was in high disapproval of it. She summed up her whole opinion with the comment that each was exactly what the other deserved, and I gathered that she thought neither one deserved very much.

I don't know why I felt compelled to prod further, because I was pretty damned sick of hearing about that dance, but I did learn that Susan Ponticorn knew something about Horatio Bunker that I thought to be my exclusive information.

"There is more to Horatio Bunker than meets the eye, Mr. Bill," said Susan. "He is talented, almost bordering on being exceptional, but he is also somewhat mixed up, and I don't mean exclusively in his political views. I think the man is terribly insecure in some way, although I would hate to have to prove it on the basis of his performance—business, political, or social." Susan smiled at her own paradox. "The right woman could make a really valuable man out of Horatio Bunker," she concluded, with that serious look that indicated an irrevocable pronouncement.

"I kind of think you might be the woman to do the job," I said.

Susan blushed in a pretty little-girl fashion but didn't lose her vocal equilibrium. "Mr. Bill, hell is only about half full, and I'd rather help fill it up than spend another day with Horatio Bunker."

"Didn't know that you had ever spent a single day with him," I said.

Susan turned crimson this time. "Oh, I ran into him while I was down in Tarvania City working on Dad's old voting records in the Legislature. I'd consider it a real favor if you didn't mention it to anybody, Mr. Bill."

"Don't worry, honey. I wouldn't embarrass you one second to save the life of that scheming Yankee," I said.

The dinner party at the Opulants' that night must have been a really colorful event. I didn't get the surplus of descriptions that I had for the dance, but enough information was available to give me a good picture of what took place. In addition to Mr. and Mrs. Grandin Opulant, Gran III, and Susan Ponticorn, Judge James Ponticorn escorted my chief informant, the widowed Mrs. Nosegay. The whole atmosphere must have been pretty strained, because Mrs. Stevens had obviously insisted on Horatio Bunker for her dinner partner, even though the rest of the table was at political swords' points with her escort. It wound up that Bunker was one against seven political adversaries.

I would have damn nigh busted my right leg again to have been in on the scene. Between the seven of them they must have really made Bunker squirm. While he is no fool, neither were the other men in the party. When the rest of them weren't politely raking him over for being a Republican, Susan was carrying on a side attack because he was so conservative. My esteemed informant said he hardly had time to eat for explaining his position and that of everybody from Rockefeller to Goldwater in the Republican Party. Apparently Mrs. Stevens came to his defense, but her lack of political knowledge made her rather ineffective.

Something happened during the course of that dinner, because Susan began defending his right to be a Republican. She brought Voltaire into the discussion somehow and wound up saying that Republicans had just as much right to run for office as anybody else, even if they were crazy. This got no favorable response from anybody, and especially from the Judge, who was in no mood to have his daughter on any kind of good terms with his determined opponent.

While Susan was momentarily supporting Bunker, Gran III was exercising his charm on Mrs. Stevens. My informant speculated that more would come of this.

Bunker's version of the dinner was succinct, and right forceful for him.

"I'll beat those damn Democratic bastards if I have to import northwest South Dakota to do it."

21

IN
mid-October it was obvious that we were not in absolute control of Tarvania, any more than we were certain of winning in Jefferson County. We had had early warning of trouble when Nixon picked Tarvania for a major speech. Republican presidential candidates have rarely fooled with the South, but 1960 was different.

The Greensedge Nixon Rally was something, featuring ice skates, a dozen choirs, and enough coffee and doughnuts to choke the voters. They had turned out in volume despite rain, clogged roads, an overflowing coliseum, and the onus of being seen at a Republican powwow. You'll remember that it started the Nixon drive for Southern votes, and if it hadn't been stalled by a lot of frightened Southern Democrats, he would have carried most of the Southern states.

By October both sides were pouring in big-name speakers at the rate of two or three every week. They didn't just visit the big towns either. Adlai Stevenson, for example, wound up in Sampsonia for a major rally, and Sampsonia is about the size of Jeffersonville.

That's what caused Grandin Opulant to send me to Tarvania City in his big Cadillac. We couldn't get any promises by telephone, and I knew Dymo McCallom as well as anybody.

You never see or hear of Dymo McCallom except during campaign time, and I don't know yet whether he smuggles opium or sells sleds in Saskatchewan between political seasons. He has no official capacity in the Democratic Party and nobody seems to authorize his employment. Yet along about the time headquarters opens in Tarvania City along comes Dymo McCallom. He agrees to straighten out the confusion for $1,000 per month plus expenses, and he's back in business for the season.

Nobody likes Dymo McCallom and everybody wants to be his friend. While it is the job of the Executive Committee, the State Chairman, the Governor, or somebody in authority to decide where money is to be spent, Dymo McCallom always winds up deciding who gets how much. He makes the final deals for advertising, he decides where votes can be corralled in blocs, and where to put our best in-state speakers. Although he can claim no personal ties with the wheels in Washington, as can our Senators and Congressmen, Dymo McCallom somehow decides how those big guns are going to be used. Sure, the Governor can veto or change any plans, but he's so busy making speeches he hasn't time to fool with plans. Besides, anybody who sets the schedule is a son-of-a-bitch to everybody except the ones who get the big name, and even they are disappointed because they didn't get a bigger name.

Dymo McCallom was in his glory when I rolled into headquarters at the Sir Johnson. Three telephone lines were in use: Dymo was on one, a girl was holding a party on another, and the third was ringing persistently.

"Kennedy will be doing a miracle if he gets all five stops in one day. It's definitely set for Jamestown, Tarvania City, Greensedge, Mecklenton and Alpine, and that's it. Now I can give you FDR, Jr., if Brightburl will let me off the hook, and I wouldn't do that for anybody but you, Joe." Dymo started listening, so I broke in.

"Howdy, Dymo. See you're still at the old stand, lousing things up as usual," I said.

Dymo held his hand over the head of the phone. "What the hell you doing in a wheel chair, Mr. Bill? I knew somebody would beat you half to death sooner or later," said Dymo and resumed his phone conversation. "No, you can't have Truman. He's going from here east and he won't do but two rallies."

I told the girl to tell anybody calling in that McCallom would be in conference for the next twenty minutes. She didn't know me from John D. Rockefeller, but I must have sounded authoritative because she followed instructions. Dymo finally hung up and the party on the other end of the line had settled for FDR, Jr.

"I hear strange things of you, Mr. Bill," said Dymo. "They tell me you have fallen to the lure of Republican gold and have thrown high principle to the wind."

"If I didn't want to get a good speaker for Jeffersonville, I'd say that you would work for the Mongolians if they'd pay you enough. While I may be temporarily working for a Republican, it is merely a matter of necessity," I said, lying to a mild degree. "My business here is to get a damn good speaker and I don't want Adam Clayton Powell or Kennedy's grandmother."

"She'd be the only Kennedy who hasn't been on tour," laughed Dymo. "She and old man Joe. The Republicans are claiming the old man was a roommate of Hitler and our boys in New York are scared of losing the Jewish vote. What happened to your legs, Mr. Bill?"

I told him the story, and he really seemed to enjoy getting

away from the telephone. We got back to business.

"Nothing like it since I've been in politics. They say it was this way in '28, but I know damn well it wasn't the same. Al Smith went through the state without making a single speech, and we are letting nobody out of our clutches without at least two. I've got Lyndon Johnson lined up for a railroad whistle-stop, but I'm scared to death. Think I'll put Promisom and a brass band along to beef up things."

"What's happened to the Republicans, Dymo?" I asked.

"They're putting Nixon in Mecklenton, I hear. They've had Cabot Lodge once and he's coming again. Then there's Barry Goldwater, Walter Judd, Bill Knowland, and even that turncoat, John Roosevelt. I understand they're even putting John Payne, the movie star, to help them in the Fourth District. Don't they know this is a Democratic state?" I asked.

"Things are changing, Mr. Bill," said McCallom. "I think the South's getting out of the bag and that every election will be close in Tarvania from now on. Futrell bumper stickers are outnumbering Promisom's six to one. It won't mean much at the polls, but it's the first time anybody but the candidate's wife ever admitted that he was going to vote for a Republican governor."

"We're lucky Bragery got with us. He's the smartest politician of the lot and he's supposed to be an amateur. I'll bet money that he'll be the only one who will get anything out of the campaign, and damned if he didn't go all the way for Johnson in Los Angeles," I said.

"I'll give you Congressman Ledbetter of Wyoming," said Dymo McCallom, returning to the business at hand.

"I don't want him! Who the hell is he?"

"A very able speaker. He'll make a big hit in Jeffersonville," said McCallom.

"Yeah, I know," I said, "he owns half of Wyoming, has no Republican opponent, can barely pronounce his own name, and can talk intelligently only on the control of snowdrifts. But I'll take him."

"You won't be sorry," said Dymo. "Miss Taylor, get a biog—what do you want, glossy or mat for the newspaper?" he asked.

"Mat," I said, "and I am ready to pretend we have just reincarnated FDR. This sheepherder won't recognize his own glorious eminence when he arrives in Jeffersonville."

"Wish everybody would accept the inevitable with such grace," said McCallom.

"Don't worry. When this cattle rustler leaves Jeffersonville, you'll be the bastard that gave us a cull," I chuckled.

"Miss Taylor, see if you can get through to Bobby Kennedy in New York," said McCallom.

The phones started their clamor and Dymo McCallom was on his throne controlling the lives of the great of the Democratic hierarchy. His rule might be short, but it was nearly absolute.

I was tired and not ready to drive back to Jeffersonville. To hell with Grandin Opulant. He could wait another day for his Cadillac. When I got to the lobby, Enebra Sellers gave me the excuse for stopping overnight at the Sir Johnson. I'll never say anything bad about liquor the night before, and nothing good about it the morning after.

We got to talking about old times, just as old men always do. Enebra Sellers wasn't interested, but he was a skilled listener. I talked about Jeffersonville.

In the old days, anything that happened to anybody in Jeffersonville was important to everybody else. The widening of a street, the election of a mayor, or the consideration of central sewerage disposal was mighty important, and every qualified voter took a lot of interest in anything that happened.

Today, nobody seems much to care, and I suspect that things go on just as well without their caring, but it's a lot different. The younger people don't have the affection for Jeffersonville that we old-timers have and always have had. They know there are better places to live, or at least they think they know it. Wonder what they will have when they are my age.

I understand that a lot of people are living in great housing developments in Florida. They live among strangers, every one of them; they don't have a place they know as home the way I think of it.

Whenever I look at the old courthouse, I remember when Jesse Barton was convicted and was hanged down at the sheriff's office. Whenever I cross Main Street, I remember when old Fetcher Guggencrow flipped Mayor Belmont full on the face in the six-inch mud. I can't go near the depot without recalling Bluechin Ball and the gang that used to hang around the engine house.

They're tearing down the Loftin place now for a supermarket, but I can remember when it was a show place of Jefferson County.

I can't travel a road over the county and not remember some old friend or some incident that I was engaged in or knew enough about to be part of. Anchor Ice and Coal Company still stands as a monument, somewhat decaying though it be, of most of my life's work. I helped raise the money that bought the bronze tablet with the names of those who lost their lives in the War Between the States. Hardly a man thereon whose son or grandson or nephew or cousin I haven't known.

Wonder what people enjoy who live far away from the place they were raised. Who the hell wants to play shuffleboard with somebody who can't remember when the Yatawba flooded its banks back in '19 and again in '34? How can you enjoy a checker game with an opponent who has never fought you in a political battle? I feel sorry for people who weren't born and raised in Jeffersonville, and I'm glad I'm not one of 'em. How could some stranger appreciate Nell Coggins when he hadn't seen her when she was the belle of Tarvania? What stranger could tolerate Sharster Queems if he hadn't known him when he had to swipe an apple to get something to eat? What colony of senior citizens, as they call 'em in St. Petersburg, would ever get behind Judge Ponticorn and send him to the General Assembly? They couldn't know the years that he devoted to the service of his fellow citizens.

An essential part of a campaign in Jefferson County is the "speakings." Speakings are not as popular as before television, but each Party keeps them going, mostly because they want the opposition to quit first.

A speaking consists of arranging for a schoolhouse, printing fliers announcing time and place, and getting the candidates to the appointed rendezvous. Sometimes food is added to the program and sometimes a three-piece string ensemble. If you have both, it ceases to be a "speaking" and becomes a "Rally."

I had been to several thousand Democratic speakings, but never to a Republican speaking. Horatio asked me along one night and I went. My reputation was so badly damaged already that a public appearance with Republicans couldn't hurt it any more. I thought a Republican speaking might be different, but it proved to be the same. As usual, barbecue sandwiches and lukewarm cokes made up the bill of fare. About 7:30 things got going when the Precinct Chairman rose.

"Friends of Faith Township, I want to welcome you to our new high school to meet this fine group of distinguished Republican candidates for County office. But first let me thank the ladies for the fine fixin's. Never tasted anything better," said old man Pritchard.

Applause.

"As precinct chairman, it is my honor to welcome this fine ticket to the community. All except one are candidates for County Commissioner, and from other parts of the county. The other one is Big John Satterthwaite; he lives here."

Laughter and applause.

"The Republican County Chairman is here and he will introduce the candidates. Let's give Bowen Brown a big hand."

Not much applause.

Bowen Brown had been handling Eisenhower patronage, and for every rural route carrier he appointed he'd made a half-dozen unsuccessful applicants furious.

"Friends of Faith, it looks like a Republican year in Jefferson County. The organization is in tip-top shape and your candidates are working from dawn till dark. Our candidate for Chairman of the County Commissioners is the kind of Republican we want leading other Republicans. He was born right here in Jefferson County, over near the Penelope Baptist Church on the edge of the Yatawba River. He attended the public schools right here in Jefferson County and married Nancy Mull from this very precinct. Y'all know old man Jeff Mull, so you know she was born a Democrat, but she's right now. Ain't that so, Bob?"

Laughter and applause, with Bob Greer looking none too sure of his wife.

"Bob's a Baptist, and a Mason. He's a member of the Yatawba Fishing Club. He and Nancy have three young'uns and Young Bob is starting college this year, so you know Bob Greer will take care of education in Jefferson County. Y'all know

Bob runs Greer Hardware and Furniture Store and is a good honest businessman, the kind we need to replace those grafting jobholders around the County Courthouse. Most of all, I guess the way to describe Bob Greer is that he is a fine Christian gentleman. Say a few words, Bob."

When in doubt, describe a candidate as a fine Christian gentleman. It was just like a Democratic speaking. Of course everyone knew that Bob Greer made most of his living by out-of-pocket loans at usurious interest rates. Bob made the usual speech.

"Folks, I'm not much at speaking in public, but I do want to tell you that this latest tax revaluation in Faith Township is the worst yet. And it seems the Republicans got their values upped the most."

Applause.

"Now, when we get in, the first thing we are gonna do is get these values back in line, and the second thing we are gonna do is reduce the tax rate. No, friends, we aren't goin' to cut back on school funds, but we are sure goin' to get rid of those Democratic loafers who have had their noses in the public trough for a lot too long. Thank you, folks."

And so it went. Through five County Commissioners, a Clerk of Court, and a Register of Deeds. Most of the candidates on the County ticket were relatively inarticulate, right embarrassed to be on their feet speaking before an audience, and delightfully short in their presentation. But one candidate for County Commissioner was an orator of the type who likes infinite detail.

This man stood there and for a full twenty-two minutes expounded on the waste of money in construction of an addition to the tax office, describing in precise detail how every bit of material from the bricks to the copper piping could have been installed at a lower cost to the taxpayers. He really knew something about building in that he went into such explicit detail as to describe that a reputable contractor would have put two coats of sealer over the concrete before laying the asphalt tile instead of the niggardly one coat used by the man who got the job. In addition, he claimed that the whole addition, amounting to about $8,500, was not only unduly luxurious and exorbitantly expensive, but that the rafters were made of green lumber. He predicted ominous cracks and likely disintegration of the roof and the entire structure as a result of these practices.

Of course, what he didn't mention was the fact that a competitor had won the job and he was so mad about the decision he decided to run for County Commissioner so he would be in a more advantageous competitive business position.

While this exposé was being detailed, a number of other things were going on. Three infant children put up such a clamor that their parents had to take them out of the hall. Youngsters in further stages of growth made periodic trips out of the auditorium for water and other activities required of active children. One old loyal Republican, who had been listening to these speeches for about fifty years, couldn't quite make the end of the contractor's gloomy descriptions and went to sleep, emitting loud snoring noises. These were interrupted by sporadic grunts, groans, and wheezes, all of which were considerably more interesting than the speech in progress. But most everybody stayed because they wanted to hear Horatio Bunker. The Republican County Chairman stood up once again to present the Republican candidate for the House of Representatives for Jefferson County. Maybe Bowen Brown was just real tired from the long proceedings, but his introduction lacked the sparkle and the enthusiasm of a proper master of ceremonies.

"Friends of Faith Precinct, the final candidate we are presenting for your consideration tonight is a man not known to all of you. He came to Jefferson County about two years ago, and, as you may have heard, was the man who did so much to keep Opulant & Company running when a lot of other hosiery plants closed down. Just because this man is—pardon me, was—a Yankee, is no reason why we shouldn't give him our full support. He can't help where he was born, but there's one thing for certain—he's a real good Republican. Horatio Bunker came to my office about six months ago and told me he'd like to run for the House of Representatives on the Republican ticket. You know we haven't had anybody elected to that office in about a dozen years, but this year it looked right and we had two or three people lined up as possible candidates. But we didn't push these other folks, because we had faith in Horatio Bunker. He's got a real good education and knows how to speak the English language as it should be spoken. I can assure you that when we elect him to the General Assembly we will know that we've got a real representative down there. He will certainly be a lot better than Old Judge Ponticorn, who can barely stagger from one day to the next. It gives me a great deal of pleasure to present to you Horatio Bunker." Bowen Brown didn't sound optimistic about his winning.

Bunker got to his feet.

"Fellow Republicans of Faith Precinct, I am very glad that I had an opportunity of joining with these other candidates in coming out here tonight and meeting with you all. I've heard a lot about the good folks who live out this way, and I want to say that Tom Hatfield and Sam McComb, who are sitting right out there among you, work at the same plant that I do and are two of the finest men I've ever met. I didn't know they were Republicans until tonight, and I'm mighty glad to find out that we are on the same side.

"One thing that they didn't tell me about the folks of this

Precinct was that the women folks were so pretty. Of course, I knew that the food was to be good because your County Chairman has been bragging about it, but he didn't say anything about the women folks. Maybe that's because his wife is mighty alert to such matters."

Laughter.

"In any case I want you to know that I am a widower and I hope to have the opportunity of meeting some of your fine young ladies when this campaign is complete. Wouldn't mind meeting a few of the older widows either."

Bunker had picked up a lot of skill at political speaking. I don't believe he had uttered a sentence so far that had one word of truth in it. He was doing fine.

"You heard our County Chairman say that I was from the North, and he spoke the truth, as he always does. I'd like to apologize for being from up in Massachusetts, but I'm mighty fond of my deceased mother and father, and I am not going to be critical of their judgment as to where I was born. Why, I didn't even know how wonderful it was down here until I came down for the first time, but you can bet your bottom dollar that I hadn't been here very long before I got a house and made it my home. I also want to tell you that I wasn't a strong Republican up in Massachusetts, although I voted that way, as did my mother and father, but I hadn't been in Tarvania very long before I realized that I wanted to be an active member of the fine Party to which most of you belong. I feel highly honored, and regardless of whether this election is won or lost by our Party, I want to express my appreciation and thanks to the County Chairman and all you other fine folks who are helping me. Especially since I wasn't born in Jefferson County. Of course, in a sense none of us originated in Jefferson County, since your forebears, just like mine, came over here and formed the colonies from England and other countries across the seas. But we are all Americans now. My only regret is that my folks didn't settle in Tarvania instead of Massachusetts.

"I don't know a great deal about Jefferson County or a great deal about Tarvania, but I do know that when I am elected I'll be able to count on you folks for the advice and help I will need to represent you properly in the General Assembly. I want to tell you now, and I'll want to tell you after the election is over, that the door will always be open in Tarvania City for you to come to visit with me and talk over things. My mailbox will be looked at every day in case you want to write me. I know that the only way a man can win an election is through the help of his friends, and when the election is over, he is a pretty sorry man if he doesn't remember his friends."

Applause.

"As I said, while I don't pretend to know all there is to know about the problems in Tarvania, I do know something about our biggest problem. That's the matter of properly educating the fine young boys and girls I have seen in this room and throughout Jefferson County. It is my opinion that they are not getting the kind of education they need to live a prosperous and happy life, and it is time something was done about it. I think you all know that the Democrats have been in power for sixty years and that we have about as poor a record in the field of education as can be found in any state in the union. I'm not going to quote a lot of statistics, but it's general knowledge that we rate near the bottom in every respect and that the number of our fine young men rejected from the armed forces on account of inadequate education is one of the worst disgraces in the country.

"For example, we have to turn down folks coming to the plant simply because they can not read and write. These are good Jefferson County people, the kind of people we want to hire, and the kind of people who would make good employees and make good wages. But today, in the hosiery business, and in every other business, we are into the time when education is needed for almost every job. We send out instructions on changes in dyeing operations, stretching operations, and countless changes in patterns. We need men and women who can quickly assimilate these changes, and we need men and women who can handle insurance contracts and numerous other documents that every employee should read.

"Just to give you a case in point, I want to refer to a fellow we have down in the shipping department. He is about nineteen years old and one of the best young men I have ever met; in fact, he is one of the few who can keep all those thousands of cartons from getting mixed up. Now many of you know old Jim Hobbs, who is superintendent of the shipping department, and that just a few months ago he came of retirement age and we had to find a replacement. The young man I was talking about was the one we had in mind to replace old Jim Hobbs. We knew he was all ready for a good job that would bring him a better income. It was almost an accident that we asked him to come up to the office and read a set of instructions we had received from the box manufacturer as to the easiest way to fold the cartons. I was dumbfounded to find that this good, alert, and energetic young fellow couldn't read well enough to follow the instructions and, of course, we had to give the promotion to another boy who was able to handle the written word as it should be handled.

"This, ladies and gentlemen, is a tragedy, and it is a tragedy for which every Democrat in this state is responsible in permitting the truancy laws to be so flagrantly ignored. I read in the Jeffersonville *Democratic Bugle* where over one-fourth of our children don't go to any school. Of course, some of these are necessarily out of school because of ill health or for other legitimate reasons, but, until we are ready to send all of our able children to school and give them a good education once they get there, we are going to have to be a backward state, and I might add that Jefferson County, in many ways, will continue to be a backward county with a pitifully low per capita income.

"Of course, we have one educational problem on the local level, and that can only be solved by action of the General Assembly. It is one of the things that I am most determined to do when you send me to Tarvania City. I refer to the election of your County Board of Education. When I first came here, I asked why there were no Republicans on the County Board, even though we had had Republican County Commissioners and occasionally send somebody to Tarvania City representing the Republicans of this County. I was amazed to find out that it is, for all practical purposes, impossible for a Republican to be elected to the County Board of Education. Oh, yes, he can be nominated and he can even be voted on favorably by a majority of the people of this County, but it doesn't make much difference, for once he gets to Tarvania City the Democrats ignore the wishes of the people and select Democrats as the members of your County Board of Education. Some Republicans can do a mighty good job."

Applause.

"There's another thing I feel touches every home in this County and that is the matter of a minimum wage for the people not covered by the one-dollar federal minimum wage. What I want to see is a dollar state minimum wage, because any employer who can hire a man at all should pay him a dollar an hour under this present economy. The young men and women seeking work and trying to raise and support their families deserve this minimum amount in order to get along, and a great many people in this County, and every other county in the state of Tarvania, are not even given this small pittance by which to meet their daily needs."

This I thought to be a really ridiculous contrast with the national Republican Party line. It was decrying the need for an increased federal minimum wage and had historically fought all minimum wage efforts. Now the Republicans in Tarvania were preaching a state minimum wage, and Horatio Bunker, of all people, was going through with the hoax all the way.

"Friends, I'd like to talk about taxes a little bit and let you know that one of the reasons our people can't have new cars, as they do up North, is because of the excessive tax load by which you are burdened. You know, back in the thirties the Democrats passed the sales tax as a temporary tax, and today it is about as solidly entrenched as every other tax they've passed, and let me tell you, these taxes are numerous. We advocate the repeal of the sales tax, which most hits the ordinary working man who has to buy shoes for his kids and tires for his automobile.

"And why are these taxes so high? I ask you to go out and watch for half a day the number of state cars rolling down the highway, occupied by one state employee who is coming from nowhere and going to nowhere. Those big new cars are expensive, and those employees are well paid. That gasoline they're burning doesn't come free either, and that's part of the place where your tax money is going. If you ever go down to Tarvania City and wander through the various offices over in the Education Building, or in the Agriculture Building, or in the Justice Department, or in the Revenue Building, you'll see for yourself the amount of work that you're getting for your dollar. I am not saying that all state employees are loafers, but I say that some of them who have been there forty years or longer aren't real energetic and it is time that something was done about it."

I thought to myself that this indeed was hypocrisy at its highest level. There is nothing that one Republican can do to change things at the Capitol. In fact, there is not much that elected Democrats can do when they come to grips with Tarvania bureaucracy.

"A lot of people have asked me why I wanted to run for this office, and I'd like to answer that question. In the first place, I think that the employees down at Opulant & Company know that I am concerned with their welfare and, although we had some pretty hard going at first, it looks like everybody down there is going to be able to make a good living for some time to come. More important than that, though, was an incident that happened maybe six months ago when I got to complaining so bitterly about the conduct of the government of this state. An old acquaintance of mine told me what I could do about it. He made it clear that howling at the moon like an old hound dog was no way to change anything, and, if I wanted some changes made in this state, it was my duty to offer myself as a candidate for public office, to express my views to the public, and to get elected so that I could make some changes. This is what I am in the process of doing now, and, if each of you helps me, as I know you will help all the candidates on this Republican ticket, I am confident that we will win the victory.

"Now I'm not going to spend a lot of time during the campaign circulating among the Republicans, but I will spend a lot of time seeking support among the Democrats. We all know it is impossible to win in Jefferson County unless a candidate gets the support of many right-thinking Democrats. But don't forget for a moment that I am a Republican, and if I am elected I'll know that it was the interest and the work of people such as you that made my election possible. You can count on me one hundred per cent, as I know I can count on you. Thank you for your kind attention."

There was a good applause for Horatio Bunker's speech, and I knew that he had gotten across enough points to sell the folks in Faith Precinct on his ability and sincerity. He was a dangerous candidate. I knew there was a good deal of trouble ahead for the Democratic Party in this election if it couldn't slow this man up. He had developed the skill of identifying himself with the people to such a degree that even I believed him. The son-of-a-bitch was mighty slippery, but Horatio Bunker didn't tell lies.

Driving home that night, I asked Horatio what his real reason was for running for public office. Some people like to be in the limelight just for the sake of being in the limelight. Others like to see positive proof of their popularity. These politicians are not too effective once they get into legislative committees. I suppose every politician has some of that need for self-glorification, but Horatio Bunker didn't seem to be the type.

"Mr. Bill," he said, "I delivered a lot of damnfoolery to that meeting back there and I know you recognized it for what it was, but beyond the silly words I have the deep belief that, if this country is to survive, the people who are slightly more talented than the average must devote themselves to service beyond their immediate self-interest. Many people are doing this in that they give their time and their energy to worthy church work, worthy charities, and such worth-while programs as the Boy Scout movement and the like. Yet, the area in which they could be most valuable, they ignore. It is in the political field where the vast majority of decisions affecting the welfare and future of our people are really made. And they aren't all made in the halls of Congress, nor by the President or his administration. Down on the state level, and even on the county level, men and women are making the decisions that increase or decrease the moral fiber of this country. Today one little old vote might decide whether or not the schools in certain parts of Tarvania close down or stay open because of the Negro integration issue.

"I'm not saying that I wouldn't have joined with every other Southerner in seccession from the United States at the time of the question of state sovereignty and the decision that our Negro people should not be chattels. Things are different today, and if those who, by natural endowment and the lucky break of a good education, fail in their responsibilities on a governmental level, this country is most certainly doomed to disaster. Possibly, it is doomed in any case. There seems to be a tremendous lack of old-time flag-waving patriotism and a lack of desire by the majority of our individuals to make current sacrifices for the long-range security of our country. The decline in the strength and character that were characteristic of generations gone it may not be possible to reverse. Yet it is the duty of those who are aware of this decline to put forth their best efforts to change the course of events. Maybe nothing can be done to reverse the trend, but I'd hate to come to the end of my life and feel that I hadn't done my part."

I had very little to say. Horatio Bunker was speaking my language.

22

THE
last week of a close election is always more like two
groups of children throwing snowballs at each other than like
exchanges of logic. Most of the missiles are wasted, and when
one does connect it doesn't bother anybody but the receiver. The
public doesn't pay much attention to the ruckus.

Charges are hurled by the Party chieftains from the national
to the county levels. Candidates join in the fray until the air is
full of flying objects. Indeed, it is so full that people trying to
sell soap or get customers to re-cap tires can't find radio space
for their messages. American tradition permits almost any kind
of slander in political exchanges. Opponents call each other
everything from barefaced liars to perverted thieves. Yet rare
is a court case. They operate under political license, which re-
sembles poetic license, except that vilification rather than ethe-
real exaggeration is the dominant characteristic.

One of Judge Ponticorn's loyal supporters was using the
local radio station:

"Friends of Jefferson County, I speak in support of a fine
citizen of this county who seeks your support as Representative

to the General Assembly. Judge Ponticorn is a man experienced in legislation. His callow opponent is ignorant of lawmaking and his election would be a criminal affront to our people.

"Judge Ponticorn is a man born and bred right here in Jefferson County. He is a man who understands our problems. On the other hand, Mr. Johnny-come-lately-upstart neither knows, nor cares, about our problems.

"Judge Ponticorn is a man of known character with a life of distinguished public service behind him. Against him runs an opponent in whom the people have little reason to trust.

"Judge Ponticorn is the man that you, the people of Jefferson County, can send to Tarvania City with complete confidence. Cast your vote for Judge Ponticorn."

Meanwhile, Horatio Bunker also filled the air with missiles:

"Vote for Horatio Bunker, man for the future. Jefferson County has been by-passed in progress, and only when it gets a fresh approach can we hope for better things for our people.

"Horatio Bunker is a man of energy, and it takes a man of energy to get things done in Tarvania City or any other place. His aging opponent has done his job well, but the time has come for a new generation to take the reins.

"Horatio Bunker knows how to get your money's worth. He has demonstrated this in business and he will demonstrate it in government. You know the taxes of Tarvania are a national disgrace and the value received in education and other government services is a worse disgrace. Why return a man to the General Assembly who was part of the plan of inefficiency? Send Horatio Bunker as Representative from Jefferson County."

So the harangue continued. It's a wonder that either side can get anybody worth a damn to run for public office. If political jobs paid well, the public abuse might be endurable. Anybody can stand a little character assassination at the right price. But the economic reward for victory is negligible, barely covering the cost of living, and never adequate to defray the cost of a campaign.

Oh, it's not too difficult to get good people involved in politics up to a certain point. Young people get interested in the Young Democrats or the Young Republicans and sponsor rallies, have conventions, and pass resolutions which nobody reads. It's all good political training and good fun—and a good catalyst for matrimony for the youngsters.

Women's political clubs are formed by ladies of high ideals and limited practical experience. Often as not they deteriorate into exclusive social clubs and reverse their original purpose of bringing more people into the Party fold. Sometimes, with a little political know-how, the women's clubs have become powerful vote-controlling forces. They ring doorbells for registration, provide lunches and socials to help a candidate show off his virtues. The women telephone, haul, and baby-sit a substantial number of voters. If they can be incited by the immorality of an opposition candidate, or even better, by the undesirability of the candidate's wife, the women can readily swing an election. Personally, I think they should vote with their husbands and keep out of politics. In fact, I'd like to see the repeal of the Nineteenth Amendment, although this possibility is pretty remote for the moment.

The regular party organizations have little trouble rounding up able leadership on every level from the precinct to the national committees. Some give their help to seek public recognition, some to rub shoulders with political royalty, and some in hopes of appointment to some public office, great or small. Though these are many, most serve their parties because they feel it a public duty and are glad to do their part. The same men and women can be found assuming other responsibilities in churches and civic clubs.

When it comes to running for election, these same people are not available, and I guess I've fallen into that category. Who the hell wants to have the public reminded that you were among those accused in the Jupes pregnancy case, or that you failed to graduate from high school because you stole the principal's umbrella? Everybody has something just as well forgotten. Even if you have a clean record, you play golf, that is, gamble; or play cards, that is, gamble; or fish, that is, get drunk up at the lakes; or something. If there isn't a real fault to be found, the opposition will manufacture one.

"Did you hear about Horatio Bunker and that marble statue in his house? Well, I couldn't swear it's true but I heard that he bought it for a tremendous price because he had compromised the sculptor's wife."

As you can imagine, this may have cost him a few votes among the virtuous ladies. He probably picked up a few among other citizens who more admired him than condemned him. While candidates may not like malicious gossip, it never seems to hurt them much. One of our governors was accused of owning a bawdy house near Tarvania City, which wasn't so bad until it was proved. He got elected to the Senate by a bigger majority than he had had in his previous race. Another governor was well known as a part-time drunkard. I can hear him yet as he stumbled through his inauguration address on a bad day.

Another thing that makes candidates hard to find is the full-time hypocrisy it takes to win. You have to promise everything to everybody. I remember when Thaddeus Barethread ran for the U. S. Senate. He promised old man McCorkle, who controls things in Stonewall County, that he would give him anything in his power when he got to the Senate. After he got to Washington, Senator Barethread got a letter:

"Dear Senator: You are as good as your word, that I know. I heered that the post for Ambassador to France is open and pays pretty well. I want it.

"By the way, Stonewall County went for you two-to-one in the primary and seven-to-one in the general election. Sincerely yours, Eugene McCorkle."

Senator Barethread had run for the short term and would be running again in two years. He replied:

"Dear Eugene: I'm mighty pleased to hear from my old friend and am delighted to hear that there is an opening in the Federal Government that might be of interest to you.

"Actually, the President appoints Ambassadors, and the Senate merely approves his recommendation, but even if I could influence his choice, it might be best for you to reconsider your request.

"I really don't think you would like living in Paris far away from your kinfolk. Besides that, they speak in a strange tongue which would cause you to be mighty lonely. Most of the time you would have to dress in fancy clothes and smell like a barbershop. Furthermore, there is nothing but foul wine in France and you'd nearly starve for a drink of Stonewall County white liquor. In addition, the climate is terrible over there. If you still want me to see what I can do, let me know. Sincerely yours, Thaddeus Barethread."

The return mail brought a reply:

"Dear Senator: I got your letter and I got to thinking and maybe you're right about my not being happy as Ambassador to France.

"The postmaster is retiring and I want my son, Jake, to be

the new postmaster at Dog Hollow. Truly yours, Eugene McCorkle."

Postmaster Jake McCorkle has long served with distinction. Barethread always got a good vote in Stonewall County.

Republicans in Jefferson County always stage one real big Rally during every campaign, and they went all out in 1960. They rented the armory down by the depot and got it decorated with flags and bunting and pictures of Ike and Nixon and Lodge. Those Republicans were using Eisenhower about as hard as we use Franklin D.

If you've never been to a big Jefferson County political rally, you've missed something. Any woman who can fry an egg cooks up her specialty, and it is put on a big table in the center of the armory. Altogether there is enough food to feed a regiment. I believe some of the people who go to the big rallies never get a square meal any other time. A bunch of white tablecloths are spread over the long table, and on it are placed pies, casseroles, meat loaves, potato salad, barbecue, more pies, candied yams, corn on the cob, home-cooked bread, and innumerable pieces of fried chicken. For those who don't drink coffee there's a sickening grape-flavored drink.

Of course, a lot of the folks who come to the rallies go to both Republican and Democratic affairs and vote for neither. They usually aren't even registered to vote and don't give a damn. But they sure do like the food. Neither Party tries to exclude them because they swell the crowd and it looks mighty good in the newspaper releases. Of course, it is hard to keep these parasites in attendance throughout the Rally. If the music is started judiciously between speeches, you don't lose too many before it's all over.

A Rally always features some out-of-state Congressman, or

something more if you can get it, which isn't usually possible for Jeffersonville. He is supposed to make the main oration, and the local candidates are limited to standing up and waving to the crowd, which is a good thing since most of them would lose more votes by speaking than they would win.

The most thunderous old party war horse gets the honor of introducing the speaker, and it's a rare rally when the man introducing the speaker doesn't take longer than the speaker. This might seem insulting to the speaker, but actually the folks would rather hear their local talent cuss out the Democrats than some notable stranger talk about the high principles of the Republican Party.

I love to hear a political speech, and it doesn't make much difference which side of the fence the talks are originating from. Some people like symphony, and they say there are various movements to it, but to me a political speech has a more complicated formula than anything Beethoven ever thought about. Naturally, I wouldn't be seen dead at a major Republican Rally, but I could listen to the speaker over the radio. He was Congressman Westmoreland and came from some safe Republican district up in Ohio. He had been sent down by the National Committee to bolster local morale in various Southern states.

True to form, the Congressman began by trying to prove that he was really a son of Jefferson County.

"Fellow Republicans and wide-awake Democrats of Jefferson County, there is no pleasure that I have that is greater than to come to a beautiful community in a beautiful country such as I have seen along the Yatawba River. I have been away from my home in Ohio for some weeks now but somehow I feel back at home."

I got real comfortable to hear Congressman Westmoreland go into his routine, for the same reason people like to lie on a sofa to hear a symphony. The speech began with the usual self-effacement concerning his introduction.

"You have been much too kind in your words of introduction, Mr. Chairman, and I am genuinely flattered. I wish my wife could have heard what a wonderful fellow I am."

Laughter.

The next movement properly tied the speaker with his audience by whatever community of interest appeared plausible.

"For several weeks I have been traveling away from my home, and I might add, my campaign for re-election in Ohio. It is my pleasure to serve the Republican National Congressional Committee in any way I can, but before I landed at the Yatawba airport I was yearning to be back home. As I was driven to Jeffersonville by your capable County Chairman, I came to feel at home. These rolling hills and small woodlands are like those that I love so well. Indeed, even the people are the same, in that the same kind of sturdy pioneers who settled here in western Tarvania were at the same time settling in Ohio. We all enjoy a common historical heritage, just as many of us share the same political ideals."

Next should come the prayer for unity.

"Sharing the same political ideals does not mean that all of us shared in the same preference for our national ticket. I understand that some of you wanted Senator Goldwater to be our candidate. Many of my friends in Ohio wanted Governor Rockefeller. Now the convention is past and we are united behind one of the greatest Republican teams in history. No Republican can fail to be proud of Dick Nixon and Cabot Lodge."

Applause.

The Congressman spent three minutes in exultation over Nixon and one minute on his "distinguished running mate." Now it was time for humor. It became apparent that this public servant would never earn a living as a comedian.

"You think things are difficult in Tarvania, and I can assure you that things are very difficult in Ohio, but if you think we have it tough, you ought to go to Mississippi. I've just left there and I can tell you firsthand that a Republican Congressman was looked upon as an oddity. They tell a story down there about a fellow who ran for sheriff on the Republican ticket in one of the Delta counties. Out of about five thousand votes cast, old Jeeter poled only twenty-six. The day after election found him downtown with a pistol strapped on either hip. One of his friends asked him, 'What are the pistols for, Jeeter? Don't you know you lost the sheriff's race?'

"Old Jeeter answered, 'Anybody who don't have no more friends than me ought never to go out in public without arms.' "

Polite laughter.

Congressman Westmoreland told one more joke and then went into the business of making the rest of his speech more impressive.

"Now this has not been published to my knowledge, and I would appreciate the press here tonight keeping it off the record, but things have not been going well in New York until just recently. Dick Nixon told me himself that it was our big trouble spot. From what Len Hall and Thruston Morton told me early this week, things have taken a turn for the better, and if the trend continues we should carry the state.

"I have been especially assigned to give an opinion on things in Tarvania, and if the rest of the state is fighting the battle with the enthusiasm of the Republicans of Jefferson County, I shall make a most optimistic report to Dick when I return to Washington."

Applause.

"Confidentially, I am also willing to predict Republican victory in Florida, South Carolina, and Texas. Especially with Lyndon Johnson in the second slot."

Laughter and applause.

Now that there was no doubt as to the importance of his distinguished self, Congressman Westmoreland got into the business of the evening, namely, giving us Democrats all kinds of hell. He started his low-level attack with high-level hypocrisy.

"There is one thing that has gotten completely out of hand in this campaign, and that is the Democratic Party's repeated implication that we are trying to beat Kennedy on the religious issue. This is an absolute falsehood. There are a hundred other issues by which we can beat this candidate without talking about his religion."

Westmoreland was just reminding our good Protestant people that their chief opponent was Catholic.

"Now if I wanted to go into the character of the Kennedy family, I would start with the old man. I don't suppose the complete story of his operations in the liquor traffic will ever be known, and I'm going to stay away from character assassination."

I wondered if he would cover the deal between Promisom and Kennedy. He did. He then went into the mistakes of the Democrats and the virtues of Republicans in great detail, in just about the same style as our accomplished speakers. A lot of statistics had been supplied him to prove beyond any doubt that the Eisenhower and Nixon administration had brought about "peace, progress, and prosperity," each itemized with absolute evidence.

This was a wonderful campaign year for both parties, in that Democrats blamed all ills on a Republican administration; all popular and pleasant developments were credited to a Democratic Congress. Now I was hearing the technique in reverse, and it seemed impossible for any fair-minded person not to vote Republican in 1960. I had thought the same thing in favor of the Democrats at the last Rally I attended.

"All these promises on the Democratic platform remind me of a few words by Abraham Lincoln," Westmoreland continued.

Republicans can't deliver a speech without dragging poor old Abe out of his grave. Maybe we should not censure them too much, since I can recall Jefferson and Jackson being reincarnated upon occasion.

"The Democratic platform is, as Lincoln said, 'like the pair of pantaloons the Yankee peddler offered for sale, large enough for any man, small enough for any boy'! He said that one hundred years ago. Now doesn't that remind you of the Democratic platform today?"

Laughter and a few yeses.

Congressman Westmoreland had a responsive audience and decided to steam them up thoroughly. "Fortissimo," I think they call it in music.

"Have you good people had enough of inflation and waste?"

"Yes," responded the sheep.

He went through a few more questions, all designed for the answer, "Yes." It was a nice variation to hear the positive in contrast to the usual "No" response. He wound up with the clincher.

"Do we need men proven by action? Do we need Richard Nixon and Cabot Lodge for eight more years of good government?"

The Republicans dutifully responded in the affirmative.

Having completed the main theme of the symphony, having laid Democrats low and raised Republicans high, Westmoreland was ready to wrap up for the night.

"But despite the justice of our cause and the perilous road

espoused by our opposition, we can not expect the people to see through the barrage of Democratic propaganda unless we each give our utmost. Few days remain, and each of us must spend every available moment telling the facts to his neighbor and fellow worker. The housewife must do her part, and indeed I know of no more formidable weapon of truth than a good talkative woman."

He went on to mention the precinct leaders, the haulers, the watchers, the judges, the registrars, the county chairmen, and finally wound up with President Eisenhower. I gathered he felt that Ike should be spending more time on the campaign trail.

Now that the prayer for action had been completed, it was time to end the masterpiece on a note of optimism.

"As I conclude these informal remarks, let me make a final request. Please invite me back to Jefferson County to join in your victory celebration. Now I must leave to go to Richfolk, but I shall never forget the inspiration I've found this night in Jeffersonville, Tarvania."

The radio left the Rally with the usual sign-off that the speech was sponsored by the Republican Executive Committee and that the views therein were not necessarily those of station management.

I could see the scene from many memories: The children were being awakened, the old folks painfully unbending to head home from an eventful night, and the women scavenging the remains of the food. All agreed one to the other that this had been an inspirational Rally and that the speaker was a true statesman, certainly headed for greater things in the future. The sergeant in charge of the armory surveyed with distaste the task of cleaning up the littered floor, much of it discarded brochures, unneeded by those who could barely read. He wondered why people wouldn't empty their paper cups if they were stupid enough to drink that damn purple punch in the first place.

Congressman Westmoreland would be shaking hands and accepting the congratulations of the faithful. He would be hurrying to head to Bunker's home for about three good slugs of whiskey. It was about the only relief on the grueling hunt that seeks nothing but votes. Even if he were succeeding, there would be no bag of tangible evidence to take home to a wife whose patience would be exhausted. She had probably sworn to leave her husband every two years.

Westmoreland's schedule next included a women's luncheon in a fashionable suburb of Richfolk, followed by a fifteen-minute television tape, which would be cut to thirty seconds by the time it reached the air. Then there would be a press interview, the only significant part of which would be a forthright prediction that Nixon and Lodge looked awfully good in the South, even in Mississippi. As to details, he had been asked to report only to the presidential candidate himself. Yes, the Republican Party was very confident in Tarvania, but was taking no chances on a reversal.

After the press interview he would take a shower, a twenty-minute nap, and go to a reception in his honor. He would have to limit himself to two thin drinks or his articulation would get sloppy at the rally. He would change a few paragraphs for the slightly more sophisticated audience of Richfolk, but most of it would be another recitation of the Jeffersonville speech. Thank God he got only local newspaper coverage. He would wonder how Nixon managed a new one every day.

Congressman Westmoreland would be very tired and Sunday would be a needed day of rest. Likely he would drink several more than par after the Saturday night rally. Another long week would be ahead and then a long flight to Alaska, even though the state was hopelessly Democratic.

He would wonder why he had to leave his safe Ohio district, where he could easily feign political emergency and cancel out the rest of his schedule. Somebody else would take his place, maybe not as well, but how many votes would be changed anyway?

Westmoreland wouldn't quit, I could tell by his voice. He preached a lot of damn foolishness, but the Republican Party would stay in existence as long as men like him really believed their Party line. Beneath the oratorical camouflage, I suspected this was a man who was convinced that the Democratic Party is actually destroying the freedom of the individual.

I'd never vote for a Republican, but I admired Congressman Westmoreland. Bunker would likely develop into another of his ilk.

It was only a week before election, and Horatio Bunker was showing a lot of signs of exhaustion. His lean frame was leaner than before, a deep frown left his face only when he was shaking hands with a prospective voter, and his hands shook like those of an old man. Where he had once walked with the straight shoulders of a Marine drill sergeant, he now seemed bent and as though each step was tiring. His most loyal supporters at the plant had come to dread his brief appearances, because he had lost the patience and good humor that makes a team operate smoothly. Although I can't say that I was sorry for Horatio Bunker, I certainly can't say that I wanted him to drop dead in this hopeless campaign. I have no fondness for what he represents, and yet suppose it's a good thing that somebody does represent something other than the pattern of Tarvania's politics.

I had never seen Horatio Bunker even slightly drunk, but I thought it was time he got that way if he were going to relax for even one night. Fetcher Guggencrow, in his capacity as a bootlegger as well as a taxi driver, and both professions go together pretty well in Jeffersonville, brought me a fifth with only half of the usual markup. I even had a bucket of ice brought over from the drugstore so that I could put forth a maximum inducement. Bunker was really tired that night, and when he slumped across a chair and a half, he looked like he'd never get up again. Knowing him, I knew that in ten minutes he would be walking around plotting against the people once more. Before that time, I had gotten about two ounces of bourbon in his stomach and had started off on a subject which is universal to men of all ages, regardless of race, color, or previous condition of servitude.

Actually, my old-time adventures in Brightburl and in France were not as flamboyant as I pretended, but after listening to varied descriptions for sixty years, I am capable of telling some pretty juicy stories about ladies of questionable decorum. I can't say that Bunker entered into the spirit of the discussion wholeheartedly, but it wasn't long before I got his mind off the campaign and on to more pleasant subjects. After three drinks poured by my hand, unaccustomed though it may be to being generous with my liquor, Horatio loosened up a little bit, and the first thing I knew he was talking about the esteemed Mrs. Virginia Burlcone Stevens.

"Mr. Bill, I'm not dead certain I want that woman for a wife," said Bunker.

"Hell, son, that's just liquor talking. You're damn lucky to have a woman that good who would marry you."

He said, "I know, I know, I know . . ." and Bunker's voice trailed off. It looked like he was about to go to sleep.

"She would make you Governor of Tarvania someday."

"Who the hell wants to be Governor?" asked Bunker with slur-tongued vehemence.

"Any politician who ever went for anything higher than constable," I answered. "It's just normal, like wanting to be bank president instead of a small loan shark."

"You've met the exception," muttered Bunker. "It's damn peculiar that nobody wants to do a job for the people for its own sake. You go to war and don't want to be a General, don't you?" he asked belligerently.

I was thinking about this when Bunker started snoring loudly.

I don't know whether Susan Ponticorn came to see me or Horatio Bunker on Challenge Day, but I guess it wasn't me, since Bunker's campaign car was out in front of the office. He often left it there when he was at the plant. "It's more than a portable billboard, Mr. Bill," he had remarked. "It is a vibrating testimonial that the old and infirm shall not be forgotten by Horatio Bunker."

Susan inquired as to getting rid of some names of people on the books who existed only on tombstones. I asked how they were registered. Since they had been loyal Democrats, I recommended no tampering with their right to vote. It looked very much as if Judge Ponticorn might need them Tuesday.

"You are getting deliciously plump, Susan. You almost look like a prospective mother," I said with no more than good humor, and a wish to keep her in the office a few more minutes.

Susan turned pink, which was not characteristic. Gathering her wits, she said, "Mr. Bill, I am afraid that the years have made you a salacious old man, and I wish you would keep such outrageous thoughts to yourself." She added, "I guess I'll have to go on a diet sure enough if a man your age thinks I'm overweight."

"Now, Susan, I didn't say that, and I meant no offense. You'll just have to forgive an old curmudgeon for his undisciplined tongue," I said contritely.

"O. K., Mr. Bill," said Susan. "By the way, is Mr. Bunker aging much with the rigors of his campaign?"

"No, he's tired but still looks revoltingly fit. What's more, unless we do some highly unethical things, with the presidential race and all, he's likely to beat your father," I said.

"I know," said Susan. "There isn't much more we can do."

"About two thousand dollars might buy enough, but we haven't that kind of money, and I couldn't guarantee it anyway," I said. Something was funny about me, because I was supporting both opponents at the same time. It wasn't hypocrisy. I had come to want both to win, which is politically ridiculous.

"About all I can suggest is that we publicize Bunker's relationship with Betty Ray Cline. Of course, we would have to add something ugly like a miscarriage to make it effective," I added.

Susan flushed. "We don't want to win that badly," she said. "It isn't true, is it?" she asked.

I assured her it was only a political idea not to be confused with the facts.

23

THE
history of every close election is pretty much the same.
Six months before the day of voting, plans are laid and candidates selected. Platforms are formulated with the intention of appealing to the judgment of the voters.

As the campaign proceeds, the appeal to reason decreases and the emotional pitch increases. Candidates who would never vilify any acquaintance become more and more intemperate in their statements. Then, towards the end, they are accusing their opposition of everything from horse-stealing to advocating germ warfare.

Party leaders become even more irresponsible, using every device that might somehow sway the undetermined vote. Defamatory pamphlets are printed in direct violation of the law and bear no signatures. The contents are such that nobody wants to claim authorship.

"Negro citizens of Jefferson County: At last we have a chance to really get something for our vote. Democratic leadership has promised that we will get two Negro deputies, who will be paid the same as other deputies serving under the sheriff. We will get the janitorship for the courthouse, and this is the highest-paying janitorship in the county. We have been guaranteed a Negro nurse in the Welfare Department. For obvious reasons no public statement has been made, but we have been privately guaranteed that the Democratic County Commissioners, if elected, will actively push integration in Jefferson County. We have no choice but to vote Democratic in this election. Signed: Negro Citizens Voters League."

There is no such thing as a Negro Citizens Voters League in Jefferson County. The message was not intended for Negro citizens anyway, but was distributed among white citizens. Authorship was not Democratic but rather Republican. Of course, their official Party leadership would deny any connection with this message. In fact, they were the first to denounce it as a scurrilous political trick. I might add that we have pulled a few such capers from time to time ourselves.

As the fateful day approached, absentees started flowing in by the hundreds. Of course a few absentees are legitimate, but with a little skill it is not difficult to vote the dead, deceased, and deserted.

People who would ordinarily be unaffected by disaster, pestilence, or the second coming of Christ get extremely excited towards an election. They pay not the slightest attention to government in the interim, but as election day approaches they become fantastically enthusiastic about their preferred candidates and libelously derogatory about their opponents. Good friends become alienated because of ridiculous statements made with such conviction that they sometimes remain enemies long after election day, long after the cause of the quarrel is forgotten.

When the final day approaches, tempers are aroused to a warlike pitch. The battle lines have been drawn and level heads are few. Surprisingly, the activities of the election day itself are relatively mild compared with the feverish preparations of the weeks before. Of course, a few fights break out, a few votes are bought, and a few votes are stolen, but most people are satisfied to get the vote out and count the results.

Part of downtown Jeffersonville is roped off election night. There are hundreds of people standing around watching the big blackboard outside the office of the Jeffersonville *Democratic Bugle*. There, in blocked off columns, are the tabulated results as they come in from each precinct. There, weary from weeks of activity far beyond their normal pace of living, and exhausted from a long day of working at the polls, rally the faithful.

The polls close at 6:30 P.M., and the first returns come in about an hour later. We have no voting machines yet in Jefferson County, so the tallying procedure is slow. Each ballot must be counted, and when a precinct is large it takes three or four hours to determine the results. Smaller, rather insignificant returns from small precincts are the first to be posted.

The bitterness of the campaign is already disappearing as people wend their way towards the big board. Although the outcome is unknown, the battle has been won or lost and only waiting is left.

Each favorable set of figures brings forth a shout of approval from the party faithful. The opposition is glum and unspeaking. Actually the early figures prove very little. Almost every precinct has a tradition of going Democratic or Republican. It is a close and unusual situation indeed when a traditionally Democratic precinct goes Republican, or the other way around. What is significant, and usually forgotten, is the degree of change. For example, if Jeffersonville Number Nine, which normally goes three-to-two Democratic, should come in with a small Democratic majority, we can be pretty certain that the Democratic

Party is in serious trouble in Jefferson County. A near even outcome in Jeffersonville Number Nine spells disaster. Meanwhile, our supporters are overjoyed, just as if Number Nine had decided the election by going Democratic by a slight margin.

Partisan animosity disappears as more and more precincts are heard from. Winners, joyful in victory, are increasingly ready to concede that the losers fought a good, clean, hard fight.

"Joe, you really should have carried Lazy Creek. I never saw you folks work any harder. If the national trend hadn't been against you, you woulda beat us to death."

"Yeah, we worked hard all right. Your boys just wanted to win too bad. I never saw so many haulers dragging in the aged and infirm as we saw in Lazy Creek today. You can tell me now: how many votes did you actually buy?"

As the evening wears on, pints of whiskey are drawn from underneath car seats. No good, steady, partisan worker fails to save one for himself. Winner and loser swig out of the same bottle while one hopes for an increased majority and the other hopes for a reverse. The next two years will be spent in crowing or alibiing over the election. It is a lot more fun to say "we swamped you" than "we just squeezed through that one."

By eleven o'clock the outcome is pretty well decided. The area around the blackboard becomes less and less crowded. Only a few die-hards stay on to hope against the figures. The police work very little, for although alcohol is plentiful, the consumers are so tired that they tend to pass into sleep instead of inciting scrimmages. By midnight the streets are deserted. Jeffersonville becomes once again a little Southern town that is as deserted as it would be on any other night.

So it would be on the night of November 8, 1960.

If Bunker won, Jeffersonville would never feel the same about old Bill Anchor. Although everybody would be polite enough and they would all speak to me election night, they would feel a lot different from the way they had always felt about Bill Anchor. Fellow Democrats would feel that I had deserted the Party, and this was to be expected.

What had already surprised me was that old Republicans, whom I had fought all my life, greeted me with suspicion. I don't know whether or not they respected me as a lifelong opponent, but they sure had been used to it. That I might be their confederate in this election made them uncomfortable. They didn't laugh, and joke, and accuse me of stealing votes the way they always had.

How easily my mistakes had multiplied. It would have been much better to have lived my remaining years as an undoubted member of the Party for which I had worked and fought the best part of my life. It would have been better never to have known Horatio Bunker. This everybody knew. It would not be long before they knew even more. Events were to follow that might cause me to resume my old place in the community. At least Bunker's victory could not be blamed on me.

Election day broke cold and dreary. Tarvania looks like it's about to snow most of the winter. Actually it rarely snows except in the mountains, but it gets awfully cold and nasty, just like up North.

Most of us don't usually get up as early as the polls open. I guess the hours were set when most folks farmed for a living. Even before the polls open, the members of the Board of Elections are distributing ballots, neat little packages of five hundred each. There is the Presidential Ballot, the State Ballot, the County Ballot, and any special ballots, such as Constitutional Amendments.

Enclosures have to be established. If the polling place is one long established, there is usually little discussion, but if a new area has to be roped off a foot or two one way or the other, it nearly causes a riot. Republican judges may be outvoted by registrars and Democratic judges, but they sure can be cantankerous.

The enclosure is designed to keep persons not actually voting far enough away from the ballot box to avoid congestion that would lead to brawls and misuse of the ballots. We don't have much trouble downtown, but out in the county it is accepted practice that the drunks go into full action on election day. The enclosure is a light rope that represents the line between going to jail and being tolerated in a lot of precincts. Also outside the "ropes," as we call the enclosure, are the markers. These people are undisguisedly partisan, yet enjoy a semi-official status. They must be sworn in just like election officials, but can't come inside the ropes except with permission of the judges. All this is subject to local ground rules, but that's the general idea.

Each designated partisan has pinned upon his lapel a paper tag printed DEMOCRATIC MARKER, or REPUBLICAN MARKER. A lot of folks are registered Independent, but I've never heard of an INDEPENDENT MARKER. Neither have I ever seen the theoretical need for markers in conducting an election, although nobody could fail to see their real function. Tarvania law requires that the electorate be able to read and write the state constitution in order to vote, a reasonable provision for everybody and especially convenient if too many darkies attempt to register. Markers are supposed to be authorized to assist voters in marking their ballots. Since the ballots are in English and rather simple, the actual need for markers is somewhat mysterious. The feeble and blind are allowed to have relatives assist them, or one of the judges if need be. Thus the need for markers becomes even more incomprehensible.

That's the legal point of view. From a practical standpoint, markers are essential. By their mere presence at the entrance to the voting place they let the voter know that he is under surveillance. I might add that we Democrats always try to have more markers than the Republicans. Just good psychological warfare.

Markers serve another function in ensuring that state employees vote right. Some of them ostentatiously mark their tickets Democrat against the walls of the polling booths. Others hand them unfolded and most obviously to the judges before they are put in the ballot boxes. The rest ask for a Democratic marker and he, in effect, witnesses to their loyalty in the privacy of the voting booth. Markers are invariably selected for their Party loyalty. They talk friendly to everybody as they enter the polls, hoping to influence by that little final gesture the action of the voters.

Susan was a Democratic marker at Jeffersonville Number Three, which is at the courthouse and right across the street from the Bunker headquarters. Horatio had passed the word that all election workers were welcome at the office throughout the day, and I was to be personally in charge of the big coffeemaker. The more Horatio Bunker kept Democratic markers drinking coffee, the fewer would be at their posts. As cold as it was, the pot would be refilled often.

Bunker himself could serve in no official capacity because he was a candidate. He was planning to spend the day roving the precincts and giving encouragement to Republican workers. I was also certain he had a bankroll of dollar bills and a trunkful of half-pints in case they should be of advantage at some of the boxes.

There is a tremendous excitement when the polls open. No matter how many elections you have fooled with, it's always like the first day of vacation for school kids. As the day wears on, the excitement decreases until the hour when the plants let loose their flood of voters. Towards closing time, fatigue sets in, and then tension mounts again to a fever pitch as the ballots are counted.

The activity of the days before the election found me mighty tired when I rolled out of bed at 5:00 A.M., election day. Like an old cavalry horse I responded to the call to arms, even though my heart began throbbing ominously. Doc Bernhardt had told me at the time of the accident that broken bones wouldn't kill me but that my old ticker was the thing to watch. Of course he had said the same thing for ten years and damn near forced me to undergo cardiographs to prove it.

Anybody who hasn't fooled with an election has missed a lot of fun. It's the biggest and most spectacular semi-peaceful event in the world, and no matter how many times you've seen one, you get excited about the carryings-on. When I was a boy, the circus came to town once a year, and for at least ten years it was the biggest thing that happened. That's the way with elections, only you keep getting excited until you draw your last breath.

It's little wonder that the big day is so big. Literally for years beforehand, every newspaper writer, every politician, and nearly every other person, even if he doesn't vote, expresses opinions on the next President. Aside from the free publicity, the side-kicks of the candidates on both sides spend fortunes trying to create a favorable impression on the public. When the National Conventions finally meet, you have a show unequaled by show business.

I was an elected delegate when we nominated Al Smith back in 1928. Of course, there wasn't television back then, but I wish there had been. We had better fist fights than you'll ever see among professional boxers. There was a lot more freedom of invective. The opposition was referred to as "liars, crooks, blasphemers, and curs" as casually as we now refer to the "errors of the worthy opposition."

The words might be different but the game is still the same. The rules of the game may be slightly refined, but the only thing that really counts is victory. There is no second prize when you are running for President of the United States, or for Representative from Jefferson County.

All the explanation of funds, all the evasive tactics of the "ins," and all the attacks of the "outs" rise to their climax on election eve. Then everything quiets down.

It reminds me of the Battle of the Champagne Sector. We had pulled French 75's, beaten mules, cursed the weather and the Heinies until the day battle began. But the most talkative got quiet that morning. Of course the fear of death was in our hearts in France. The awareness of the immediate prospect of battle ended our claims of easy victory. It's something like that on election day, at least in Jefferson County.

Although Democrats outnumber Republicans, victory is never certain. They know every trick in the trade, and while we are no angels, we are still guardians of the election machinery, and we are not all without honor. The opposition thinks we are using our preferred status to steal the election anyway, so they will do damn near anything to win. Sometimes they succeed.

As election day wears on, you see people you haven't seen for two years, maybe four. We have often written up absentee ballots for people we thought safely under ground, only to find them stumbling to the polls on election day. I could have sworn I had actually been to old Mrs. Troy's funeral and got a helluva shock when she was brought in by ambulance to vote. I was relieved to learn that her sister actually had died the previous year.

Drunks, who wouldn't ordinarily be spoken to at any other time, become big men on election day. From experience I know that the last half-pint gets their vote and they had better be toted there in person. Many's the slip between the bottle and the ballot box. In fact, all our ne'er-do-wells are sought after on election day. These votes are bought clean and simple. Republicans somehow have a lot of cash on Election Day in Jefferson County.

The weather got worse instead of better in the morning. Dawn broke cold, foggy, and dark grey. Midmorning was colder, drizzling, and light grey. The voting was light, most people hoping for better conditions under which to perform their civic duty.

Markers of both parties trooped in and out of the office. Not even the most rabid Democratic hauler objected to the "Vote for Bunker" sign, even though it was well within the legally prohibited distance from the polls. Political posters are supposed to be at least fifty feet from any enclosure.

About 11:00 A.M., I had a seizure. It's hard to tell anybody who hasn't had one the terrible pain of a heart attack. You think you've been hit in the chest by a locomotive. You gasp for breath and more than likely pass out. I was able to steer the wheel chair behind the partition and maneuver onto my cot. I was half-conscious and ready to die.

Voices could be heard through the thin partition after a while. Election workers were gulping coffee, prognosticating, and bitching about the weather. They couldn't see me and I knew there was little they could do if they had. Doc Bernhardt would just throw me in the hospital, and I would just as leave pass over the hill with my shoes on.

Then I heard Bunker's voice. He didn't even speak loudly, but I could always hear him within seeing distance.

"Come in, Susan," he said. "There is no sense in freezing on a misconstrued sense of loyalty for your father."

"Where is Mr. Bill?" she asked. Her voice was difficult to hear, even though the plywood partition was almost like an amplifier.

"I guess the old gent's down at the Grill getting something to eat. He was here before the polls opened, and I don't suppose he had any breakfast," said Bunker.

"You tricked him into helping you," said Susan. "He's always been close to Papa."

"He still is, Susan, and always will be. Bill Anchor has been paid to do a job and he's done it, that's all. I'd bet money he's already voted for the Judge," said Bunker.

I hadn't thought about voting myself, and now I wasn't sure the Judge should represent Jefferson County. I would never make it to the polls anyway.

"Maybe so," said Susan. I knew she was sipping coffee and thinking of something else.

"Well, if you go to Tarvania City, watch the calories," said Bunker. "I believe you're putting on poundage, although it's still becoming. Let me see you often after today." His voice was earnest now.

"I think not, Mr. Bunker. I'm going to Washington tomorrow and will not be back to Jeffersonville for at least six months. My baby will go through the Children's Home in Greensedge for adoption," Susan said without a whimper or audible emotion.

There was an absolute silence. I should have made my presence known before, but it was too late now. I hoped they didn't discover me. I knew no one would ever discover my overhearing them.

"Like hell you are, Susan. I want you to make a journey." He probably was on close terms with an abortionist, the bastard.

I couldn't hear the rest. They must have been quite close and talking in whispers.

"I'll pick you up at your house at six tonight. Bring enough clothes for at least a week. Some warm-weather clothes, if you please." Bunker was tense and not very successful at being casual on this one occasion.

"Yes, Horatio, I'll be ready," she said softly. I could feel Susan's terrible insecurity.

By midafternoon I was feeling better. Nobody had detected my condition. I look so damn aged anyway that my post-attack appearance would differ little from the way I usually looked.

The election didn't seem important now, but people kept coming in and I kept refilling the god-damned machine with coffee and water.

About 3:00 P.M., Horatio came in again.

"A half-dozen precinct chairmen have called for you, Horatio. They've been expecting you and they're looking for money and liquor," I said.

"Sorry, Mr. Bill, I've had something to come up, at the plant," he lied. I didn't question him.

"There is something I want you to do, Mr. Bill, and it is terribly important to me. I'm not offering to pay you, and I can't blackmail you. You'll be violating the law, and I can only help keep you out of jail should you be caught," Bunker said.

"All right, Horatio, let's hear it."

"I want you to steal the election for Judge Ponticorn," he said.

For six months Horatio Bunker had done little besides fight for victory over Judge Ponticorn. I knew now it had been more than a desire for a personal victory. Bunker somehow felt he was championing the rights of the forgotten man, and the General Assembly was to be his forum. Until this moment he had been willing to do damn near anything to win, including buying and stealing. A complete reversal was impossible, some kind of trick to ensure victory.

"Get them any way you can," he said. "I'm confident that I will win this election, but I don't want it. I think six hundred extra ballots for the Judge would win it for him. Three hundred switched ballots would do the same thing, but I don't want to torpedo the rest of the couny ticket unless I have to. If only I get robbed, only I could request an investigation. I will not investigate the outcome, so help me God." Bunker never had to put such emphasis to make a statement absolute.

"All right, Horatio," I said. "I'll fix it, if I can." I wondered what I would have done if I hadn't overheard the earlier conversation. "Now get out to the precincts, Horatio. You won't change many votes your way this late in the day, but we don't want any suspicion that you're taking a dive." Funny, we always referred to it as "selling out" in elections. The usual phrase didn't fit here.

I was sweating now, and a glance at my reflection in the office front window told me I looked as bad as I felt. It wasn't far to the office of the Board of Elections, but getting up those stairs to the second floor would be nearly impossible.

I rolled up to a couple of Democratic markers and told 'em to get a few other old cronies and meet me at the office by 4:00 P.M.

I had to do the next job alone, unobserved if possible. I made it to the stairway without trouble, but getting up the seventeen steps about finished me. Step by step and lifting my bottom up backwards, I dragged myself to the top. The casts on my legs pulled like two iron cannon.

Blackton Shepard, Chairman of the Board of Elections, was

at his job. A few late absentee ballots were the order of business. A lot of people don't vote at all, but let an old Party war horse fall sick election day and somebody will rush fifty miles to get him a ballot.

"What are you trying to do, Bill?" Shepard asked. I must have looked like death itself for him to show such concern.

"Help me to your office," I said. Shepard half-dragged, half-carried me and dumped me on the old leather sofa that had once been the pride of a more successful Shepard attorney.

"I want a thousand county ballots, Blackton," I said.

Shepard didn't answer. He just looked at me as if he neither believed that I were alive or sane. Then he thought over the years behind us. I guess I was one of the few who had never turned on him, even when most of his friends had written him off as an objectionable drunk. He made up his mind.

"I'm going to the men's room and I'll be gone five minutes. I'll drop two unopened packages on the floor. If you get out of here alive, I've not seen you all day. Good luck, Bill," said Blackton.

The trip downstairs was not too tough. My wheel chair was where I had left it, which I hoped meant nobody had noticed it.

Back at the office, seven men awaited me, including three markers from across the street. Two of my recruits were questionable. I asked them to leave and the door was locked. I couldn't have declared "conspiracy" more clearly if I had used the radio station, but the time remaining was short. My own strength was ebbing as fast as time was running out for the polls to close.

The instructions were simple. It was $50.00 apiece for an hour's work. We marked ballots rapidly, single-shotting only Judge Ponticorn. Questions came fast.

"No, the number won't be checked against the poll books.

Trust me that there will be no challenge of the outcome. That is, if all of you refrain from cheating for your pals on these ballots. We want to beat Bunker, that's all."

I wondered what these scoundrels thought of me. What skulduggery I had done over the years was mighty mild compared to this wholesale fraud.

"Get 'em in the boxes any way you can. Bribe the judges, sneak 'em in, start a riot, anything that's necessary," I said.

"No, take care of Smoky Creek first. You can get eighty in that box. More that twenty-five would look odd in Maidendale Number One." I was thinking well. A lifetime of experience came in handy.

"I know the total count will look funny, but we won't vote more for State Representative than we do for President. There's been a lot of interest in the race, and only the County Commissioners will be curious. I'll handle them," I said, with a lot of bravado and little real sureness.

I was kind of proud that these boys trusted me. Not just money would cause them to risk a jail sentence if they thought I wouldn't protect them. Of course I couldn't, if it came to court. Anyway, I'd probably be dead and it would be hard to link Shepard and the conspirators without me in the middle.

"Oh, should I forget, gentlemen, there's an extra $50.00 apiece for you if Bunker is beat."

I passed out the money, and when they had left I collapsed. Somebody carried me away this time.

24

IT

was five days before Doc Bernhardt let anybody see me, and at that I was barely conscious. Effer Vestal, who is the chief and only reporter at the Jeffersonville *Democratic Bugle,* got to me first. He had to poke his head under the oxygen tent to talk to me.

He wanted information, but I demanded a complete account before I would say a word. Of course Doc Bernhardt had given me the results, but I wanted to hear 'em again. Catholic or no Catholic, Kennedy is a Democrat, and oh, how good it was to know we had beat 'em. Not much of a popular majority, but enough electoral vote, and we had a Democratic majority in Congress. The Republicans had been noisily confident of carrying Tarvania for Nixon. They hadn't talked about it, but the radicals had had a lot of faith in Baptist loyalties. They called it intolerance. We didn't beat "squirrel-jaws" badly, but there would be four years of peace from Tricky Dick.

Of course Promisom handily beat the Republican candidate for governor, Optimo Futrell, who is a pretty good guy. It showed in the voting too. We had been beating them by four hundred thousand, and Futrell had cut Promisom to a one-hundred-thousand majority. I hoped I wouldn't live to see a Republican in the Governor's Mansion. Now might be a good time for a lifelong Tarvanian Democrat to go to his eternal reward. The Republicans had re-elected Cary Plunder Jones for the fifth time, and the races were awfully close in two other Congressional Districts. We might even be losing our grip on Tarvania.

The General Assembly didn't go to our taste. The Republicans more than tripled their seats there. I know we stole three of the mountain counties, besides the one with which I was personally familiar. Still, they had only ten per cent of the Legislature. It was worse back in '28.

Effer Vestal had been at the newspaper office when the returns came in. So were most of the candidates and everybody else who could squeeze into the building. The blackboard which normally reported results outside was out of use because of rain. Brinkley's Insurance Agency, across the street, got the overflow of the crowd, and messengers scampered back and forth across the street.

The main interest was in the national race, and WTVR in Mecklenton was giving it better coverage than the Jeffersonville *Democratic Bugle*, so most folks at the newspaper office were primarily concerned with the County ticket.

Judge Ponticorn looked old, tired, and worried. He needed to win if he were to spend his last years with the respect of the community in which he had spent his life. Defeat would mean that his life's work was refuted.

The first boxes' returns showed that the race would be close. After each count was made, the registrar or judge brought in the returns. Shepard received them unofficially and Effer Vestal tallied and reported the cumulative returns. The smaller boxes came in first, since their counting was completed earlier. When about half the returns were in, it looked as if two of the Democratic Commissioners were safe, and the other three might be beaten by Republicans. The Clerk of Court was safe, but the Register of Deeds was definitely lost. What a rat race it would be for the next two years. One Party in control of the courthouse was confusing enough. Two made it a veritable madhouse.

Judge Ponticorn was losing his race. Only one of the early boxes had given him hope. For some reason, Maidendale Number One gave him a considerable majority over Bunker and a much larger vote than the rest of the Democratic ticket.

About that time a long-distance call from Gaffney, Salabama, came through, and Judge Ponticorn was called to the phone. He turned pale as he listened and muttered a few inaudible words. He asked Effer Vestal to phone results to his home and left the newspaper office.

Apparently Bunker's secretary knew the whereabouts of Horatio Bunker, because the Doc had received a phone call from her within an hour of my collapse on election night. Doc Bernhardt was also the family physician of the Ponticorns, and he hadn't had to guess about Bunker's and Susan's hasty flight from Jeffersonville. The Doc had played down the seriousness of my attack to keep the newlyweds from rushing home.

I got two letters postmarked "Sea Island, Salabama."

"Dear Bill: Just heard about the heart attack and hope it is no more serious than Doc Bernhardt has told us. Losing the election was a terrible blow to my pride. I suspect the Democrats cheated us again, but I am now involved with something more interesting than politics, so I won't press the issue. Thanks!

"Of course I consider you responsible for the wedding trip,

having led me beyond the normal area of political endeavor. I am married to a stubborn woman who thinks Democrats are just as good as humans.

"Am counting on you to act as my full-time campaign manager for the 1962 election, and I sure would appreciate your changing your registration in the meantime, but am prepared for hell to freeze over while waiting.

"Incidentally, I am happy for the first time in many years. There are no windmills to topple here, but I'm not forgetting the one that you knocked over election day.

"Will be home in a week, and sooner if need be. Listen to Doc Bernhardt just for a change. Good luck, Bill. Horatio Bunker."

That boy will probably run again, and when he does, I pity our good Party of the People. Times change, perhaps, but damned if I ever will.

Susan's letter was in the same envelope.

"Dear Mr. Bill: How wonderful it is here, and there are just loads of other honeymooners. We are often mistaken for old married people, we are above the usual age, and I wish we had started earlier.

"We might never have gotten together if it had not been for you, you ole dear. We talk about you all the time.

"Please be good till we get home. While it's most wonderful here, I can't wait to get home. Of course I want to see you, but I will also be glad to go back into the old homestead where I was born and raised. Isn't it wonderful to return to a place that I thought I had left forever? I hope we raise a passel of youngsters and that the Belmont-Bunker home will survive for generations.

"Incidentally, and this will come as a terrible surprise, we are planning to start a family right away. If it's a boy, he will be named William, after you. Horatio says that if it isn't a boy, we'll keep trying until we hit pay dirt. Men are very crude at times, and that doesn't exclude you.

"Papa seemed terribly shocked and offended at first. Winning the election must have helped, however. He's already bought two new suits to show off in Tarvania City. We understand announcements have already gone out about our wedding, so he must be reconciled. He might as well be, because Horatio and I are hitched for good.

"I love Horatio completely, Mr. Bill. Can I keep you for a second love? Sincerely, Susan (Ponticorn Bunker)"

An old man has the right to shed a tear. Besides, I felt awfully sorry for myself, which was reason enough.

Effer Vestal explained that there were a lot of unanswered questions about the election. Shepard had admitted that one thousand unmarked ballots were stolen. Judge Ponticorn got about five hundred votes more than the average on the Democratic ticket, and then carried the election by only 289 votes.

What had I done in deliberately thwarting the will of the people? Despite my occasional political shenanigans, it had never amounted to more than a few votes and never really changed the outcome. Had I committed an unpardonable sin against the county to which I owed such a happy life? Anyway, when, or if, I should go to hell, I hope it is divided along Party lines so I will be with some old friends. Couldn't stand nothin' but Republicans.

Vestal went on to say that haulers, well known to me, were seen to be handling ballots outside of several boxes. Rumor had it that they had met in my office late election day. Republicans were howling "fraud," and if Bunker pressed charges, Democrats were afraid he could prove it. Even the Governor-elect,

Madison Promisom, had called up Vestal to get the straight story. Newspapers outside the county were curious as to how the lopsided vote had taken place. Nobody gave any answers, but everybody said Bill Anchor knew them.

I could barely talk, but I wasn't dead either.

"Vestal, I'll make a deal. If you do a noncommittal and succinct job of reporting, for once in your life, then I'll tell you the whole story. But you must not print a word until the snow is an inch deep in Jeffersonville."

It rarely snows in Jefferson, and we had some snow on the ground twice last year, so it was a pretty good gamble for a few years.

Effer Vestal looked hopefully at the grey November skies. He had to agree or get nothing.

"O. K., Mr. Bill. I'll do it your way. I've got pen in hand. Let's go," said Vestal.

"Not so fast," I said. "I'm pretty tired now, but if you'll get a dictating machine up here you'll have every word. I'll get it on record as fast as I can."

I talked into the machine from time to time, and wasn't always sure whether it was night or day.

Doc Bernhardt had prohibited all visitors by this time. Besides, he was being carefully solicitous and had stopped giving me good conduct sermons. I didn't need these external signs to know that Bill Anchor was close to the end of the road.

Breathing was difficult, even though eased by an oxygen tent. Blackouts became frequent and longer. It's right disturbing to learn that you've missed a couple of days. I had a hard time keeping up with the absentee ballot votes in California. Nixon seemed to be picking up votes, and I can't get it clear if he is about to beat Kennedy or not.

One visitor got through Doc Bernhardt's protective cordon.

I pulled a dirty trick on Judge Ponticorn. I got my nurse to put a newspaper over the tape recorder and she mixed the microphone in with a lot of similar-looking gadgets attached to the oxygen tank.

"Good morning, aged friend. Your appearance belies the onerous reports we have heard of your condition. Our worthy practitioner has never been a harbinger of good news."

"Morning, Judge," I said weakly. "You know damn well I'm nearly dead, and I'm in no mood for the grandiose hypocrisy for which you are ill-famed."

"Seriously, Bill, all MD's feel obligated to paint a hopeless picture. If the patient dies, he was beyond the scope of medical science; if he survives, it is the result of medical genius. Such skill should have its financial reward, incidentally," said Ponticorn.

"Glad you won the election, you old phony," I said.

"True, my victory was deserved, as the people have in their wisdom chosen well him who shall once again devote his life to their service in those hallowed halls of the Legislature of this great state of Tarvania. Indeed, no state can yield to its fellow states less, if at all, in the quality of those who are elected to public office." The Judge rambled on like an old phonograph record, sometimes repeating and sometimes skipping parts of an old refrain.

"To you, Bill, I really owe victory. I know not how you accomplished the accumulation of extra votes, nor do I care to know if there might have been something irregular. Naturally I would refuse to serve in such a case." The old Judge wasn't lying. He would just prefer not to know all the facts.

"Don't worry, I have no intention of letting the wood pussy out of the bag, until later on." I laughed, thinking of the recording of this talk.

The Judge smiled benignly, knowing that there wasn't going to be a lot of "later on" for either of us.

"Something happened towards the end of the campaign. I got to realize that Bunker was the better man to represent the people," the Judge said, almost to himself. "A good thing, now that I've acquired him as a son-in-law. Republican though he be, he will make a good husband for Susan. And guess what?" asked the old man brightly.

"You've sold out to Enebra Sellers and the liquor lobby," I replied, with effort.

"No, senile cynic, this is important. I'm going to be a grand-father," said the Judge with gusto.

"Horatio and Susan have barely taken the vows," I said with feigned horror at the so-called news.

"In the history of Jefferson County it has happened, is happening, and probably will continue to happen, that our best families go through marriage formalities for the most excellent of reasons. Such may have been the case here, although it is difficult to believe of little Susan. I am sure that all will accept the time-honored fact that the percentage of premature babies is very high in this area. Our peculiar water brings this about," said the Judge.

"Remember when Fetcher Guggencrow had his first-born four months after wedlock? That baby established an all-time record weight of eight pounds, four ounces." I chuckled malevolently.

"Someday, Bill, your withered old body may depart from this world. But you can go with the assurance that the malicious gossip you have broadcast for a lifetime will live on for generations," said Judge Ponticorn, virtuously.

"Your remarkably inept decisions as a Judge for most of your life will make far more notorious recollections than any of my activities," I said. "What scheme have you got to immortalize yourself while you are in Tarvania City this session?" I asked. I was having trouble speaking, but I didn't want to go into a coma until I'd talked a little more with my old friend.

"Bill, you know I was very much opposed to the court reform which was brought up in the 1957 session. Having our JP's and allowing the method of reimbursing them by the costs they assessed seemed a necessary evil. I've changed my mind now, and I'd like to be of maximum assistance to whoever proposes a real court reform bill. I'd propose it myself if I had enough prestige down there, but I know better, and I really would like to see some corrective legislation," said Ponticorn.

"Don't get carried away by your own virtue," I said haltingly. "If we ever started electing judges within the districts that they serve, we'd likely as not get a bunch of Republicans in. As long as we keep electing 'em by the state as a whole, we're safe," I said.

"Don't think a Republican son-in-law is going to influence me," said the Judge haughtily. "While I wish him no ill in other phases of life, for my daughter's sake, I have no intention whatsoever of giving the Republicans any additional opportunities to succeed in the State of Tarvania. You can count on me, Bill," said the Judge with unnatural simplicity.

I knew I was very tired and I don't remember any more. The recording showed that my part of the conversation ended with an inaudible murmur. It did pick up a few final words by Judge Ponticorn.

"Good-bye, old friend. It won't be long before I'll be joining you," said Judge Ponticorn. The tape recorded his closing the door and the quick footsteps of a nurse as she hastened to my oxygen tent.

Things forgotten come to mind:
Our ice is dirty water; our business is destroyed.
You'll be President, Senator Calhoun.
This country is bigger than any of us.
Your feet are so small, Emmy Lou.
The lanyard's blown off. Give me your boot strings.
Blackstone is essential; learn it well.
Pa, I can't throw up another pitchfork.
Children aren't everything, Emmy Lou.
You're *supposed* to vomit on *this* troopship.
I swear to uphold the Constitution of the State of Tarvania.
The nigger-lovin' Republicans are finished in the South.
Why did you get started in this, Sally?
To hell with Smith. I'm going for Underwood on the next
ballot.
Gendarme, you only get a purple heart once in a while.
Don't go for Senate now; stick to Congress.
Cherie, there're none half so good back home.
Educate 'em and you can't vote 'em.
Education needs men more than money.
He gave us a paved road right through the County.
You have a duty to offer yourself for public service.
The soreness is a little higher, Emmy Lou.
It's biggest and best, but get rid of Hoover.
Pa said to bury him here on the homeplace.

Now the light in the room keeps coming and going. This
morning it is very grey. Snow is falling, and it must have fallen
most of the night.

END